As Olivia burst through the door of her room, she stopped short and stared.

"I know, I know," Zach snapped, catching her look of dismay, then turning back to his task. "Don't worry. It'll grow."

"What on earth happened?" Slack jawed, she stared in wonder at the three ragamuffins who stood looking back at her, eyes wide.

His heavy sigh was laden with self-deprecation. "I let the Colonel talk me into allowing him to give the kids a trim. That's what he called it anyway. A little trim. Said there was no sense spending good money on a barber when he had the tools to do the job himself. At the time it made sense, so I agreed."

Olivia shook her head and tossed a pained glance at the ceiling. That was a man for you. But she couldn't chastise. Zach already looked as if he felt lower than a snake's belly in a wagon track. Her heart went out to him. And to the kids. Oh, the poor kids.

Our **Giggle** Guarantee

We're so sure our books will make you smile, giggle, or laugh out loud that we're putting our "giggle guarantee" behind each one. If this book fails to tickle your funny bone, return it to your local bookstore and exchange it for another in our romantic comedy line.

Romantic Comedies from WaterBrook Press

SUZY PIZZUTI
Say Uncle...and Aunt
Raising Cain...and His Sisters
Saving Grace (Summer 2000)

SHARI MACDONALD
Love on the Run
A Match Made in Heaven
The Perfect Wife

BARBARA JEAN HICKS
An Unlikely Prince
All That Glitters
A Perfect Stranger (Spring 2000)

ANNIE JONES
The Double Heart Diner
Cupid's Corner

SUZY PIZZUTI

Raising Cain....
and His Sisters

WATERBROOK
PRESS

RAISING CAIN...AND HIS SISTERS
PUBLISHED BY WATERBROOK PRESS
5446 North Academy Boulevard, Suite 200
Colorado Springs, Colorado 80918
A division of Random House, Inc.

Scripture quotations are from the *New Revised Standard Version Bible*
© 1989 by the Division of Christian Education of the National Council
of the Churches of Christ in the United States of America. Special
thanks to Tyndale House Publishers, Inc. for permission to quote from
The Complete Book of Practical Proverbs and Wacky Wit by Vernon
McLellan, 1996. All rights reserved.

The characters and events in this book are fictional, and any
resemblance to actual persons or events is coincidental.

ISBN 1-57856-141-8

Library of Congress Cataloging-in-Publication Data
Pizzuti, Suzy.
    Raising Cain—and his sisters / Suzy Pizzuti.—1st ed.
       p.   cm. — (Halo Hattie's boarding house ; 2)
    ISBN 1-57856-141-8 (pbk.)
    I. Title.   II. Series: Pizzuti, Suzy. Halo Hattie's boarding house ; 2.
PS3566.I93R35   1999
813'.54—dc21   99-10755
                                                        CIP

Printed in the United States of America
1999—First Edition

10 9 8 7 6 5 4 3 2 1

*For my darling new daughter, Olivia,
our angel baby on loan from heaven*

*Thank you, dear Lord,
for giving us laughter
with which to face life's valleys.*

*Special thanks to
Noreen Sauer for sharing her story
with our congregation. Her bravery and loving heart
were the true-life inspiration for this novel.
Also, thanks to my wonderful neighbors
at the Butteville Community Church,
especially the Lewkowskis and the Wiggers,
for Jungle Jam and character sketches.
You guys are the best!*

1

Zach Springer cast a frustrated glance at his surroundings. It had been raining like Niagara Falls for the better part of the month now, which was not exactly typical for October in McLaughlin, Vermont. Usually, there were plenty of crisp, sunny fall days, with a brilliant blue sky acting as a backdrop for the dazzling colors of autumn. But, alas, not this October. This October was one foggy, soggy dishrag from beginning to end.

Made his job a living nightmare.

Slowly, his gaze traveled over the landscape of the project he'd been hired to do. As a building contractor specializing in the renovation of old houses, Zach was looking for a way to beef up the eroding soil around one of Vermont's many historic landmarks, the McLaughlin House. Sitting up so high on the hill the way it did, the old place needed a retaining wall around much of its perimeter.

As he surveyed the site, water sluiced over his yellow rain hat, and from there the rivulets drizzled down over his slicker and puddled at his feet. Zach passed an icy cold hand over his eyes in order to better stare at the dismal situation.

Just how they were going to pour concrete in this weather was beyond him. *What am I doing out here?* he wondered, longing for the thermos of hot coffee that lay in his rig down the hill a piece. The weather was definitely turning unfriendly.

As if the threatening sky could read his thoughts, lightning, like so many fiery fingers, reached out of the clouds toward him, causing the little hairs at the nape of his neck to come to attention. Then, mere moments later, a great clap of thunder roared across the sky, sounding like a stampeding herd of buffalo.

"Yep," Zach muttered to himself, "it's time to head for shelter." He stood for a moment, peering through the sheets of rain at the old house on the hill and then down at the ground beneath it.

Bad situation.

"Hmm." A suspicious note rumbled in his chest as he leaned forward to get a closer look into the backyard. *The wind must be blowing something fierce, because it almost looks as if...as if...well, as if that little tree behind the house is...moving.*

Zach blinked.

Yes, he was certain now. The soil around that area had begun to crack. Funny. Even the old McLaughlin House looked as if it were beginning to list on the downhill side. He stood there processing this information for a moment before the warning bells went off in his head.

Uh-oh. Landslide!

"Uhh...uhh...uhh...ohhh!" Willing his shock-leaden legs into action, Zach began running back toward his truck. He had to get out of there. He had to get out of there fast!

"O Jesus! O Lord! O Lord Jesus, help me!" The earth beneath his feet began to ooze down the hill. Stumbling, bumbling, fumbling, he dragged his feet through the

sucking, waterlogged mud and headed as if in slow motion to the safety of his truck.

• • •

"Yoo-hoo! Olympia! Where are you, dearie?" Hattie—elderly owner and proprietor of Hattie Hopkins's boarding house—yodeled as she wobbled toward the back of her Victorian home.

Behind the large old country kitchen, Olivia Harmon had been sitting in the sunroom, reading a good novel, and listening to the incessant rain drum on the roof above. She loved to read there, enjoying the view through the large expanse of windows. From her favorite seat she could see Hattie's rose garden, the hillside beyond crowned by the beautiful old McLaughlin house and the lake next to that.

A smile tugged at Olivia's lips at the sound of her darling old landlady's voice. "I'm in the sunroom, Hattie!" Setting aside her book, she stood and folded her afghan.

"No," Hattie warbled, her voice reverberating off the mahogany paneling in the giant hallway. "No, no. She's not in the front room, I looked there."

Olivia's smile blossomed. It seemed everyone knew that Hattie had a hearing problem, with the unfortunate exception of Hattie herself.

"Olympia? Dearie? Where have you run off to?"

"I'm in *here,* Hattie!" Olivia lifted her voice.

"Oh! My stars! *There* you are!" Winded, Hattie made her way with her cane into the large, glass-walled sunroom. "Why didn't you say so?" Wreathed in a mass of smile lines, the old lady's beaming face appeared around the corner. Her gray hair was falling loose from the clip that held it in a bun at the crown of her head. The flyaway wisps, coupled with her bright pink cheeks and two sparkling raisinlike eyes, gave an oddly youthful look to her eighty-plus years. "Olympia, darling girl, you have company."

"I do?" Olivia looked around, puzzled. No one was with Hattie.

"Well now, that's funny." Turning in a circle, Hattie pursed her lips. "She was right here behind me, moments ago."

"Here I am!" Nell's nervous giggle floated into the room before her. "I took a detour to the powder room, to get a cup of water. Hope you don't mind." She held up a small paper cup filled with water. More self-conscious giggling bubbled forth from the depths of Nell's generous body.

"No, of course not, Nell." Olivia stepped forward and gave her friend a light hug. "Come in! Come in and sit down. I was just sitting here, wishing I had someone to visit with." She motioned to a longer couch, away from the window, that could better accommodate two.

"Oh?" Nell twittered. "Well good." She smiled, her birdlike gaze darting here and there and settling nowhere in particular.

Now that she'd accomplished her mission, Hattie slowly worked her way to the door. There, she paused and smiled at the two young women as they took their seats near the glass wall. "It is lovely to see you again, Belle."

Nell colored. "Thank you, Mrs. Hopkins."

"Olympia dear, I'll have Bonnie bring you ladies a bit of tea and some cookies. We can do better than paper cups of water around here."

"Thank you, Hattie," Olivia called after her, sure that there was no way the woman heard.

"Who is Bonnie?" Nell smoothed her wiry auburn hair away from her face and, arching a brow at Olivia, shrugged out of her coat.

"Rahni. You remember her. Hattie's household assistant. From the Middle East? She goes to school at night, to learn English."

"*Rahni!*" Bubbly laughter danced past Nell's lips. "Oh yes, of course."

"So, Nell, what brings you here on this dreary Saturday afternoon?" Olivia studied her friend's face with curiosity. She could sense that Nell was strung as tightly as Scarlett O'Hara's corset.

"Oh, nothing really." Her words rang hollow.

Olivia was skeptical but she remained silent, waiting.

"Actually," Nell confessed, "I had to stop at the pharmacy to pick up a prescription for myself and, since I was in the neighborhood, thought I'd drop by so that we could chat for a few minutes."

"A prescription? Are you all right?" Olivia leaned forward and peered at her friend. *Come to think of it, she does look a little green around the gills.*

"I...guess."

Nell rummaged around in her purse with her free hand. The water in the cup she held in her other hand sloshed about, dampening her skirt until finally she set it down and concentrated on locating her new bottle of pills. Once she found them, she busied herself extracting a letter opener from the mysteries of her voluminous leather bag.

"What are those?" Olivia leaned across the white wicker settee to watch in amazement as her friend and coworker began a vicious assault on the childproof lid with her letter opener.

"These?" While she stabbed and clawed at the top of the stubborn vial of medicine, Nell's rounded shoulders bobbed to and fro as more agitated laughter issued forth. "These are my nerve pills."

"Nerve pills?"

"Yep, for my anxiety," Nell grunted. When the letter opener proved useless, she slipped off a shoe and hammered at the unmoving lid with the heel.

Jaw dropping, Olivia watched Nell's energetic attempts and after a moment could hold back no longer. "Nell, honey, that's a good way to break a shoe."

In spite of Nell's best efforts, the cap wouldn't move, and she eventually threw her hands up in exasperation. "Oh, for pity's sake, if I didn't have a problem before, this…this…*lid* will land me in the nuthouse for sure."

Olivia bit back a smile and took the bottle from her flustered friend. She pushed on the top with the palm of her hand, easily opened it, then handed it back. Nell gave her a grateful smile.

Olivia and Nell had worked at the Vermont Department of Tourism together for at least a half-dozen years now, and they were as close as sisters. Still, Olivia had no idea that someone with such rock-solid faith as Nell had would ever suffer from any kind of anxiety problem. While it was true that Nell continually lapsed into fits of nervous, twittering laughter, for the most part she was as stable as the Rock of Gibraltar. *Salt of the earth, good old Nell.*

As Olivia thoughtfully considered her friend's life, it seemed to her that Nell had very little to be anxious about.

Nell, unlike herself, had a loving husband and two wonderful children to go home to every night. Not to mention a very close relationship with the Lord, a beautiful house complete with the latest decor, three newish cars, and a charming little dog.

Now I, on the other hand—Olivia thought with irony—*should be the one on nerve pills, considering the tragedy I've lived with for the past five years.*

"You're suffering from anxiety?" Olivia adjusted the pillows between them on the settee and leaned toward her friend. She watched Nell study the directions on the label, her warbling giggle braying through her nose as twin spots of crimson stained her plump cheeks.

"Mm-hmm. And panic."

"Panic?"

"Oh, lately, yes. All the time. That's me! Worry, worry, worry. Panic, panic, panic. It seems...well."—thoroughly embarrassed, Nell glanced up at Olivia—"that I have somehow or another, developed something called 'panic-anxiety syndrome.' Ever heard of it?"

"No..."

"Me neither." Snorting, Nell slapped her thigh. "Not until last month anyway."

Outside, a clap of thunder rattled the windows.

"Yiikkkessss!" Pills spilled into Nell's lap and she gripped Olivia's arm, clutching it in a hold that would do the World Wrestling Federation proud. When the sound had rumbled by overhead, she slowly opened her eyes and shot a sheepish glance at her friend. "Sorry." She giggled, released Olivia and, sitting up, found a pill among the ones scattered across her skirt. Quickly tossing it into her mouth, she chased it down with what was left of the water in her cup.

"Oh, Nell. I didn't know you had an anxiety problem! Why didn't you tell me?"

"Ha! Oh, well, I guess because I didn't really have a problem, until about a month or so ago. Plus, it's more than just a little embarrassing, being terrified of everything this way. I just kept hoping it would go away. Silly me!"

"You should have told me."

"And said...what?" Nell's grin was self-deprecating.

7

"Hey, Olivia, guess what? The phone rang and I think I'm going to faint? A customer came in and my heart is pounding a mile a minute and I can't catch my breath?" Rolling her eyes, she slapped her forehead with her open palm. "Hello! Basket case."

"You know, I kind of thought you hadn't exactly been yourself at the office lately."

"I know. That's why I thought I'd better stop by and come clean. It's a relief, really, to confide in you."

"I'm so glad you did. What can I do to help?"

Nell clasped her hands together and lifted her shoulders in a light shrug. "Nothing really. Just pray for me."

"Oh." Olivia couldn't remember the last time she'd prayed. It was high on her list of activities to avoid. "I...I will." Her promise was tentative. She hadn't exactly been on the easiest of terms with God since the accident, but for Nell, she would try to humble herself. Besides, there were one or two other items that she'd thought about bringing to God's attention, but she never seemed to find just the right moment. May as well break the years of ice with a request for Nell.

"Oh, bless you, Livie, hon. I know I'll get a handle on this dumb thing. Eventually. I hope."

Olivia cast a tender look at her dear friend. "I don't think it sounds dumb at all. It sounds kind of scary actually. How and when did this thing start?"

"Well, that's the weird part. It just hit me out of the blue! No reason that I can pinpoint. One minute I was up there singing away in the soprano section of the church choir, and the next minute I was being carried off the stage by the bass and baritone sections." Nell patted her well-rounded hips. "A few tenors pitched in for good measure. It was the single most mortifying moment of my life."

"I can imagine. I wish I'd been there for you." In the last five years, Olivia's church attendance had been sporadic at best.

"Oh, it's okay, hon. The doctor thinks it's simply something I have to work through. He says it's a chemical imbalance in the brain and it can happen to anyone. Sometimes stress brings it on. But not always."

Olivia nodded. "It has been pretty stressful at work, since the management changes. Wow. I hope your thing isn't contagious," she teased, then sobered. "I guess you simply have to keep telling yourself you have nothing to be afraid of and try to believe it."

"That's what I've been chanting over and over in my head. 'Nellie, old girl,' I say, 'get a grip! God is with you! You have nothing to fear.'"

"That's the spirit." Olivia patted Nell on her back. Still, she wondered if Nell's self talk was true.

God hadn't exactly jumped in and fixed anything for her lately.

• • •

It looked as if the earth beneath his truck was ready to give way any second. Grim faced, Zach had the sinking feeling it was too late to reach the driver's-side door. Luckily he'd left his tailgate down, because at this point he surmised his only chance at survival was to reach *anything* solid. Immediately.

As the mud swirled and slid past his heavy feet, Zach slogged toward his pickup, closed his eyes and, taking a deep breath, leapt into the bed of his truck, praying out loud all the while.

"Lord, help me! Get me...through this...alive! I'm...too young...to die." He grunted as he rolled into his toolbox, banging his head and bruising his shoulder. Rattled as he was, Zach had the presence of mind to reach behind him and yank the tailgate closed. Just in time.

He'd no sooner heard the lock click shut than his truck began to move. Zach blinked in disbelief as he watched the scenery go by. At first, the rumbling movement was slow. Then as the earth—and his truck—built momentum, raw terror gripped his throat, making it impossible to scream for help. Before he knew it, his trusty pickup was turning in lazy circles, then faster and faster until it was spinning and careening out of control down the hill. In the back, Zach was being tossed about like a marble inside an empty coffee can.

"Ohhhh, Looorrrddd!" he cried when he could finally catch his breath. *"Thave me, God!"* He lisped over the tongue he'd bitten until it was numb and bleeding. He prayed like a madman that his truck wouldn't roll and, scrambling to his knees, tried to grab his toolbox before it rendered him unconscious.

A quick glance over the side of the bed told Zach that he was now bouncing down the hill at a pretty good clip, heading directly toward an old boarding house that lay at the bottom. *Aw, man.* He stared with morbid fascination at the passing landscape. *Maybe jumping into the back wasn't such a bright idea after all.*

· · ·

"You know," Nell continued as she sipped on the tea that Rahni had brought only moments before, "for some reason, that verse in the Bible about the faith of a mustard seed keeps running through my brain."

"Oh really?" Olivia reached for one of the homemade cookies. "Why is that?"

"I guess I find it comforting that if I have the faith of a mustard seed, which is the least of all the seeds, that maybe I can beat this thing. After all, God promises that with that much faith it's possible to move mountains."

"Then I must not have much faith." Olivia's tone was dry. "I'm sure that if I ever told a mountain to move, it would just lay there and mock me."

"Have you ever tried?" Nell, an ever-perky smile on her face, peered at her friend.

It was amazing to Olivia how Nell could be so chipper, considering what she was going through. "Well, no," Olivia confessed.

"You should try sometime. All you have to do is point at your 'mountain,' whatever that may be for you, and in faith order it to"—Nell pointed dramatically out the window to the hillside beyond and commanded—*"move!"*

"Somehow, I doubt that it's that simple, Nell. For years now, I've been wondering why my prayers went unheard when it came to...John and Lillah and...uh, Nell?" Leaning forward, Olivia peered into her friend's suddenly ashen face. "What is it, honey? You look as if you've seen a ghost."

Mouth gaping, eyes bulging, Nell pointed a shaky finger out the window behind Olivia.

"Ahhbbaa...Ugghhh..." Nell gasped through lips that opened and closed like a dying carp.

"What is it, honey? Are you having a reaction to your pill?"

The fearsome look on Nell's face sent great waves of goose flesh rippling down Olivia's spine. Something awful was happening. Nell couldn't control her speech or her arm! This was simply terrible. She grasped Nell's hand as the woman pointed out the window and appeared to be going into shock.

11

"*Ieesshhh…Gaaaa…Ohhh!!*"

"Nell, do I need to call 911?" Rattled, Olivia groped behind her for the phone on the wicker coffee table and yanked it into her lap. Staring at the buttons on the phone, she frantically tried to remember the numbers.

Dumbly, Nell nodded.

Numbly, Olivia dialed.

"Nine-one-one operator." A nasal voice buzzed into the room mere seconds before a handsome, mud-coated man—looking like a hapless bronc buster on a runaway mustang—rode his bucking pickup through the glass wall and into the sunroom of Hattie Hopkins's boarding house.

2

By the grace of God, the shattered glass, the truck, and the mountain of mud that Zach rode in on slid to a stop just shy of the wicker grouping where Nell and Olivia had—only moments before—sat sipping their tea.

Huddled together, the two women stared in shock at the battered truck, now parked in Hattie's sunroom. Olivia attempted to comfort the shrieking Nell, though she was too stupefied to say much herself at the moment.

"Nine-one-one operator!" The nasal voice continued to buzz into the room. "Police, fire, or medical?"

"Uhh, I...I...uh..." Olivia gazed dazedly at the phone she still held in her hand. "Yes, please."

"Augghh!" Nell sank into her chair and fanned herself with frenzied hands. *"Ohgoodheavens! Ohgoodgrief!"*

A cacophony of indignant and fearful squawks and screeches filled the air as the rest of the boarders came scurrying to see what all the racket was about. First to arrive were Hattie's three oldest boarders, the two elderly Ross sisters—Agnes and Glyniss—and their next-door neighbor on the second floor's west wing, the ancient Colonel Milton Merryweather. Well into their eighties, the sisters wobbled to a stop when they reached the door and stared agog. The

13

Colonel, older by several years than the ladies, stumbled fearlessly into the wreckage.

"Great galloping grenades!" The Colonel's high-pitched tenor filled the room. One too many scrapes in the war had skewed the Colonel's sense of reality, and the old man tended to revert to his military days in times of stress. The retired officer peered through watery blue eyes past his bifocals and into what he perceived to be a war zone. "Someone quick"—agitated, he fell into one of the fits of wheezing that plagued him when he grew excited—"set up a command post!" His shrieks echoed about, once he could breathe again.

Ignoring him, Agnes Ross pushed past the Colonel and planted her hands on her hips. The slighter and more dignified of the two sisters, Agnes had a commanding presence that Olivia knew could be formidable when the situation warranted, as apparently this situation did. Never married, Agnes had been a schoolteacher for many years. To this day, the world was her classroom, and the population at large, her student body.

"What is the meaning of thisss?" She peered accusingly down her pointed nose at Olivia and Nell. Tottering into the room, she cautiously stepped over some of the smaller boulders that had come in with the mud slide. "Whatt on earth have you girls been up to?" Nostrils flaring, she sniffed the air. Her rubbery mouth was pulled so far down at the corners it nearly melded into the folds of her neck.

The swirling wind blew rain sideways into the room through the gaping hole in the wall of windows. Curtains flapped, mud continued to ooze, and Agnes's severe hairdo began to droop under the inclement onslaught. A stop sign that had wedged into the truck's wheel well flapped in the squall.

"Ladies, man your stations!" The Colonel's thin, reedy voice squeaked with exuberance. Wispy gray hair sprouted in all directions from his age-spotted and balding pate. His sagging lips opened and closed rhythmically as he sucked his ill-fitting dentures. Then drawing his bony shoulders back, the old man surveyed the mud-covered truck. "Looks like a suicide mission! Better get down! The bomb may still go off." In slow motion, he hunkered down behind the couch and covered his head with his hands.

"Now, Agnes..." Glyniss, the younger, more easygoing of the two sisters, placated her suspicious sibling as she maneuvered around the cowering Colonel. "Whatever happened, I'm certain it was an accident. Surely the girls couldn't have meant for this to happen." Sidestepping some debris, she beamed at the shaking women. "Isn't that right, girls?"

Glyniss had been widowed for many years, and to stave off the loneliness, she and her sister had moved in with Hattie.

"Ohhh." Nell buried her head in her hands.

"Nine-one-one operator!" Still on the job, the operator shouted, hoping to glean some information that would help her do her job. "Please respond! Police? Fire? Medical?"

"Oh my!" Hattie gasped, as she stepped into the room, clutching Rahni's arm. "When did this happen?" She looked with dismay at her once beautifully appointed sunroom.

Rahni, eyes bulging, muttered something in her native tongue.

"Get down, Hattie!" The Colonel beckoned her over to the relative safety of his position behind the couch. "Suicide mission in progress." To Olivia he shouted, "Radio your commander to send the bomb squad!"

"My commander?" Perplexed, Olivia looked at the phone and frowned. "The bomb squad?"

"Ohhh!" Nell shuddered.

"The *bomb* squad?" The 911 operator was suddenly all business. "What's your location?"

"Hold on a minute please." Covering the mouthpiece with her hand, Olivia looked to the little group for direction. "Before we do anything, shouldn't we check to see if there is anyone in the truck and determine if they need medical attention? I thought I saw someone in the bed of the truck, although"—she squinted at the pile of mud and rocks in the back of the pickup—"I could be mistaken…"

She must be mistaken. Why on earth would any sane person be riding in the back of a truck on a day like today? She must have been imagining things. Besides, from the look of things, nobody was back there now.

"Don't do it!" The Colonel—lost in his time warp— once again tucked his head upon his knobby knees. "The enemy is hoping we will fall for his ploy!" A loud coughing attack exploded from between the old man's legs and for a long, fearsome moment, he lay crouched in silence. Finally, he reared back and glared at Olivia. "What are you waiting for?"

"Holy moly!" Ryan Lowell burst into the sunroom. He'd been conducting a puppy obedience class in his third-floor room, so a half-dozen puppies trotted into the room after him and immediately began to explore the mud mountain.

"Get those hounds off that disgusting pile," Agnes roared. "They'll track mud everywhere!"

"Oh, Aggie." Glyniss snorted. "At this point I hardly think that matters."

Harried voices and hurried footsteps sounded from down the hall.

"What on earth happened in here? We heard the noise clear up on the third floor! Sounded like a...bomb...went off..." A very pregnant Julia Flannigan and her husband, Sean, rounded the corner and arrived on the scene shortly after Ryan. Coming to an abrupt stop, they stood behind him and stared in amazement at the truck.

Julia and Sean, Ryan, Rahni, and Olivia—all in their late twenties or early thirties—constituted the five members of the younger generation of the boarding-house population. Sean and Julia would be moving out as soon as the house they were having built was complete, probably a few weeks after their baby was due in February.

Hattie, the Ross sisters, and the Colonel brought the number in residence to nine. There was nothing Hattie loved more than a bustling household, full of people for which to pray.

"No ma'am." Olivia hastened to reassure the 911 operator. "I don't believe the bomb squad will be necessary at this point. I...well, I guess we will need a policeman." Stretching the cord on the phone to its limits, she picked her way through the mud and peered into the empty cab. "Just a policeman. A driverless truck just slid down the hill behind our house and crashed into the sunroom."

As she proceeded to give the operator details, a muffled groan could be heard from the bed of the truck. Olivia froze. The murmuring, head-scratching crowd that shuffled around the perimeter of the mess went suddenly still. For a moment, everyone stared at one another, wide-eyed, wondering what to do.

Someone was in the back of the truck.

Olivia was the first to regain her faculties. "Hang on just a moment please," she whispered to the operator.

Quickly setting the phone on the floor, she hiked her slim

fitting skirt up to her knees for better mobility and cautiously proceeded up the mud pile toward the rear of the truck. Her pumps sank into the ooze up to her ankles and beyond. As the moans increased, so did her dogged efforts. Someone was trapped back there, under a pile of mud. She had to help.

"Hello? Hello? Can you hear me?" Olivia called.

Muffled grunts and some thumping came from up near the cab. Huffing and puffing, Olivia clawed at the rocks and mud with her bare hands, trying to find the source of the noise. Snapping out of their stupefaction, Ryan and Sean sprang into action, rushing up the slithering mountain to her aid.

"Careful, soldiers!" the Colonel cried, unfolding his bony body and beginning to take command. "Keep your heads low." Arms outstretched, he stumbled toward them.

Finally Olivia, Sean, and Ryan had scraped enough dirt away to dislodge the human form, wedged behind a good-sized toolbox.

Zach, now looking as if he'd been away to an expensive spa and had been dipped from head to toe in a body mask, slowly sat up and blinked gratefully at the angel of mercy who stared at him.

"Hi." He grinned a lopsided grin. Unbeknownst to him, his eyes and teeth sparkled white through the layers of mud that caked his face.

"Hi." Olivia sighed with relief. "Are you all right?"

"Think so." He grunted, rubbing at the tiny, merciless construction crew that jackhammered within his brain. *Where on earth am I?* Zach blinked at Olivia. Had he died and gone to heaven? That couldn't be right. There was no pain in heaven. And right now, he hurt like…well, like the other place. His entire body felt as if he'd gone one too many rounds with a steamroller.

Olivia pointed to the red octagon that flapped in the wind. "Guess you didn't see the stop sign." Her grin told him how happy she was that he was alive.

"Nope."

He studied her lovely features through blurry eyes. Her smile was mesmerizing.

Wow.

Her flaxen, shoulder-length hair lifted and fell with the frigid breezes, framing her face in a silky halo. An errant strand clung to her full, lower lip. He longed to reach up and tug the golden thread free, then cup her heart-shaped face in his hand. Something in her eyes—an inexplicably tender compassion mixed with a minxish twinkle—drew him into their sea blue depths. A roaring in his head prohibited him from further analyzing the connection he suddenly felt with this celestial apparition. If he wasn't dead, sometime he'd have to ask her who she was. Lifting his hand, he reached through the long, long fuzzy tunnel of light toward her face. So beautiful. So...perfect. So...so...sweet.

"Heaven. I'm in heaven..." The lyrics to a long-forgotten song echoed in his brain.

Eyes rolling back in his head, he slumped against the toolbox as the world went black.

• • •

After the paramedics had assured Nell that her palpitations were most likely not the fatal variety, they loaded Zach onto a stretcher and lowered him down the mud pile and over to the floor near the wicker grouping where they could check him over. Huddled into a clump for warmth, the curious group of residents looked on with curiosity.

"How many fingers am I holding up?"

Zach squinted at the paramedic's hand. "Six." He

frowned. No, that wasn't right. He blinked to clear the mud that floated in his eyes. "Three."

"Good." The paramedic nodded as he focused on his watch and, with probing fingers, took Zach's pulse.

"Is he going to be all right?"

Kneeling beside Zach, Olivia cradled his head in her lap and stroked his mud-caked hair in a soothing manner. Her hands were strong and comforting. Though his head felt as if it were caving in, Zach lowered his eyes and gave himself up to her gentle ministrations. She really was an angel.

The paramedic smiled. "Can't be positive, but I think he's in pretty good shape." Turning his attention back to his patient, he looked into Zach's eyes. "What's your name, sir?"

"Zachhh," Zach moaned. Man, his head throbbed. His eyeballs throbbed. Even his hair throbbed. "Zach Thspringer." His tongue was still mangled and swollen.

Nell twittered in disbelief. "Zach?"

"Huh?" Zach grunted.

Leaning forward on her wicker perch, she scrutinized his face. "Zach Springer, it *is* you! Well, I'll be! What are you doing here, scaring the tar out of me?"

Attempting to lift his head, Zach shot her a weak grin. "Oh, hey there, Nell. Just thought I'd crash your...uh"—he gestured at the wicker table, amazingly still set with china—"tea party." He laughed, then regretted it.

As the paramedics worked, one of McLaughlin's men in blue, Police Officer Menkin, arrived on the scene. An air of gruff impatience preceded him as he strode into the room. His protruding brow sported a single fringe of wiry hair that topped both of his piercing eyes. His mouth, a formidable slash that curled down at the corners, lay above a jaw that was as angular as a brick. Occasional growls and grunts from deep inside his throat could be heard as he surveyed the scene with a fearsome expression.

After deducing that Zach was going to make it, he began making notes.

He noted the stop sign that was lodged in the wheel well. He noted the damage to Hattie's property, the pile of mud, the broken windows, the dents in the truck. He noted and sampled the cookies on the tray that Rahni had brought for Nell and Olivia.

After this cursory inspection and culinary testing, he lifted his radio to his lips and mumbled some clipped, explanatory sentences back to headquarters. Then, without ceremony, he flipped open his ticket book and began to furiously scribble. When he'd finished, he tore out a ticket and stuck it on Zach's muddy forehead.

"Next time," he instructed, with something akin to dry humor in his voice, "don't run the stop sign."

Nell giggled, then noting Olivia's frown, whispered, "He's teasing, hon."

Olivia didn't care. This was no laughing matter.

With a nod at Nell, Officer Menkin snagged another of Rahni's freshly baked cookies, allowed a rare grin to crack his stony expression, then ambled out the door.

Olivia stared after Officer Menkin, unable to believe his lack of compassion. Couldn't he see that it was not this poor man's fault? A wave of protectiveness toward this stranger swept over her as she peeled the silly ticket away from his forehead and tossed it on the floor.

Finished with the preliminary checks, the paramedics packed up their equipment, hoisted Zach's stretcher, and carried him to the waiting ambulance. On the way out, they explained to the concerned residents that they were taking him to the hospital. Interested parties could call for an update, but to give them some extra time to travel.

"Several of the roads between here and the hospital have been affected by the mud slide," one paramedic explained. He scratched his head, a puzzled look on his face. "Funny. It wasn't a very big slide." He pointed up the hill to the streets between the McLaughlin House and Hattie's boarding house. "Just straight up behind the house here really."

Olivia exchanged wide-eyed glances with Nell.

"Anyway, it'll take us a little longer to get up to the hospital than usual. Haven't heard anything more on the radio, so hopefully there were no more injuries." As they maneuvered Zach down the porch stairs, the medic smiled at Olivia. "Don't worry about him, ma'am. He's strong. He'll be just fine. He's one lucky guy." He winked.

Olivia's smile was uncertain. She had the distinct impression that the young man was somehow referring to her relationship with this mysterious Zach person. A telltale warmth flooded her cheeks. How silly.

"Thank you," Olivia called, moving down the steps and watching as they loaded Zach into the back of the vehicle. Oblivious to the driving rain and searing wind, she pushed her whipping hair out of her face and waved at Zach. Their eyes connected for a moment, just before he disappeared into the belly of the ambulance.

Nell's voice came from over her shoulder. "Of all people to come crashing into your sunroom!" Her shoulders bounced with her mirth. "I never would have guessed that swamp thing was my neighbor."

"You know him?" Olivia wondered aloud, turning to Nell with interest.

Something about Zach and his disarming grin fascinated her. Attracted her. Olivia hadn't felt such feelings for a long, long time. She'd thought those kinds of emotions had died in the car wreck with her husband and daughter. Although why she should feel such an interest boggled her mind. It wasn't as if he was anything more than a mud-caked concussion to her at this point. Still...there was something there. She had felt it when their gazes had collided a moment ago.

She thought maybe he did too.

"Oh yes," Nell chirped. "Ted and I went to his and AmyBeth's wedding about eight or nine years ago. He's been a neighbor of mine for close to a decade now. In fact—"

Nell nattered on, regaling Olivia with Zach's history, oblivious to the glazed look that had filled her friend's eyes.

So. Olivia sighed. *He's married.*

Ah well.

An annoying curl of jealousy tightened in her stomach for a moment before she dismissed it.

As Nell's voice continued to burble on about heaven only knew what, a decided chill shivered down Olivia's spine. Gracious, it was cold out here. What on earth were they doing standing on the front walk this way?

"Come on, Nellie." Olivia wrapped her arm around her friend. "Let's get out of this weather. I thought I saw Ryan building a fire in the parlor."

Nell gratefully obliged. "Good idea. I'm a bigger wreck than Hattie's sunroom." Her peals of giddy laughter preceded them into the house.

• • •

Much later that evening, as Olivia prepared for bed, her mind wandered back over the events of the day. Sitting at the antique vanity, she stared unseeing into the mirror and brushed her hair. Outside, the rain continued to hammer mercilessly from the sky against the multileveled roof of the old Victorian.

It was nearly midnight, but the excitement of the day had kept her up past her usual bedtime. Undoubtedly, everyone else in the boarding house was asleep by now, or on their way. A soft smile graced Olivia's lips.

She was glad for the heavy flannel of her nightgown tonight. The chill in the air was unmistakable, partly due to the new air-conditioning system installed by the runaway truck. That afternoon, down in the sunroom, Ryan and Sean had done their best to board up the walls and windows damaged by the mud slide. No doubt it would take a crew of landscape experts the better part of the summer to put Hattie's rose gardens back into any semblance of order. But the window and wall replacement would have to begin immediately.

Odd, Olivia mused as she stared at her reflection, how that mountain had come slithering down the hill just as Nell had commanded it to move. Coincidence? Olivia didn't know, but it was strange nevertheless. Very strange.

Should she take God up on his promise about faith? If she had the faith of a mustard seed, could she pull herself out of this five-year-old funk and make something of her life? That she couldn't answer. She simply knew that to her what had happened today seemed to be some kind of sign.

Inhaling deeply, Olivia held her breath for a moment, then, running her fingertips over the stiff bristles of her hairbrush, she sighed. She needed to get her house in order with God.

It would be five years in just a few days.

Five years since she'd kissed her daughter's soft, smooth, baby-fat cheek. Five long years since she'd been held by a man who had loved her without reservation. This was always such a hard time of year for her. Morbid trepidation filled the pit of her stomach as the mere thought of John and Lillah's deaths flitted through her mind. Could she possibly let go of her bitterness?

She knew it was time. Time to get on with her life. Time to come out of her self-imposed solitude and move into the light. She'd held God at bay for far too long, and she knew it.

But the pain...How could she deal with the pain? Tears threatened as she envisioned pouring her heart out to the Lord. It had been so much easier to simply turn off emotionally. To stay away from anything that made her feel. And if there was one thing she knew beyond a shadow of a doubt, it was that her relationship with God evoked powerful feelings.

Feelings of anger. Hurt. Betrayal.

Sorrow.

A sorrow so deep, she feared if she ever really allowed herself to feel it all, she'd simply bleed to death from the wounds in her heart.

Olivia pulled open the top drawer of her mahogany vanity and dropped her hairbrush inside. The golden glow from the table lamp died as she switched it off and made her way toward her bed through the moonlight that filtered through her glass veranda doors. There, she snapped on her bedside lamp and, pulling back her coverlet, climbed in and waited for her body warmth to penetrate the down.

On her nightstand, John and Lillah, ever young, smiled at her from a silver frame John had given her for their anniversary. As she did every night, she blew them a kiss and settled back against a generous stack of fluffy bed pillows.

Her eyes swept her room slowly, and she allowed her mind to drift. Her small suite was cheerfully covered in an old-fashioned paper with a wandering design of ribbons and English herb garden flora. Gauzy curtains ran from floor to ceiling, and Olivia had always loved the way they billowed in the spring breezes.

The furniture was a muddled cornucopia of mahogany antiques passed down through the many Hopkins generations. Highboy dressers, assorted chests of drawers, trunks, and delicate chairs and tables were squeezed into every nook and cranny. Her bed, a squarish canopy, was draped with the same gauzy beige fabric that adorned the many windows.

Gilt frames on the walls surrounded pictures of what had to be Hattie's ancestors. And the floor—a beautiful hardwood—was scattered liberally with Turkish area rugs of varied colors.

Olivia cherished her living quarters.

After the accident, feeling lost and lonely and plagued by depression, she'd moved into Hattie's boarding house in order to get what was left of her life back together. John's untimely death had left her saddled with staggering bills, and Hattie's place had been all she could afford at first.

Besides, Hattie and the sympathetic elderly boarders had been just the soothing balm her battered heart had needed, especially considering members of her own fractured family were scattered all over the country. A smattering of long-lost cousins and various and sundry aunts and uncles that she had lost touch with were all Olivia really had left.

She'd lived here a long time, she thought with a rueful smile. About four years longer than she'd intended.

Ah well.

She'd needed the time to recover. And, for the most part, she had. She'd even managed to find a reasonable amount of happiness with Hattie and the others.

However, she still suffered from a feeling that God had abandoned her. For the past five years, Olivia had been wondering why God had left her on this planet. Deep down in her heart, she knew John would not be pleased to see how she had been hiding away from reality.

And, to tell the truth, lately she'd been feeling restless. Unfortunately, she had no idea what God's plan was for her life. Nothing was clear. Oh, she'd done a little scattered praying, but with no success. Once in a rare while, she'd even attempted to make herself available, but God was not caring to use her, it seemed. Without a husband and child, Olivia felt about as useless as a refrigerator in an igloo. It was hard not to think that she would have been better off in the car with John and Lillah. At least then she wouldn't have to deal with the hollowness in her heart.

Her lips puffed with her heartfelt sigh. Oh, well. She was here, and there was nothing she could do about it. It was time to leave her pity party and get back into the swing of things.

But how?

Perhaps she needed to find a way to help someone in need, she thought. Hmm. Yes, that was a good idea. Perhaps that would get her mind off herself.

Reaching over, Olivia switched off her bedside lamp and snuggled down beneath her comforter. Her eyes were heavy with fatigue. However, as tired as she was, every time she closed her eyes a mud-coated man with a most engaging grin popped into her mind.

Another pang of jealousy suddenly, and most surprisingly, lodged in her throat. He'd lived through his accident, she thought in irritation. His wife was no doubt at home right now, thanking God for saving her man from disaster.

Olivia went rigid at the path her thoughts had taken.

Oh, good heavens!

How could she begrudge some poor woman the life of her husband? Olivia squirmed under her covers. She was lower than low. It was becoming increasingly clear that she had some major work to do within herself before she would ever be able to function as a normal woman again. Maybe it was finally time to pray.

Closing her eyes tightly, Olivia made the first tentative stab at communicating with God in a very long while. So long in fact, she wondered if he even remembered who she was.

"Hello, God…" Silently, she began to pray, her lips moving against the satin edge of her blanket, her eyes prickling with the beginnings of tears. "It's me. Olivia. Olivia Harmon?" She hesitated for a beat, waiting. For what, she didn't know.

"Uh…" Her uncertainty caused her hands to tremble. "I…uh…don't really know what to say to you anymore. I guess I need to ask you to forgive me. Or maybe I need to forgive you. Or maybe I need to forgive myself." Clutching the satin hem of her blanket, she murmured brokenly into the soft fabric. "Or John…I don't know."

Again, she lay silent for a moment, waiting and listening and feeling vaguely foolish. Surely she'd been out of touch for so long, God had no use for her limp attempt at prayer. A giant lump of remorse filled her throat. Nevertheless, Olivia forged ahead, knowing she owed it to Nell, at the very least. Touching her tongue to her lips, she rushed on before she lost her nerve.

"So…ah…please…oh, God. I've been away for so long. I've been so self-absorbed. So hurt and angry. I'm…I'm sorry." She sniffed. "Anyway, I promised Nell I'd speak to you about her anxiety, so here goes. Please, help Nell get well."

Once more, she paused and listened. Nothing. Straining, she attempted to listen harder.

"This is so strange. Are you there? Can you hear me? Do you care? Hello, God."

Her mind drifted for a moment. Hattie knew how to pray. Hattie was always praying. And it seemed to a lot of people that Hattie's prayers were almost always answered. Why? Olivia wondered. What did Hattie know that she didn't when it came to talking to God? Maybe she should ask Hattie for some advice on this prayer thing. With the blanket, she mopped at the tears that had pooled into the corners of her eyes. Slowly, her thoughts flitted to Zach.

"Oh, and, God, I wanted to apologize for my appalling jealousy. Zach's wife is a lucky woman. I'm sorry to begrudge her her good fortune. You know," she continued, more to John's shadowy photo than to anyone, "I don't really ever want to get married again, so why do I feel so upset when I see other people happy?"

Olivia listened to the night sounds for a long while, hoping against hope for some answer to her prayer. But there was none. Unless she counted the haunting hoot of an owl from the woods behind the house.

"Well, anyway, I'm sorry. It's just that this nice man reminds me so much of what I've lost." Her voice cracked with emotion, but she forced herself to continue, "So, please, uh, God, shower this man with special blessings. Amen."

The silence was deafening.

In the morning, she decided as she punched her pillow into shape, she would consult Hattie about her prayer requests. If God wasn't going to listen to her, surely he would listen to Hattie.

God always listened to Hattie.

3

You?" Fingers fluttering in accusation, the Colonel fell into a most debilitating wheezing spell. After honking and shouting at the ceiling like a Canada goose headed south, he eventually recovered. Then, straightening his stooped shoulders, he poked a finger into the chest of the young man who stood before him on the porch.

"Have you got papers? Special clearance? After the incident here yesterday, I'm afraid I can't let you in without the proper paperwork!" The Colonel's concerns echoed their way into the dining room from the grand mahogany-and-marble foyer.

"Special clearance? I...well, no. But I do have a contractor's license, if you'd like to see that..."

From where she sat at the breakfast table, Olivia cocked her head toward the muffled ramblings and tried to remember where she'd heard that vaguely familiar baritone before.

"You wait here, while I get my glasses." Using the door as leverage, the Colonel launched himself into the hall.

"Okay. I'll...uh...I guess I'll just wait here—" the visitor called just before the door crashed shut in his face.

Hearing the new voice, one of Ryan's pupils charged out from under the dining table to the front door. Excited beyond control, the puppy barked, jumped, wiggled, wagged, squealed, cowered, and then promptly created a puddle of welcome in the middle of the magnificent marble entry.

"Copper!" Ryan bellowed, tossing his napkin to his plate and bounding after his puppy. Ryan was in the process of obedience training a group of German shepherd puppies for the McLaughlin police force. "Oh, Copper." He shook his head upon spying the golden puddle on the foyer floor. "Bad, Copper!" He growled, making eye contact with the cowering puppy. "Grrrr, BAD, dog, rrrr."

Then, flinging open the front door, he pointed at the rolling lawn beyond the porch steps. "Okay, you. You've done quite enough damage here, buddy. You need to un-derstand who's the boss." Ryan pointed dramatically at the lawn beyond. "Get out of here and...go whiz!"

"I...I beg your pardon?" Zach's startled gaze shot to Ryan, then over his shoulder to the lawn, then dubiously back to Ryan.

Surprised, Ryan blinked at Zach, who stood just behind the door. "Oh no, no!" His surprised laughter filled the air as he threw back his head. "Not *you*. No, no. That's dog lingo. We're housebreaking."

"Oh sure. Housebreaking." Zach nodded and grinned, understanding. "I learned a little about that yesterday," he quipped, referring to the number he'd done on the sun-room. "Zach Springer." Stepping into the foyer, he held out his hand.

"Yes, we met yesterday, though I doubt you'd remember. Ryan Lowell." Reaching forward, he grasped Zach's hand and gave it a firm shake. "Glad to see you up and around so soon."

"Glad to be up at all."

"I hear that. You must have had a whole mess of guardian angels steering that rig for you yesterday."

"Yep." Zach gingerly fingered the bandage on his head. "It would have been nice if one of 'em would have held the tool chest down. But for the most part, I can't complain."

Ryan laughed, then remembered his dog. Peering up at them from the floor, Copper covered his snout with his paws, his tail thumping pathetically on the marble tiles behind him. Ryan sighed.

"Excuse us." One hand on the puppy's collar and the other on his behind, Ryan directed Copper past Zach, through the door, and to the front yard beyond.

The Colonel, his bandy-legged gait carrying him as fast as was possible, returned to the foyer. Donning his specs, he peered up at Zach, who now stood just inside the door.

"Okay, son, let's see those papers of yours. And no funny business." He squinted through his bottle-bottom lenses at Zach. Flecks of spittle flew, and the clicking of his ill-fitting dentures picked up in tempo. "I don't want to have to hurt you."

Calmly sipping her coffee at the breakfast table, Hattie looked up from the editorial page of the morning paper. "Is someone at the door?"

The Colonel's excited investigation filtered into the dining room, capturing everyone's attention. With a frown, Hattie pushed back her chair and, clutching her cane, made her way to the foyer to check on him and whoever had come to call.

"Stand back, Hattie," the Colonel instructed upon her arrival. "It's the suicide bomber, returning to the scene of the crime." Grabbing an umbrella out of the stand, the Colonel let it balloon open, then held it out to shield Hattie from probable nuclear fallout.

Hattie peeked out from under the umbrella. "Why, Jack Spangler!"

Perplexed, Zach lightly scratched his temple and looked over his shoulder. *Jack?* Who was Jack?

"What a welcome surprise! Come in, dearie, come in! Look out for this wet spot here on the floor." Hattie's brows knit in consternation. "Seems we have a leak."

Olivia's cereal spoon froze halfway to her mouth as Hattie's voice drifted through the rooms. *Jack Spangler?* Hmm. That name. That voice.

Her pulse quickened.

What was Zach Springer doing here so early on a Monday morning? And what, in heaven's name, was he doing out of the hospital, for that matter? Only yesterday, they'd carted him out of here on a stretcher, and now here he was back already? Setting her spoon in her dish, Olivia unconsciously straightened her clothing, smoothed her hair, and dabbed at her lips with her linen napkin.

"Come in, dear boy." Hattie thumped with her cane from the foyer into the enormous dining room, tugging her visitor behind her. "Join us for breakfast. Nothing fancy, just some oatmeal and toast and scones with a little clotted cream and jam. They'll be fresh from the oven in a moment. Homemade, mind you. Bonnie makes the best pastries, bless her heart."

The Colonel flapped after them, wielding his umbrella like a semiautomatic weapon and fuming under his breath about fraternizing with the enemy. The boarding-house breakfast club glanced up from their morning meal and various reading materials to see who had come to call this early Monday morning.

Delicious aromas of recently baked bread and fresh-ground coffee filled the air. The old room had a warm, bright, homey ambiance that welcomed all who entered. An ornate, hand-painted chandelier of day lilies on rose-glass dominated the middle of the room and presided over the long mahogany table and numerous chairs like a queen over her subjects. Against the wall nearest the turret windows—through which Ryan could be seen out on the lawn, lavishing praise on Copper for finally making a proper deposit on a bush—stood a magnificent china cabinet, overflowing with cups and saucers, goblets and glassware, and all nature of bric-a-brac. And Oriental rugs of all sizes and patterns adorned the gleaming hardwood floor.

Beneath the extravagantly carved fireplace mantel, a fire crackled merrily, warding off the autumn chill and giving the room a cheerful feel. That morning, all of the boarding-house residents were in attendance for breakfast.

"Everyone's in here." Hattie tugged Zach into the dining room.

Spoon dangling from her fingertips, Olivia lifted her lashes and stared at Zach as he ambled into the room, filling it with his easygoing, yet somehow commanding, presence. *Oh my.* Her heart shifted gears and began to race.

This was the infamous Zach Springer?

This Mel Gibson look-alike who'd inadvertently demolished the sunroom in a matter of seconds? This was the man whose muddied and bloodied head she'd cradled in her lap less than twenty-four hours ago? The man whose rakish grin was, at the moment, making her heart leap and whirl like Dorothy Hamill at the Ice Capades?

The man who was married to a very—no, make that extremely—lucky woman named AmyBeth?

Goodness, she mused, mentally slapping her hands and reining in her wayward pulse. He cleaned up nicely.

"Come along," Hattie chirped, nudging him farther into the massive room. With her cane Hattie pointed, making a hasty round of introductions. "You must remember everyone from yesterday?" She eyed the bandage on Zach's head and smiled. "Oh, hoo-hoo! Maybe not. Don't feel bad. We all certainly remember you!" Aiming her cane at Julia and Sean, she announced, "This is Don and Beulah, our newlyweds. They are expecting a baby in a few short months. Kids, this is Jack."

Reaching forward, Zach extended his hand. "Zzzach," he enunciated, gently correcting his hostess's mistake.

Sean grinned in understanding. "Sean and Julia."

Hattie continued. "And you met Brian at the door. He trains dogs from the Colombian rain forest."

"Ryan is a canine behaviorist." Sean winked.

"Ah."

With a swing of her walking stick, Hattie indicated the Ross sisters, whom she'd known all her life. "And you remember Miss Glyniss and Miss Agnes Ross?"

"Of course." He bowed slightly.

Glyniss, taller, plumper, and most obviously—by her clashing clothing choices—less concerned about style than her sister, preened under his charming gaze.

"And the Colonel."

"Yes...ma'am." Zach's smile was wary.

The Colonel squinted in suspicion at him.

"And last but not least, Olympia Hormone."

A blush of mortification stained Olivia's cheeks crimson. "*Harmon*. Olivia *Harmon!*"

Good grief. She was going to have to stop acting like such an infatuated schoolgirl if it was obvious even to Hattie how her hormones were suddenly running away with her this morning. Picking up her spoon, she forced herself to shovel some oatmeal into her mouth.

"Bonnie is in the kitchen preparing some more scones at this very minute. Of course you'll stay for one." Hattie patted Zach on the steely biceps that bulged through his work shirt.

"I...uh..." Zach's glance around the table told Olivia that he hadn't planned on staying for breakfast.

"Rahni's scones are the best," Julia said. A look of rapture transformed her face as Rahni and her steaming tray entered the room.

"She's eating for ten." Sean teased his wife with a tender pat on her well-rounded middle.

Rolling her eyes, Julia punched her husband on the arm in a playful manner, then helped herself to a scone.

While this happy banter was going on all around her, Olivia doggedly dealt with the oatmeal in her bowl and donned what she hoped was a sophisticated—in spite of the vicious way she was attacking her meal—air of indifference. After all, Zach Springer was no big deal. He was just some exceedingly charismatic, unbelievably handsome—and very married—guy who crashed through the wall and practically landed in her lap. What was so unusual about that?

"I'm not interrupting?" An engaging grin played at the corners of Zach's mouth.

Everyone pooh-poohed this idea, the Colonel excepted.

Olivia gave her head a tiny shake and forced herself to keep chewing. "No no, you're not interrupting." Gamely, she stuffed half a piece of toast into her already full mouth. She chanced a peek in his direction and then quickly averted her eyes.

Okay.

It would be impossible for any woman with even a barely discernible pulse not to notice the way his still-damp-from-the-shower hair curled in such an appealing manner at the back of his neck. The way his mouth quirked at the corners when that easy grin spread across his handsome face. The way his lashes drooped, hooding his gaze as he shot Olivia an appreciative glance of recognition.

Even the Ross sisters were gaping.

The Colonel, on the other hand, took the seat opposite Zach and stared hard at him through watery, ice blue eyes. He dared not even to blink, lest he miss some subtly subversive activity.

Olivia's eyes traveled from Zach to the Colonel and back to Zach. Though Zach had an endearing, boyish countenance, she judged him to be in his mid to late thirties. There was a quiet maturity behind that minxish grin of his.

"I hate to just drop in unannounced," Zach said.

Agnes snorted. "Should have thought of that yesterday."

Zach threw back his head and let his easy laughter flow.

"Agnes!" Glyniss gasped, then tossed Zach an apologetic—yet coquettish—look. "How's your head today, honey?"

Gesturing to the white bandage taped to his forehead just below his hairline, Zach lifted and dropped his shoulders. "I have a hard head, Miss Ross. My truck now, that's another story."

Glyniss clucked in sympathy. "Oh, dear, whatever will you do?" She motioned for him to take the empty seat between her and Olivia. "And please, sweetie, call me Glyniss."

Olivia felt her heart stop, shift gears, and begin beating in reverse as he lowered his body into the seat next to hers and favored her with another charm-filled grin. She could feel the warmth radiating from his body, where his thigh rested ever so lightly against hers.

Grabbing a piping-hot scone off the tray that Rahni offered, Olivia broke it in half and poked a large chunk into her mouth. By the time she realized what she had done, it was too late. Her eyes began to water as the scalding bread seared her tongue and blistered the roof of her mouth. There was no way she could gracefully rid herself of the fiery lump. She darted a dismayed glance at Zach and, blinking madly, grabbed her mug and gulped. Unfortunately, Rahni had just made the rounds with the steaming coffeepot.

"Oh, don't worry, Miss Glyniss, soon I'll have a new truck—"

"Ohhh." Exhaling, Olivia was sure that flames must be shooting past her lips. "Ahh haaa…"

"—uh, yeah, it's a lucky thing for me," Zach continued, responding to Glyniss but returning Olivia's dewy-eyed smile, "I have really good insurance, so I should have my own rig again in a matter of days."

"Ooo, ahh," Olivia breathed, and dabbed at her streaming eyes.

"Yeah, that will be nice. In the meantime, I'm using a rental—"

"Ohhhh, haaa." Her tongue felt as if it had been used as a razor strop and then sandblasted to perfection. She knew she must sound like a blithering idiot, but was in too much pain to explain.

Zach favored her with a warm smile. "Yep, should be interesting."

"Ahh, ahh, ahh." Her answering smile was weak. Fumbling for her water glass, she grabbed her spoon, fished out an ice cube, and stuffed it between her lips. She sighed with relief.

Beady-eyed, Agnes zeroed in on Zach with a raised brow. "What I want to know is, just what do you plan to do about the sunroom, young man? The draft alone is enough to freeze me up tighter than the Tin Man. I can barely talk, my teeth are chattering so," she harrumphed.

"Praise be to God." This from Glyniss.

"Actually—" Zach began, dragging his gaze from Olivia, then training his attention over toward the head of the table where Hattie sat straining to catch snippets of the conversation. "That's the reason I'm here. I'd like to set up a schedule to begin rebuilding the sunroom. I am a contractor, after all. If that's okay…"

Hattie beamed, interpreting to the best of her abilities. "Why, certainly dear, you may come over next Sunday and bring someone. Anytime, my door is always open. And these days, the windows too!" Sapphire blue eyes twinkling, her laughter yodeled up and down the scales.

Obviously perplexed at her response, Zach's smile was tentative. "Uh, I usually don't work on Sunday, ma'am."

"Someday is fine, sweetheart. But just keep in mind, one of these days is none of these days."

"Ahhh…" Zach looked from face to friendly face around the table, clearly looking for a translator.

Leaning toward Zach, Olivia swallowed several times, blotted her lips, and injected what she hoped was a mature, nay cultured, note into her voice. Unfortunately, her burned and frozen tongue had other ideas.

"You're going to have to shpeak up. Hattie is quite hard of hearing, unlesh you pretty mush yell."

She felt her cheeks tingle and grow warm as his twinkling brown gaze focused on her lips. Curiosity tugged at his brow. *Gracious,* she thought, battling a wave of hysterical laughter, it sounded as if she'd spiked her orange juice. It was a good thing this guy was married and she didn't have to worry about making any kind of long-term impression on him.

Ever charming, Zach nodded in understanding. "Oh. Thank you. I was beginning to think it was me." Pushing his chair back, Zach winked at Olivia, then made his way to the head of the table where Hattie was sitting.

And so, after a rousing conversation, complete with hand gestures, pantomime, and dozens of misunderstandings on both parts, it was agreed that Zach would begin work on repairing the sunroom right away.

"I hope you aren't planning on charging this woman any money for your dubious services!" The Colonel gesticulated wildly in Hattie's direction. "I smell a plot! I know what you're up to! First of all, you come crashing into her house, and then you rob her blind to fix the damage!" He paused to wheeze for a moment. "I'll have you know I was not born yesterday. I've seen *20/20* and *thirtysomething* and *60...*" the Colonel paused and reflected.

"Hattie, what's that thing we watch on Sunday? *Sixty...* something or other..."

Hattie's smile was sanguine.

The Colonel grunted. "No matter. Point is, we watch all those investigative shows. Not all of us with snow on the roof are gullible to you crooks!" He shook a gnarled finger in Zach's direction. "I've had the same dollar bill in my pocket for over a month now, and it's because I'm hip to flimflammers like you!"

Olivia winced.

A smile threatened Zach's lips, so he pulled them between his teeth for a moment before speaking. "No sir, I have no plan to charge a single penny for my services. Like I said, I have comprehensive insurance coverage. Everything will be fine. No need to worry." This comment, he directed to Hattie.

"No, dearie. No hurry. You just do things as you have time."

The Colonel, only semi-placated, emitted some skeptical sounds.

Olivia pushed back her bowl and fussed with her cuticles as she listened to Zach go over his plans.

Miraculously, he told them, damage to the McLaughlin House property, up on the hill, had been minimal from the mud slide. Zach explained how his crew would have to spend the next month or so building a retaining wall behind the historic home before they could shore up the foundation and begin the interior restoration anyway, so the timing was perfect. He and his business partner, Mike, would put Hattie's sunroom back to rights, and by then the McLaughlin House would be ready for his attentions.

After Zach had made the preliminary arrangements and shaken hands with Hattie, he ambled back over to where Olivia was seated. Leaning casually on the back of the chair he'd been using, he bent forward and favored her—and Miss Glyniss—with his heart-stopping, pearly-toothed grin.

"I never had a chance to thank you for taking such good care of me yesterday." His low murmur, resonating in that velvety voice, had Olivia's insides suddenly in a dither.

"Oh, pshaw!" Miss Glyniss twittered. "Don't be silly, honey. I didn't do anything any other compassionate human being wouldn't have done in the same emergency."

Agnes snorted.

Taken aback, Zach blinked, then turning, smiled at Olivia. "Thank you, too, Ms. Harmon."

"Call me Olivia," she suggested, relieved that her tongue was back in working order. A pleasing warmth filled her from head to toe.

"Olivia it is then."

Ah. Her name was a melody on his lips.

Olivia sighed, then frowned. What a gooberball she was. The man was *married,* for crying out loud. It was becoming increasingly obvious that she needed Hattie to

41

help her begin a fresh prayer life. Immediately, if not sooner.

After pushing away from the back of the chair, Zach bid everyone farewell, with a promise to be back a little later that morning to begin taking some measurements, making supply lists, and unloading the tools he'd need in the weeks to come.

Olivia bit back the giddy feelings of anticipation that she would have allowed to surface had he been single. With another heavy sigh, she watched him leave.

AmyBeth was a lucky woman indeed.

• • •

"Hattie?"

"Yes, my dear heart?" Hattie's smiling eyes greeted Olivia as the younger woman entered the parlor. Putting her needlepoint aside, she patted the cushion on the delicate settee and invited Olivia to sit for a spell.

Olivia moved over to—and perched upon—the delicate, springy, buttoned-and-tufted settee that her landlady indicated. From the smell of dried lilacs and the lemon furniture polish and the way the morning sunlight filtered through the voluminous lace curtains, to the porcelain knickknacks and musty old books and most especially the elderly woman who smiled so brightly at her now, Olivia felt a peace come over her. A peace she hadn't felt in years.

The breakfast dishes had been cleared away and the dining room put back to rights. It was nearly 8 A.M., and Olivia would need to leave for work shortly.

But first, she wanted to have that little chat with Hattie on the subject of prayer.

"What is it, dearie?" Hattie queried, once Olivia had settled into her seat.

"Hattie, I wanted to ask your advice on prayer." She raised her voice to a near shout so that the older woman could comprehend. "I think I'm still having some problems getting over John and Lillah."

"Ah yes." Hattie sighed and clasped her hands to her bosom. "What is it you need to know, dear one?"

"That's just it, Hattie. I don't really know."

Hattie smiled and nodded, encouraging her to continue.

Unsure of exactly how much was getting through to Hattie, Olivia plunged ahead. "I think I need to get back on the right track with God, but I'm not sure exactly how. I feel so useless most of the time, without my family. Not," she hastily assured Hattie, "that I want another family. No no. No one could ever replace John or Lillah, I understand that."

Not even someone as wonderful as a guy like AmyBeth Springer's husband. Not that Olivia even knew any available men. But still, the idea of remarriage held no appeal.

Eyes bright with empathy, Hattie nodded.

"And since this month will mark five years since the accident, I guess it's time I stop feeling sorry for myself and make some changes. Especially concerning my relationship with God."

"It's not the outlook, but the uplook that counts," Hattie quoted sagely.

Olivia nodded. "Yes! Exactly. That's why I need...I want to learn how to pray so that my prayers will be answered. Like you do. I know I must be doing something wrong. I...I don't feel like he hears me at all."

Adjusting her spectacles, Hattie peered at Olivia, her mouth drawn into a contemplative bow as she did her best to read Olivia's lips.

"I feel like I've been stumbling in the dark for the last five years. I'm tired of lying around and feeling sorry for myself, Hattie." Seeing the quizzical look on the older woman's face, she lifted her voice. It was so easy to forget that Hattie didn't always catch everything she said.

"Surely," she emphasized, "there must be more to life than grief. There must be *some way* for me to contribute to society."

"Certainly there is. Child, the best place to find a helping hand is at the end of your own arm, I always say!"

The older woman's rather muddled words of support suffused Olivia with a wonderful warmth. "Hattie," she enunciated carefully, "would you mind praying for me? I know that God listens to you."

"He listens to you too, child, even when it doesn't seem that way at all. Nevertheless, I should be pleased to speak to him during my morning devotions on your behalf. Now then. Where would you like me to begin?"

Perplexed, Olivia's eyes glazed over as she thought. "Well, I don't know. Life is so complicated. Sometimes," she mumbled under her breath, "I wish I could simply go back to being a child again."

"Mmm," Hattie murmured, making mental notes for her prayer. *You're wishing for a child again.* She mouthed these words, searing the wishes into her mind for future reference.

Focused inwardly, Olivia continued to gather wool aloud, forgetting her audience. "Life would be so much more uncomplicated then."

You're wanting a complimenting man. Hattie mouthed again, somewhat confused by this unusual request.

"I've been thinking I should volunteer."

"I see you are sincere, yes."

"Maybe I could do some knitting of sweaters for the poor now and then. Of course I'd have to learn to knit…"

Baby-sitting in the ghetto for poor children? Hmm...that's quite brave.

"Perhaps I could read to the elderly."

Get them to bed early...

"Or, I don't know—" Olivia continued, training her glassy-eyed stare out the window to the brilliant oranges and golds of the autumn trees. The possibilities were endless really. Why hadn't she thought of this volunteer thing before? Perhaps she was only now emotionally ready to come out of her cocoon. It felt wonderful, she thought, as a seed of hope began to germinate within her breast. To be needed again. How exhilarating! "Maybe I could cook for the hungry..."

*Why, of course you'd want to look for a doggy...*Hattie mused under her breath. *Hmm. Surely Brian could give you some advice on puppies for children.*

"...or minister to the sick."

You want it to happen quick.

"I know there must be some little needs out there that I can attend to."

Little ones to be a friend to...Hmm, yes...yes.

Snapping herself out of her self-induced reverie, Olivia smiled at Hattie. "Well, I'm sure you don't need to be told how to pray. I trust you to say all the perfect things to God!"

A tender smile pushed at Hattie's paper-thin, time-weathered cheeks. "Well, luckily for us, though the askin' may not be perfect"—her eyes rose reverently to the ceiling above—"the listenin' is."

Olivia felt relief wash over her in a nearly palpable way. "Thank you, Hattie." Leaning forward, she kissed Hattie's delicate cheek.

"You're welcome, Olympia, dear. You'd best run along.

You don't want to be late to work. I shall begin on your requests to the Lord straightaway."

Heaving a sigh, Olivia stood and, with a bounce in her step, strode purposefully toward the door. Everything would be all right. Hattie was praying for her.

• • •

As she promised, Hattie bowed her head after Olivia had left for work, her brows knit in concentration.

"Oh, Lord Jesus, Olympia is seeking your will. And, Lord, since none of us really knows exactly what your will is for Olympia's life, she would like me to offer you a few suggestions." Lifting and dropping a tiny shoulder, the old lady began to recount the list for God.

"Well, Lord, it would seem that Olympia is ready to try her hand at family life again. Right away, if possible. Though," she hastily amended, "she wants you to know that no one can take the place of her precious Ron and Sheila. So if you could see your way clear to send her a man, Lord. A"—Hattie cleared her throat—"*complimenting* one. Perhaps she needs reassurance..."

Hattie sniffed.

"Although, to my mind, too many compliments a swelled head make, but who am I? I'll simply keep my nose out of it. Besides, Olympia could certainly use the moral support.

"Let's see. A complimenting man...Oh, and a few poor children from the ghetto to baby-sit, Lord. She would like to have them stay with her—which would be safest to my way of thinking—so that she can be a friend to them and put them to bed early and so forth. This would be fine with me, Lord, for as you know, we have the space here in the house. Poor children would be more than welcome. And,

Lord, they will be needing a puppy, so if you could see your way clear to handle that little detail, I'd be much obliged.

"Well, Lord..." Hattie ticked her mental list off one last time on her fingers. "I think that should do it for Olympia. I knew that if you and I kept working together, we'd get her back in the saddle. Hoo-hee-hee!" Her laughter warbled, as she handed this burden to her heavenly Father.

"Now, to change the subject, thank you also for protecting that nice Jack Spangler from real harm on his way down the hill yesterday. I like him, Lord. Seems like a sweet fellow. Kind of...a complimentary guy, too, don't you think?" Hattie chuckled easily, as she often did when she and God whispered together. "He made quite a fuss over the scones and coffee.

"Well, Lord, my most high and precious dearie, I thank you for taking care to hear these simple requests today. And, Lord, in case I haven't mentioned it yet today, I love you. Amen."

4

*O*hmystars!"
Olivia jumped on the brakes of her compact car and clutched at her thundering heart. She'd nearly run someone over, and she wasn't even out of the driveway yet. Rolling down her window, she poked her head out and came face to face with Zach Springer's wide grin.

"Oh! Hello there. I thought you'd gone back to…ah…" Olivia struggled to regain her composure. "Get some tools and such."

Hand dangling, Zach draped a casual arm on the roof of her car and leaned forward. "No no. Not yet. Nah," he lifted his thumb, loosely pointing, "I was just looking in the backyard. I'm gonna need some earthmoving equipment before I can even get close to the house. And this weather"—he squinted up at the rain-laden clouds—"is certainly not helping matters."

"It's pretty bad back there, huh?"

He lifted his hand in a kind of shrug. "Worse than I originally thought, but doable."

"You're lucky to be alive."

"Somebody up there likes me." Zach's grin was infectious.

"How are you feeling?"

"Not much like working, to be honest."

"I'm sure. You should probably take it easy for a few days."

"I plan to. Actually, today I was just going to do some measuring and ordering. I won't be doing any real work till the end of the week. My partner, Mike, will be giving me a hand, so that will make life easier."

"That's good."

"Yeah." A lazy grin stole across his face. "Say, listen. I'm glad I caught you. I wanted to take a moment to thank you again for calling 911 and digging me out of my rig yesterday. I owe you some new clothes and a pair of shoes."

"Don't be silly. Those were old shoes. And the outfit was washable."

"Well, anyway, I really appreciate your presence of mind."

"Any time."

They smiled at each other until the moment grew awkward. Olivia's gaze drifted to her hands as they lay in her lap. Tugging at her skirt, she wished she'd bothered to buy a new pair of pantyhose last time she'd been at the store. These ones had a wide run from knee to ankle. He probably thought she was a real slob. No doubt his wife was one of those June Cleaver types, never a hair out of place.

"Well." Zach gave the top of her car a friendly slap. "You'd probably best be getting to work. I don't want you to be late on my account."

"Oh, no problem. I'm just glad I didn't run over you."

"Probably wouldn't have done my headache any good," Zach joshed and, taking a step back, tucked his thumbs through his belt loops. Again, that rakish grin of his stole her breath.

Olivia laughed and shifted the car into reverse.

"See ya later." He stood watching as she backed out of the driveway.

"Bye-bye." Olivia tossed a jaunty wave, then proceeded

to bounce clumsily over the curb, scraping the bottom of her car. Befuddled, she slammed on the brakes and inadvertently tooted her horn. Flames of embarrassment engulfed her cheeks. She couldn't look at him. Grinding gears, she shoved the car into first, popped the clutch, stomped on the gas, and promptly shot out into the morning traffic.

• • •

As Zach stood watching Olivia disappear from sight, he felt that familiar lump of loneliness settle in his stomach. Olivia Harmon was a neat woman. Something about her sweet countenance and fresh-faced beauty reminded him of his own AmyBeth.

Eyes glassy, he wandered over to his rental rig and, reaching inside, grabbed a pad of paper and a pencil for notes on supplies he'd be needing. Leaning against the side of the truck, Zach stared off into space, deep in thought.

Why would a woman like Olivia Harmon be living in a boarding house? Why didn't she have a husband and some kids? Slowly, he rimmed his lower lip with the eraser end of his pencil. Not, of course, that everyone had to be married to be happy and fulfilled. But still, he couldn't help but wonder. She was so sweet. And so pretty.

Zach's mind drifted back to AmyBeth.

Meeting Olivia reminded him of just how acutely he missed his wife.

• • •

A few minutes later, in a convenience store off the beaten path, Olivia juggled a slippery handful of pantyhose packages. Deep in thought, she tried to calculate her height and weight and assign it the proper letter of the alphabet on the sizing chart. This took every bit of concentration she possessed, so the commotion taking place in the next aisle was not appreciated.

Juvenile whisperings, the sounds of paper tearing, bickering, arguing, a little shoving, and other noises finally had Olivia fuming in exasperation. Why weren't those children in school yet? She snapped a look at her wrist. Surely it was past time.

Selecting a pair of hose that she hoped would cover her long legs without a battle, Olivia tossed the rejects back into the bin and decided to investigate the noises in the next aisle on her way to the register. As she rounded the corner, she paused and watched in surprise as three raggedy children—who looked to be somewhere in the neighborhood of three to five years in age—gobbled food right off the shelves. Quickly shoveling potato chips, cupcakes, and cookies into his mouth, the boy shot covert looks over his shoulder now and again while he shielded what must have been his sisters—judging by their looks—from the storekeeper.

Olivia's heart caught in her throat. It was obvious that the boy had packed a lot of life into his few years. Jaw jutting defiantly, eyes glittering, he tucked candy bars and gum into his pockets while his sisters ate. It looked as if several months ago someone had attempted to shear a trendy style into his tangled and dirty hair, but that—and his personal hygiene—were a thing of the past. A small hoop earring dangled from his left ear, and his clothing was tattered and in need of a good washing. Or burning. The girls were no better off.

Her heart twisted. What kind of mother would allow her babies to run around unsupervised this way? Her blood began to boil. What kind of woman would allow them to become so gaunt with obvious undernourishment? Who was this...this *person,* that she didn't have the common decency to provide her children with a clean set of clothes and an occasional bath? Olivia quelled the urge to scream as she watched the children.

Her own precious Lillah had been very near in age to the scraggly-looking older girl. Clutching her pantyhose, Olivia shot an outraged prayer skyward. *Why, God?* she asked, silently venting her frustration and anger. *Why leave this woman her children and take mine? I was a good mother!* Tears of frustration burned the backs of her eyes. It didn't make any sense. Her talents at motherhood were moldering while some sluggard who obviously didn't care allowed her children to run wild.

Olivia filled her lungs, then blew out a weary breath. Just another of life's bitter pills. The sound of her ragged exhalation drew the boy's suspicious eyes, and before Olivia knew what happened the children had scattered.

"Hey! You kids! *Wait!*"

Tripping after them in her slippery pumps, she slung her purse over her shoulder and did her best to balance her purchases. Her commands only served to fuel the children on and, before she knew it, they had burst out of the store's large, double-glass doors and vanished. A mantle of disappointment and melancholy settled over her as she backed away from the doors and sagged against the cash-out countertop.

"Those your kids, lady?" the cashier demanded.

Olivia looked up. "No."

He grunted. "Brats. When I get ahold of their folks, I'm gonna give 'em a piece of my mind."

"They've been in here before?" Setting her pantyhose and other sundries on the counter, Olivia rummaged through her purse for some money.

"They sneak in every once in a while and rob us blind."

He rang up her hose, breath mints, and the various cosmetics she'd purchased on impulse and stuffed them in a bag. "Usually they wait until I'm in the back before they come in. Haven't been able to catch 'em cuz they generally eat and run." His stony expression cracked a bit at this.

"They must live nearby," she mused, handing him several bills.

The clerk jabbed at the buttons on the register. "No doubt. This ain't exactly the best neighborhood in town. I expect their folks are just more of the riffraff you see hangin' out on the streets around here. I've called the cops and children's services, but nobody's been able to catch 'em yet. That boy..." The clerk sniffed and shook his head. "He's a wily critter." He counted Olivia's change and held it out to her.

"No, that's okay. You keep it. Breakfast"—she gestured in the direction the children had run—"is on me this morning."

• • •

"You *what?*" Nell's eyes bulged as she watched Olivia wrestle her pantyhose out of the package. "Are you trying to give me heart failure? You know better than to go to *that* neighborhood. You could get killed shopping there! Or worse!"

Nell's nervous twitterings echoed hollowly off the tiled walls in the women's washroom that was located just outside their office.

"I know." Olivia's lament came over her shoulder as she disappeared into a stall to change her stockings. "But I desperately needed some new hose. I almost died of embarrassment this morning when Zach poked his head into my car and my stockings were in shreds."

"Zach?" Her attention diverted, Nell grabbed on to this juicy new bit of information. "Zach Springer poked his head into your car?"

"Well, after I nearly ran him over." Olivia's tone was sardonic.

"Gee, I didn't think he'd be up and around so soon. You know, Olivia, Zach is a really special guy. You'd love him if you got to know him."

Olivia grimaced. No doubt. Therein lay the problem.

"Isn't he cute? I just love that little dimple in his chee—"

"Nell, could you throw this away for me?" Wanting to change the subject, Olivia tossed the empty pantyhose package over the stall door. The last thing she needed was to focus on the wonders of Zach Springer.

"Oh!" Nell's twitters reverberated as she discarded the plastic.

"Nell?"

"Yeah?"

Grunting, Olivia struggled within the confines of the tight stall, to remove her old stockings. Once that was accomplished, she held up her size-*A* hose. Should have gone with size *B*. Oh well.

"This morning, while I was in that store I was telling you about—"

"Oh, my land!" Nell's shudder was audible. "Don't ever go there again! My nerves simply can't take it. Next time, take Park to Alder. There's a little store on the corner there. Never take Twenty-second. That area scares me to death. Especially lately. I'm always seeing on the news how bad that neck of the woo—"

"You're right." Olivia's tattered pantyhose came sailing over the stall door. "It's really bad. In fact, while I was there I saw three little kids. Couldn't have been much older than my Lillah was. They were so raggedy, and, Nell, they were eating food right off the shelves!"

"Oh, dear Lord, no." Clucking and tsking, Nell snagged Olivia's hose off the floor and proceeded to clean the mirrors.

"That's...what *I* said!" Olivia kicked her pumps out from under her feet and bent to poke her foot into the re-inforced toe of the new hose. "I...just...can't believe...that God would let stuff like...that...happen to those...poor kids."

"You never know. God may have plans for those kids."

"Maybe." The jury was out on that, as far as Olivia was concerned. Snorting, she shifted this way and that in the stall. What kind of a contortionist did one have to be in or-der to get these stupid things up over her hips? "Oops." Rolling her eyes, she fished her purse strap out of the toilet bowl. Yech.

"Hand me a towel, Nell? My purse strap fell in."

A germ-killing moist towelette, accompanied by Nell's nervous giggles, came sailing over the stall door. "You might want to throw that purse out. Lately I've developed this annoying fear of germs."

"I'll be all right. Thanks."

Dismayed, Olivia sighed and peered down at the cotton crotch of her new hose as it hovered between her knees. This would never do. She couldn't totter around the office all day Morticia Addams style. The death grip she held on the waistband as she tugged finally proved too much. Her fingernails popped through the fine material, sending runs zigging and zagging down both legs. Doggone it. With a snort of disgust, she let her head fall back on her shoulders while she rolled her eyes at the ceiling. "Nell?"

"Yeah?"

"You wouldn't happen to have any clear nail polish?"

"No, hon. The fumes make me dizzy lately."

"Of course." Double doggone it. Olivia slumped against the stall. Hattie's prayers must not have kicked in yet. This was definitely not her day.

• • •

Much later that same day, as he looked up from his task, Zach noticed Olivia hovering just outside the sunroom. She obviously hadn't spotted him yet.

"Hi," he called. An unexpected jolt of delight jumped down his spine at her dazzling smile.

"Oh, hi!" Taking a step back, she clutched the doorframe.

He could tell she was surprised to see that he was still here so late this Monday afternoon. Mike, his best friend and partner, had called it a day and gone home over an hour ago. Truth be told, he was a little amazed to still be there himself. Especially considering the ever-present pain that had throbbed in his head for the better part of the afternoon. However, pain aside, he'd had a productive day and, with one thing and another, simply hadn't found the need to rush home to an empty house. Something about Hattie's boarding house beckoned him. Made him feel curiously at home. Warm. Welcome. Couldn't have anything to do with the lovely blonde that hovered in the doorway...

The sun had already set, and it was dark as midnight outside. He could smell the delicious aromas of dinner emanating from Hattie's kitchen. His stomach growled, and he wondered what stale and moldy bits and pieces he could fish out of his fridge and toss in the microwave. Cooking had never been his forte. Plus, he hated eating alone.

"You've been busy." Olivia took a tentative step into the room, her eyes drifting over the wheelbarrow, the shovels, the planks out the back door, and the stack of supplies he'd carted in from his truck. Bats of insulation and sheets of plastic had been stapled in a temporary fashion over the broken and boarded windows, affording the room a bit of warmth. "Are you sure you should be doing so much so soon after your"—she gestured to the broken wall—"accident?"

Zach puffed his chest and affected a mock he-man pose to make her smile. It worked. "Aw, nah. I'm fine. Just finishing up actually. Truth be told, Mike did most of the work today." He waved toward a stack of broken boards he'd torn out of the wall. "I told him I'd load these, then I'll be on my way." His stomach growled again. Man, he wished somebody would ask him to stay for dinner. Whatever they had cooking in that kitchen, it smelled killer.

There was a moment of silence as they both groped for something appropriate to say that would either prolong or wrap up the conversation in a graceful way. The house was alive with the typical sounds of evening. The Ross sisters could be heard bickering from the parlor, Hattie and Rahni's pleasant laughter, a harmonious contrast. From somewhere upstairs a dog's sharp bark sounded with Ryan's admonishing growls and stern instructions following.

"Well." Olivia finally broke the silence, her flickering gaze landing on the boards. "You probably shouldn't...you know...try to do too much. Should you be carrying such heavy loads?" Golly, she hoped she didn't sound like she was trying to tell him what to do.

His smile was reassuring. "Probably not. Maybe you wouldn't mind giving me a hand with these longer ones? They're really not that heavy, but I'd sure hate to knock over one of Hattie's little glass doodads. They're everywhere."

Olivia, who was still hovering behind the doors, cast a worried glance down at her knees. Would her pantyhose be up to the task? While she debated the issue, Zach took her silence as acquiescence and began to gather boards.

"Here." He swung a stack in her direction. "You grab this end and lead us through the house. I'll bring up the rear."

Left with no choice, Olivia caught the boards, about-faced, and shuffled as fast as her drooping hosiery would allow. Finding her way through the house was no real problem as the mahogany-and-marble floors were smooth and obstacle free. It was the front porch that presented the...situation.

How it happened, Olivia could only speculate in the days that followed. Perhaps it was the way her pantyhose slithered down around her ankles just as she began descending the front porch stairs. Perhaps it was the fact that she hesitated at the top of the stairs and Zach did not. Perhaps it would have been helpful if the Colonel hadn't chosen that precise moment to conserve energy by slamming the front door and snapping off the porch light.

However, the real reason became a moot point as Olivia lost control of her footing—not to mention the boards and her dignity—and tumbled down the steps.

"Oh my gosh!" Zach dropped his end of the boards and bounded down the steps to where Olivia lay in a crumpled heap. "Are you okay?"

Dazed, Olivia peered through the stars that danced before her eyes and tried to make out his face. "I...I...think so."

"Don't move," he ordered, quickly taking off his jacket and covering her. "At least not until we figure out if anything is broken."

"Okay..."

With deft motions, his gentle fingers probed her forehead for lumps and bumps. Once satisfied that she wasn't bleeding there, he lifted her arms, one at a time. "This hurt?" He lifted her arm and slowly rotated it.

"Uh, no. I think I scraped my elbow though."

"Okay. Anything else hurt?" Setting her arm down, his explorations moved to her legs. "Any pain here?" His warm hands enveloped her knees.

"I...uh..." *Uh-oh.* His hands were moving toward her ankles. She closed her eyes and grimaced. Her pantyhose. Drat.

"Wow."

She could hear the puzzlement in his voice. Giving her shoulders a sheepish shrug, she could think of no graceful explanation.

"That was some fall." He chuckled as she sat up. "That's what I call knocking your socks off."

Olivia groaned, but giggled in spite of herself. Accepting his outstretched hand, she allowed him to help her to her feet. His large hands were warm and callous, and now that her eyes had adjusted to the lack of light, she could see the concern in his face. He didn't make her feel a bit silly for her inexplicable stocking situation. Nor for falling down the stairs in such an undignified manner. What a wonderful man. AmyBeth was such a lucky woman.

"I'm so sorry. I never should have asked you to help. I'm such a goon. I didn't even give you a chance to change your shoes or anything—"

"No no, it's okay." Swallowing back the mirth that bubbled into her throat, Olivia attempted to explain. "I...uh," she squeaked, biting her cheek to keep the laughter in check, "I bought the wrong size pantyhose this morning, and...oh." Her eyes squeezed shut for a second. "All day, I've been fighting these dumb things..."

Her giggles must have been contagious because, as

she kicked off her shoes and stepped out of her hose, Zach began to laugh. Soon, they were both slapping their thighs and howling with laughter.

The Colonel, hearing the commotion, whipped open the door and peered into the shadows. "Who goes there?"

Zach stepped into the blinding beam of light that lasered from the foyer. "It's me, sir. Zach Springer."

"You?" The Colonel pointed at the lumber scattered down the stairs. "What are you tearing apart now, boy?" His eyes strayed to the pair of pantyhose that lay under the spotlight's glow as it pooled in the walkway. He frowned.

"Nothing, sir. Simply getting rid of some old wood."

"Getting rid of it! Why?" The old man stumbled out onto the porch and, peering through the shadows, surveyed the broken and splintered wood. "These boards are just what I need. Stack them at the side of the house, and I'll use them later." He pointed to a shadowy pile where he stored many of his recyclables and projects in progress.

"Yes sir." Zach snapped to attention and bobbed his head in a crisp nod.

Satisfied, and not wanting to waste any more precious heat, the Colonel shot one more befuddled look at the discarded hose, then glared at Zach. Turning, he shuffled back into the house and slammed the door.

Zach and Olivia exchanged startled glances, then promptly fell into another fit of hilarity. Olivia slipped her bare feet into her pumps and, after assuring Zach that she had no more than a scrape on her elbow and a few miscellaneous bruises, helped him load the wood onto the Colonel's pile.

"I feel like we are the walking wounded, in some sort of bizarre army," Zach joked as they stumbled about in the darkness, smashing into the porch and bushes with the unwieldy boards.

This tickled Olivia's funny bone, and she had to stop walking so she could howl for a few minutes. Zach's hearty laughter only served to egg her on, and soon they were clutching each other's jacket lapels and whooping like a couple of punch-drunk hyenas. Finally, they were able to settle down enough to get back to work. And, after laboring for far longer than would have been necessary had the Colonel not doused the lights and locked them out, they had all the lumber deposited in a neat stack at the side of the house.

"Well," Zach said, dusting off his hands.

"Well," Olivia echoed.

He didn't want to leave.

She didn't want him to.

"I should probably be on my way." Zach's melancholy sigh filled the air.

"Probably." Olivia agreed verbally, but was sorry to see him go. She wished he would stay for dinner. The dinner table would be a lively place indeed, with his sense of humor. Ah, well, he had a family waiting at home.

"I'll see you tomorrow."

"Tomorrow," Olivia repeated, injecting a note of cheer into her voice that she didn't feel as she watched him get into his truck and drive off into the darkness.

• • •

Unable to get those three raggedy children out of her mind for the rest of that Monday night, Olivia found herself taking the same route to work Tuesday morning, despite Nell's ominous warning. She stopped at the same convenience store and asked the same clerk if he'd spotted those same children that morning.

"Nope," he grumbled, loading the donuts she'd requested out of the glass case and into a waxy white bag. "And

61

that's fine by me. Let 'em pick on someone else today. I got enough problems without worrying about some kid choking on stolen gum. Parents would no doubt be in here suing the pants off me in a hot New York minute. Whole world's gone sue crazy."

Olivia inclined her head and murmured in agreement, but her mind was a million miles away. Had the children eaten yet today? Where was their mother? Their father? Did they have a warm place to sleep? If they hadn't eaten and she could find them, perhaps they would accept the apple fritters and maple bars she just bought. If not, the gang at the office would make short work of them.

After paying for the donuts and thanking the clerk, Olivia went outside and made a cursory inspection of the store's parking lot. She checked behind the garbage bins and looked in the exterior rest rooms, to no avail. Disappointed, she headed to her car and, thoughts spinning as quickly as her tires, pulled into the early morning traffic on Twenty-second Boulevard.

As she threaded her way through the hustle and bustle on the road, she glimpsed something in her rearview mirror that had her heart skipping beats.

The kids!

Was it the kids?

Twisting around in her seat, she craned her neck, but only glimpsed a blurred group in the distance as it vanished down a side street. Olivia gripped the wheel and made a split-second decision.

She was going after the blur.

If it was the kids, she would figure out what to do when she crossed that particular bridge.

Horns honked and drivers shouted as Olivia rolled down her window, gestured her intent then pulled a wild U-ie in the middle of the intersection. Burning rubber, she sped in the direction opposite her office. She would worry about her boss later. Right now, she thought, her jaw grim with determination, she had kids to catch.

Tires squealing like something out of a bad chase scene in a TV drama, Olivia rounded the corner and swerved onto the side street where she believed she'd seen the children headed. No luck. Shifting down, she slowed to a crawl on the dumpy looking street and searched as she went. Ahead, on the right, lay a pothole-filled alley. As she approached, she could see children playing in a puddle.

Three children.

Three raggedy little children in need of a good meal, a hot bath, and a mother's love.

When they spotted her easing into the alley, they took off. The boy shouted at his sisters to hurry and hustled them in record time to the street that loomed at the other end. Olivia's heart hammered beneath her breast. Stepping on the gas, she bounced after them as fast as the potholes would allow.

That did it. She was going to have to get her front end realigned. No no. She was going to have to get her spine realigned. Teeth chattering, she gripped the wheel, pressed on the accelerator, and shot a prayer skyward.

"Lord!" She called out, her voice herky-jerky with the dips and ruts her shocks could not absorb. "It's m-me, Olivia Harmon. Remember? Well, anyway, I haven't asked m-much of you in the last few months. Okay," she amended, remembering to be truthful, "years. But if you are really there, then...helllp!"

Up ahead, the children ran higgledy-piggledy across the street. Thankfully, there was no traffic. Veering over someone's unmowed, appliance-filled lawn, they headed toward a house that looked as if it should be condemned. In a frantic rush they stumbled up the crooked porch steps and shot in through the front door, slamming it behind them.

Aha. So. This was where they lived. Or at the very least where they hid now and then.

Olivia slowed to a stop in the alley and stared at the house where the children had disappeared. They were peeking out the window and across the street at her car. She vacillated. Should she go talk to their mother? Offer help? Food? Assistance? Advice? Or should she take the proactive stance and inform the Children's Services Division of their condition? Then again, perhaps she should simply keep her nose out of it.

The smell of donuts from the bag on the seat reminded her that she was hungry. In her enthusiasm, she'd skipped breakfast at the boarding house. If her stomach was rumbling after one missed meal, she could only imagine what the children must be feeling. On autopilot of sorts, Olivia made a decision.

Pulling onto the alley's rutted and glass-littered shoulder, she cut the engine, grabbed the donut bag and her purse, tossed her keys in her pocket, and locked her car's doors. In this neighborhood, she doubted that her car would even be there when she returned, but what did she care? She had insurance.

Striding purposefully across the street and down the cracked and broken sidewalk, Olivia headed toward the ramshackle tract house. When she reached the steps, she hesitated. What was the worst that could happen to her? Okay, they could kill her. No problem. These days, she didn't have all that much worth living for anyway.

She rapped on the door. No answer. She knocked again. This time louder and with more authority.

"Who's there?" a little voice demanded.

"I...uh, my name is Olivia. I'd like to talk to your mommy."

"Go away."

Olivia assumed this was the boy speaking. In the background, she could hear him shushing his sisters.

"Mom's got a gun," he shouted, his bravado quavering ever so slightly.

Nevertheless, his bluff had its desired effect—Olivia was quaking in her pumps. "Oh? Well, I...I just want to talk to her. And bring her some donuts."

Silence.

"Big ones. Still warm."

More silence.

"With frosting."

Frosting seemed to be the magic word. The door cracked open, and three pairs of eyes—one suspicious, one curious, and one frightened—peered out at Olivia through the crack in the door.

5

The standoff lasted for a good minute before hunger overcame rational thought.

"Okay." The boy huffed, as if pained by the inconvenience. Pushing open the door, he stepped out onto the trash-littered porch, keeping his sisters behind him. "My mom will want me to take the donuts to her, because she is really busy in the back polishing her shotgun."

"Is that so?" Olivia attempted to sound casual, despite the thunder and lightning that exploded in her chest.

"Yeah. She has several guns. Loaded." The boy squinted at Olivia. "She don't like strangers much."

"That's okay, you can bring a donut to her when we're finished with our picnic out here." With deliberation, she lowered herself to the porch steps and opened the bag. "Would you or your sisters like a donut?"

Unable to control herself, the older sister smiled shyly and pushed in front of the boy. "I do."

"Here you go, honey." Olivia offered the bag in her direction. Rats. She wished she'd thought to bring some milk. Oh well. There was always tomorrow.

The girl reached inside and, eyes glowing with wonder, pulled out a giant bear claw. Greedily, her brother and sister followed suit, ransacking the bag for donuts of their own.

"How come you're bringin' us these?" the elder of the two girls wanted to know.

Olivia decided to be truthful. "Because I saw you in the store yesterday and you looked hungry."

"We didn't steal nothin'!" The boy's tone was defensive through his bulging cheeks.

"Just ate some food," the same girl explained. She had a dab of frosting on her nose and a sugary smear on her dirty cheek.

An intense and tender mother's love for these children crowded into Olivia's throat. "What's your name, honey?"

"You don't have to tell her that," the boy barked at his sister.

"You're not the boss of me, Cain." Turning, she moved to the step and settled down beside Olivia. "My name's Ruth. And hers," she pointed at the younger girl, who was busily licking the frosting off her maple bar, "is Esther. She's my sister. Sometimes she still pees her pants."

Olivia lifted an amused brow. "Thanks for the warning." Had Ruth not explained, Olivia's nose would have eventually detected this bit of information.

Cain, Esther, and Ruth. Three rather unusual names for children of this generation. Olivia liked the names—and the children that bore them—instantly.

"How old are you, honey?"

Through a mouthful of food, peppered with enthusiastic lip smacking, Olivia was able to gather the basic facts from Ruth. Cain scowled but remained silent for a while, busy with his own breakfast.

"I'm four, but I'll be five when it's my birthday pretty soon. Esther is three and Cain is already five, that's why he thinks he's the boss of us. But he's not. I have a doll. She's in the house. Her name is Silly. I..." Ruth's freckled nose wrinkled. "I don't know how old she is. Her hair is almost all gone, so she's kind of old. She likes to jump on the bed with me and Esther. Once her eye fell out, and that gave me baaaad dreams. Do you ever have bad dreams, donut lady?"

"Sometimes, honey. We all do, I think." Nodding and smiling, Olivia encouraged this childish prattle, gleaning as much information as she could about the kids and their folks.

For the next half-hour, Olivia listened intently, while Ruth's glib tongue rattled off the family history and some of its darker secrets. Every so often Cain would contradict his sister and unknowingly help paint a clearer picture for the woman they all began to call "donut lady."

It soon became clear that the children's parents were not at home, and seldom were. Dad had been gone since before anybody could remember, and Mom, well, Mom was gone all the time. Except when she came home with some food, which obviously was not often enough. She was always real tired and cried a lot. Someone named George, who lived across the street, would come over from time to time and check in on them when Mom was gone. But George was mean. And he had baaaad breath. And he said Mom owed him money.

"Shut up, Ruth." Cain, temper rising, and hunger now sated, remembered his role as guardian.

"You're not the boss of me, Cain," Ruth shouted, crumbs flying from her rosebud lips.

Cain heaved a world-weary sigh. "Am too."

"Are not."

As they argued, Esther climbed up into Olivia's lap and nestled against her breast. A burning lump tightened Olivia's throat as she wrapped her arms around Esther's tiny body. Nostalgic memories of moments like this with

Lillah washed over her in an emotional tide that had her blinking and striving for composure. She stroked the child's tangled and dirty hair and rocked back and forth in a comforting manner, the way she used to do, when Lillah was three.

For a long time, Ruth continued jabbering, regaling Olivia with nonsensical stories of monsters under the bed and the kid next door who threw rocks and bottles at them, and the time the bad people came looking for Mom, and Mom cried, just like this: "Waaa," Ruth wailed and ground her grimy fists into her eyes. Mom went with those mean people, and she didn't come back for a looonng time. And when she came back she was sick. Mom was sick a lot.

"Shut up, Ruth." Cain stood.

Olivia could tell Cain was impatient and ready to end this impromptu picnic. She glanced at her watch, determined to find out what she could before she had to leave for work. As it was, she'd be over an hour late.

"Where is your mom?" Olivia gently probed, remembering Cain's shotgun story, figuring it was Cain's cover when he was scared.

Ever chatty, Ruth piped up. "She is at the doctor. She is always at the doctor, getting her medicine. She's been there a looonnng time this time. I can't even remember what she looks like."

"She's only been gone two nights," Cain argued. "I'm not scared to be alone." He shot a defiant look up at Olivia.

A bizarre mix of emotions jockeyed for pole position within Olivia. Tears stung the back of her eyes, and she could feel Esther's baby-fine hair tickle her chin as the child's head bobbed. Craning her little neck, she smiled a guileless smile up at Olivia.

Olivia swallowed against her fury. What kind of mother

would leave her babies all alone this way? More than ever, Olivia was determined to do something.

"Do you kids have any food in the house?"

Cain's head snapped around, and he scowled suspiciously at Olivia.

"Come on, Ruth. Come on, Esther." Abruptly finished with social pleasantries, Cain grabbed his squawking sisters, tugged them away from Olivia, and hustled them into the house. The door closed behind him with a resounding crash.

Olivia could hear Cain shoot the bolt, and then it was silent.

• • •

"Can I get you another scone, Jack dear?" Hattie peered over her teacup at Zach as he blotted his mouth on his napkin and eased his chair away from the table.

"Oh no, ma'am. I'm quite stuffed." He felt a pleasant laziness wash over him. The only thing that could possibly make him feel any better would be if Olivia walked through the door and took the empty seat beside him. But much to his disappointment, she'd left early for work that morning.

"One is never enough for me either," Hattie chirped, sliding the plate in his direction. "How about your friend, Mark? He looks like a scone man."

"No thanks, Hattie. Mike ate breakfast with his wife and children."

"Ah."

By now Zach had pretty much fallen into a conversational rhythm with Hattie, realizing that she only gathered about half of what he was saying at any given time. Luckily, it didn't seem to hamper her ability to communicate all that much. "Help yourself to as many as you like, dear heart.

That's hard work you're doing back there in the sunroom. And you being a growing boy—well I can't have you fainting from hunger on me." Her eyes twinkled with fun.

Zach patted his stomach. "Not much chance of that."

"No! You're not fat!" Hattie clucked and tsked and pursed her lips till Zach felt obligated to grab another scone, smother it with clotted cream, and wash it down with a second cup of coffee. Mmm. How he wished they could invent a toaster tart that could rival this.

That Tuesday morning, everyone who lived at the boarding house, with the exception of Olivia, was at the table for the usual routine—eating, working on the daily crossword, bickering, barking, growling, and conversing. The Colonel wove odd-looking doilies from the used paper napkins he'd gathered off everyone's plates, and grumbled to no one in particular about the cost of living.

As Zach sat soaking up this homey ambiance, the heat from the fire warming his back, he felt drowsy and comfortable. He had no idea what set of circumstances led Olivia to live here in this boarding house with these rather eccentric, yet lovable, folks. However, he could definitely see the attraction for anyone who didn't have an immediate family of their own. He wondered absently if that were the case for her. At any rate, the home cooking was excellent, the company cheerful, and the surroundings elegant. It sure beat his messy, cold, and lonely home any day. Contented, he sipped the last of his fresh-brewed coffee.

Funny how Olivia's presence—or lack thereof—made such a difference to the feel of the room. If she were here, he doubted he'd be feeling quite so drowsy. No, even the thought of her lovely smile caused little jolts of anticipation to jump down his spine.

He darted a glance at the grandfather clock, visible from

the foyer. Eight long hours till she came home. He sighed. Well, enough daydreaming. Time to get to work.

• • •

Olivia stood at the bottom of the ramshackle porch steps. Staring at the door Cain had just slammed, she waffled. What on earth should she do? Beads of perspiration broke out on her forehead as she went hot, then cold all over. Her heart beat a frantic staccato, causing her pulse to roar in her ears. She couldn't leave those three babies to fend for themselves all day. It didn't matter that they were not her children. It didn't matter that she'd never laid eyes on them before yesterday morning. It didn't even matter that she was risking her job by standing there waffling when she should be at work.

She had to do something. Anything. But what?

"Lord," she whispered, clenching her fists into a tight ball beneath her chin. "Hello again. It's me. Olivia Harmon? Remember? From this morning? And last night? Well, I hate to bother you all at once like this. Especially when I've ignored you for so long, but this is an emergency. If you are there, God, could you please do something!"

Eyes closed, she only hoped her fervent prayer was being picked up on the other end. Her voice became slightly hysterical, and her lips nearly bled from the way she was forcing them between her teeth and her prayerful fists.

"Are you there, God? Uh, listen," she offered, beginning to barter. "If you don't want to do it for me, that's okay. I understand. But those are just little kids in there. It's not their fault that their mom is a loser. Sorry," she amended, shooting an apologetic glance skyward. "You know what I mean. Anyway, if you are there, and you care, please, *please*," she murmured, "*please*, do something. Anything. Amen."

Nothing.

Olivia sighed. Her purse slid off her shoulder and landed by the strap on the crook of her arm.

Well, what else had she expected? God never listened to her. Maybe Hattie would know what to do. With one last, longing, backward glance at the house, Olivia turned and slogged dispiritedly toward the alley where her car was still parked. At least that hadn't been stolen. That was one bright spot in her otherwise dreary day.

As she unlocked the driver's side door and tossed her purse inside, a car slowly cruised down the street. Only after it passed did Olivia realize that it was a squad car.

Her heart cartwheeled within her chest.

"Hey!" she shouted. Forgetting her purse, forgetting the keys hanging from her car door, and forgetting her dignity, Olivia chased the policeman down the street. Arms waving, hair flying, eyes wild, she shrieked at the top of her lungs. "Heeyyy! Stop! Wait!"

Finally catching a glimpse of this madwoman in his rearview mirror, the squad car's brake lights flashed on. Slowing, the law officer pulled over to the curb, just beyond the children's house. Fearing heart failure, Olivia also slowed to a quick limp, silently cursing her fashionable work shoes.

Huffing and puffing, she reached the black-and-white car and pasted on a bright smile to prove that she wasn't the lunatic she appeared. Her smile faded as the policeman unrolled his window and stared at her. It was the same grim-faced officer who had ticketed Zach the other morning.

Oh no. She closed her eyes in frustration and shot another frustrated prayer past the gray clouds. *Why? Why, God? Why did you have to send this emotional mannequin? Couldn't you have sent someone who cared?*

In answer to her heated question, the heavens chose that precise moment to open, and a torrent of rain fell from the sky. Okay. Jaws grim, she held her hands up over her head to deflect the sudden downpour. Was God trying to cool her ardor? She hoped not, because she was long past the boiling point.

Lord, she prayed in earnest, *I hope this is your will, because I'm in too far to back out now.*

Thunder rumbled off in the distance.

"Is that a yes?" she muttered, darting a glance at the sky.

"Pardon?" The officer's narrowed gaze locked in on her dripping nose.

"Oh, not you." Donning her smile again, she greeted the officer in a frenzy of charitable goodwill. "I was just...you were just...an answer to prayer," she panted. "I...think."

Maybe not.

"Can I help you?" Officer Menkin's wiry brow wrinkled, his only concession to vague interest in her predicament.

Olivia ignored his skeptical expression and deadpan tone. "Yes! Yes, you can." Obviously, he thought she was just another rebel without a clue. She didn't care. There were kids' lives at stake here.

With much passion and frantic gesturing toward the rotting house where the children hid, Olivia explained the situation to the best of her ability.

She told him how she'd come across the children in the convenience store on her way to work yesterday. She told him their names and ages. She told him that she was afraid the children were being neglected and starving. The father was missing. The mother had been gone for several days now. She even went so far as to tell him that if no one else cared, at least *she* did.

She would be *happy* to take these children.

To feed them.

To clothe and bathe them.

To *love* them!

Rain pelted down upon her, causing her clothing to cling uncomfortably to her body. She shivered, chilled to the core.

Officer Menkin looked quite cozy.

She flung her soggy locks over her shoulder, purposefully spraying his granite face. Hopefully her lips were turning blue. Hopefully the chattering of her teeth was getting on his nerves. Hopefully lightning would strike his car and jump-start his fossilized heart.

As he sat in his comfortable seat, out of the rain, warming under the heater's tropical blast, she wondered what it would take to impress this man. Perhaps she should have saved a donut for him, she thought facetiously.

Thunder rumbled again, off in the distance. She ignored it.

Her words continued to tumble over themselves in an outpouring of emotion, bouncing off the wooden-faced Officer Menkin. Was this guy even listening to a word she had to say?

Hello? she wanted to shout. *Anybody home?*

Eyes flashing and lungs heaving, she knew she must be coming across as a psychopath, so she guessed some of his skepticism was understandable. But she didn't know how else to convince him of the urgency. Swallowing her pride, she vehemently continued to try to elicit some sort of response, pro or con. She pitied Mrs. Menkin, if there was such a woman. Poor thing.

Finally, after Olivia had run out of steam and Officer Menkin had given his nails a thorough cleaning with his pocket knife, he spoke.

"Okay, ma'am. I'll have someone make a welfare check on the kids."

"Oh." Olivia was deflated. A welfare check? What in the world was a welfare check? Could it possibly be as limp as it sounded? "Is there anything I can do to help?"

"No."

"Then, I guess you won't be needing any more details from me about the kids?"

"No."

"Can I give you my card?"

Officer Menkin shrugged. "Sure."

"Will you contact me, if you find out anything?"

"You want to be contacted?"

Hadn't the man been listening to a word she'd been saying?

"Yes! Of course I want to be contacted. If the kids are removed from the home, and, uh, they don't have anyplace else to stay, *I'll* take them." Even as she spoke the words, she wondered at her sanity. What would she do with three little raggedy kids? She took a deep breath. Well, she couldn't help but do a far sight better than their mother was doing.

"Okay." Officer Menkin extended two fingers for her card then tossed it on the dash. Putting his car into gear, he eased down the street without so much as a by-your-leave.

The man could use a class in social skills. Her heart sank.

"Okay," she whispered to no one in particular. A welfare check. Big deal. She knew perfectly well that she would never hear from him again. Perhaps it had been her delivery. Someone as...emphatic as she had been could never really be taken seriously. Filling her lungs, Olivia heaved a weary sigh.

Hopefully, someone would do something.

Sounding closer now, the thunder drew her out of her soggy ruminations. Slowly turning, Olivia limped back to the alley where her car waited.

As she walked, three pairs of eyes watched from behind a broken window across the puddle-filled street.

• • •

Nell nearly swooned.

She and Olivia were in the rest room again, this time trying to dry Olivia's hair under the hand dryer and put her into some semblance of order before she had to face the music with the boss for being late. Lucky for them, their employer was rather soft-hearted and quick to forgive.

"I can't believe you went back to that horrible neighborhood again." Jittery with anxiety, Nell wrung her hands. "Are you nuts?"

"What?" Olivia couldn't hear over the roar of the dryer.

"What in heaven's name were you thinking?"

"Pardon?"

"I know, I know, you're thinking, 'There goes nervous Nellie, nattering on about safety.' But honestly, Olivia! This has nothing to do with my anxiety issues. This is about common sense! Using the brains God gave you..."

Unfortunately, Olivia couldn't make heads or tails of what she was saying. Good thing. Nell hadn't stopped harping on her since she'd finally arrived at work.

"Nell, you should see these kids. They're just babies really." Olivia talked over the top of Nell's henlike cluckings. Bending at the waist, she began to dry the locks at the back of her head. "They are so skinny and dirty. I'm sure they haven't had a decent meal in weeks. Maybe longer. It's so sad—"

"That's because they are being raised by wolves!" Red

faced, Nell shouted above the dryer's whine. Moving over to the sink, she turned on the water and began scrubbing her hands. "You should stay away—"

"Do you remember that unfeeling policeman? You know, Nell, the one that gave Zach the ticket?" She grunted, her mouth level with her knees while her hair swept the floor. "I know he's not going to do a single thing. In fact—"

"—from that area. People like them don't like strangers snooping around—"

"—I bet he won't ever get around to that welfare check he promised. Welfare check." Olivia snorted. "What's that all about?"

"—there. Why the other day, I saw this story on the news where this poor, confused lady took a wrong turn down a street over—"

"I'm sure he's already forgotten all about those kids. Why, I bet you money he didn't hear a thing I said!"

"—in that neighborhood. The next thing she knew, her car was hijacked." Nell's terrified giggles bounced off the tiles but couldn't compete with the hand dryer or the rushing water. "In broad daylight! The creep took her purse, her jewelry, her coat—it was raining, too, by the way—*and* her umbrella and even, get this—"

"You know," Olivia mused, dragging a comb through the tangles in her hair and bouncing to and fro to speed drying time, "that's the problem today. Nobody listens to anybody anymore. Not even God. You know, Nell, I finally broke down and said a prayer. I asked God to help those kids. And did he hear me? No. He paid just about as much attention to me as that...that—"

"—he even took her *shoes!* Her *shoes* of all things. They were Italian leather, after all, but for pity's sake, did he have to take her shoes? Couldn't he have left the shoes?" Nell shot a fearful glance at Olivia's feet as she shut off the water. Since Olivia was using the hand dryer, Nell flapped her wet hands in the air, then wiped them on her skirt. "Promise me, Olivia, that you'll never go to that neighborhood again without a—"

"—as that..."

The dryer clicked off.

"—policeman!" they cried in unison.

Olivia stood upright and straightened her collar. "They're never around when you need 'em."

"Exactly!" Nell beamed, satisfied that she'd driven her point home.

"How do I look?"

"Like you just stepped off the cover of *Cosmo*."

Olivia rolled her eyes. "I love you, Nell."

Nell giggled. "I love you too, honey, and that's why I nag."

• • •

For the better part of the day, Olivia felt like something the cat not only dragged in, but mauled and then buried. Her clothes were just damp enough to feel clammy and rumpled, and the chic hairstyle she'd so carefully arranged in front of her mirror that morning was now a windblown haystack. Even the rose red lipstick and super-lash-building mascara she'd bought on impulse yesterday morning were nothing but well intentioned smudges.

Ah well. Such was the life of a children's rights crusader.

When the end of her workday finally rolled around and Olivia had arrived home, she could think of nothing she'd rather do than take a long, hot, steamy shower. Then, if Zach Springer was still around, she might slip downstairs and check on his progress. Simply out of curiosity, of course. It wasn't Zach that interested her, so much as his handiwork, she told herself as she entered the grand foyer of Hattie's Victorian and closed the door.

Before she visited with anyone, however, she would take that shower.

"Hi." A cheery, mellifluous, and very masculine voice greeted her before she could shrug out of her coat.

Or not. Olivia grimaced and slowly turned around, knowing as she did, she would come face to face with the ever unflappable Zach Springer. *Why, why, why?* Why couldn't she—for once—look at least halfway presentable in this man's presence?

"Hi!" She sang her greeting and ran a breezy hand through her tangled mop. "How are you today?" Even bruised and battle scarred from his slide down the hill and through the wall, he looked like a million bucks.

"Much better, thanks." He seemed inordinately pleased that she would think to ask. "And how are you doing? The elbow holding up all right?"

Her cheeks flamed even brighter. Memories of her ig-nominious tumble down the porch stairs danced through her head. Was she doomed to always feel so completely di-sheveled and uncoordinated around him?

"Yes!" She was glad that he couldn't see the scabby patch that covered the better part of her left arm. "Good as new."

"Wow. You must heal quickly."

"Oh sure. I come from a long line of…" Where was she going with this? she wondered, disgusted with her need to jabber. "…er, quick healers." What an idiotic thing to say. She plucked at her clammy blouse and tried to make sense of what she'd just said. "Kind of like Bones, I guess." She laughed what she hoped came across as a bubbly, carefree kind of laugh.

"Pardon?" A pleasant little frown knit his brow.

"*Star Trek?*"

"Yes?"

Oh, this was just getting worse by the second. Maybe she should simply go jump off the roof now and get it over with. Doggedly, she forged ahead. "Wasn't he the one who could heal people quickly?"

"Never got into that show."

"Oh." She would just be on her way to the roof. He was staring at her. And smiling. Obviously, he thought she was a complete moron.

"Well." She couldn't think of anything else to say, which was probably just as well, considering the prattle she'd concocted thus far.

"It was nice seeing you again," Zach said.

Oh sure. Olivia bit her lip and nodded.

"I guess I'll just go put my tools up and be on my way."

"Me too." She rolled her eyes. "Of course, I don't have any tools to, you know, put away."

"Of course." The tiny frown was back between his eyes, but he was smiling.

Before she could further humiliate herself, Olivia spun on her heel and headed upstairs to look for a way to the roof.

• • •

Zach had finished putting his work space to rights and was loitering in the sunroom, hoping to catch one last glimpse of that adorable Olivia Harmon, when the doorbell rang. The pleasant tones echoed through the ground floor, but nobody other than himself seemed to notice.

The bell chimed again. And yet again.

Zach shrugged. No doubt Hattie couldn't hear it, and

the others were all probably getting ready for dinner. No biggie. He'd get the door.

He might as well hit the road while he was at it. Obviously, Olivia wasn't going to reappear anytime soon. He couldn't hang around forever. That would seem weird.

Much to his chagrin, when Zach pulled open the door, he was greeted by the stony-faced Officer Menkin.

"Oh, uh, hello, Officer. What can I do for you?"

Officer Menkin shot a quick glance at the card he held in his hand. "Olivia Harmon here?"

Zach tried not to register his surprise. He'd been sure the officer was here to write him another ticket. Perhaps this time for illegally parking in a sunroom without a permit. "Yes sir. She's upstairs."

"Could you tell her I have her kids?"

For the first time, Zach noticed the three raggedy little kids cowering behind the large man's neatly pressed trousers.

His jaw dropped. *These are Olivia's children?*

6

Pssst!"

Agnes craned her neck around the swinging door as she beckoned her sister and the Colonel to join her and Hattie in the steamy, aromatic kitchen.

"Over here!" Eyes bulging, head bobbing, throat waggling, she looked like a hen in search of grubworms. "And be quiet about it now. Shhh!" Arms in windmill formation, she herded everyone over to the kitchen table for a confab.

Rahni busied herself in the background with dinner preparations, occasionally pausing to eavesdrop.

"What's got your bloomers in such a twist today?" Glyniss demanded.

"Shhh!" Agnes's lips curled back like a braying donkey's, revealing her longish, tea-stained teeth.

"Whatever for?" Glyniss wanted to know, her voice as loud as ever. Chairs scraped against the wooden floor as the elderly foursome settled in at the table.

"Because I don't want her to know we are talking about her!" Agnes's hoarse whisper filled the room.

Pushing back the headdress that was customary in her country, Rahni made no bones about the fact that she was listening. "Who?"

"Her!" Agnes jerked her head in the direction of the foyer.

Smile benign, Hattie looked with interest from face to face. She made no comment as she absorbed what she could of the clandestine conversation.

"Egads!" the Colonel thundered, his eyes bulging with shock. "Not her!" His eyebrows seesawed dramatically, then he paused to reflect. "Her…who?"

"Our own Olivia Harrr-mon, that's who!" Nostrils flaring, Agnes posed for theatrical effect, her prunish face smug with satisfaction.

Glyniss snorted. "What about her?"

"She has *children*, that's what!" Agnes leaned forward in a conspiratorial pose that had Rahni shuffling toward the table. "It's obvious that the poor little creatures have been neglected for a *long* time. Don't get me started on the foibles of the modern parent."

"Oh, please." Glyniss sighed.

"If you ask me—"

"No one did. Furthermore, Agnes, you know perfectly well that that lovely girl lost her poor little child in a car accident five years ago."

"Well, that's the story I've always bought into. However, I'd like to know who those three motley little children are, standing in the foyer with that Zach Springer fellow. The one who came crashing through the wall the other day."

"Children?" The Colonel wheezed excitedly and rubbed his furrowed brow. "In the foyer with the enemy? Is that safe?"

"What makes you so sure that they are Olivia's children?" Glyniss wondered, ignoring the Colonel.

"The law officer said—and I'm quoting here—'Tell Olivia Harmon that I have *her* children,'" Agnes loftily informed them.

"What law officer?"

"The one in the foyer this very minute, that's what law

officer! Apparently, the police have only just now caught up with her."

"That's absurd," Glyniss groused and smacked the table. "Shhh!"

"Maybe not so absurd," the Colonel put in. "I'm beginning to wonder just how much we know about this Olivia person."

"What do you mean, Colonel?" Agnes's hawklike gaze landed with interest on the old man.

The Colonel, his reedy voice peppered with the occasional gasp for oxygen, related what he knew. "The other evening, I found her outside consorting with the enemy."

"The enemy?" Glyniss tossed a beleaguered look at the ceiling.

"Zach!" Agnes pounded her fist on the table. "I knew it!"

Glyniss stared at her sister. "Consorting?"

The Colonel pulled a thoughtful frown. "Well, I don't know what to call it exactly, except to say that she'd tossed off her knickers and was dancing about in her bare feet. The way they were laughing and carrying on, well it put me in mind of a furlough I took back in '45. Or was it '46?"

Agnes gasped, her face turning redder than a sunburned beet. She shot an I-told-you-so look at her sister.

Glyniss was taken aback. "That does not sound like Olivia." Turning, she peered at Hattie. "What do you make of this?"

"Yes?"

She shouted for Hattie's benefit. "Has Olivia been acting oddly lately?"

Hattie beamed. "Yes, yes, you could say that she has been acting godly lately. Just the other day, she asked me to pray for her."

Agnes harrumphed. "Good thing."

"Yes," Hattie went on. "It seems she's been feeling a little lost, these days. I think the poor girl simply needs to get back in touch with the Lord. That and some male companionship. And perhaps to get out and have a little fun."

"Well, she's certainly taken the ball and run with it," Agnes groused.

The grand old foyer door slammed shut, and Hattie looked over her shoulder. "Is someone at the front door?"

"The police have just brought Olivia's children home," Glyniss shouted.

Horrified, Agnes flapped her arms in frenzied circles. "Shhh!"

Hattie smiled with satisfaction. "Good. Good. I've been expecting them." Leveraging herself to a standing position, the little landlady quoted one of her sage bits of wisdom for the group, "I always say, a good way to forget your troubles is to help others out of theirs."

• • •

Fresh from her shower, Olivia came bounding down the stairs for supper, in hopes of catching one last glimpse of Zach before he left for the day. Perhaps if he saw her in a less disheveled mode, he might not think she was such a nut. Not, of course, that it mattered what Zach thought of her, exactly. It wasn't as if she were trying to make any kind of impression on him. No. However, it was a small town. Keeping up appearances was a good idea. Unless one liked being the object of gossip.

Reaching the bottom of the stairs, Olivia rounded the corner into the parlor and stopped dead in her tracks.

Officer Menkin?

What is he doing here? Her pulse picked up speed. Zach? *Why is he looking at me with such a peculiar expression on his face?* Her gaze slowly traveled between the two men and then down to the sofa.

The children! Overjoyed at the sight of them, she rushed forward and ruffled Ruth's tangled hair. Both girls looked relieved to see her but remained mute. Arms outstretched, Esther wordlessly begged to be held, but Cain sat stoic and silent, ever the brave little man of the family. Reaching down, Olivia scooped up Esther and cuddled her close.

"Hello, Officer. What's going on?"

"You did say you wanted 'em, didn't you, ma'am?" he stated in his lackluster Sergeant Friday monotone.

Olivia's mouth dropped open. Cain flinched, but remained quiet.

The only sound in the parlor was the steady ticktock of the grandfather clock as it filtered in from the foyer. The officer stared at her, and a fire began to burn in Olivia's stomach. Lucky thing Officer Menkin wasn't a doctor. His bedside manner would have people keeling over like flies.

"Well, uh, yes..." Olivia dragged her eyes from the officer and darted a helpless look at Zach.

The confusion on his face reflected her own inner turmoil.

"Good, because Children's Services is swamped. They have done a preliminary check on you, ma'am, and you are approved to take these three in until we can sort through the red tape."

"I...uh...oh!" As she battled a wave of panic, Olivia sank down to the couch between Cain and Ruth. Swallowing, she smiled at the children and tried to look delighted, for their sake. "What about their"—she studied their innocent little faces—"mother?"

Zach's questioning gaze shot to Olivia.

"In the morgue, ma'am." Officer Menkin imparted information, *Dragnet* style.

Blinking rapidly, Olivia's grip tightened on Esther. "In the *morgue*?" She whispered the word, her heart pounding. Suddenly she was transported back five years, as memories of a similar conversation on a similar night flooded her mind. A night when the world as she knew it came to an abrupt end.

Seeming to somehow understand her pain, Zach moved around to the back of the sofa and placed a comforting hand on her shoulder.

"Yes ma'am. Been there a few days now. OD'd on several different things. We couldn't tag her till this afternoon, when we finally figured out who she was. She has no immediate living family nor any relations interested in taking her kids. The neighbors tell us that the children's father passed away in a gang-related incident in another state several years ago."

"Oh." Olivia sighed, trying to digest this stunning information in a way that would not upset the children. "Nobody in the family is interested in," she chose her words carefully, "providing for them?"

"No ma'am. Most of 'em are deceased. Lifestyle."

She blinked back the tears of sorrow for the untimely death of this young mother. And for the babies she'd left behind. She swiped at her eyes with the back of her hand, and was grateful for Zach's gentle touch on her shoulder.

She lifted her eyes to Officer Menkin. "Do the children understand this?" Her gaze traveled first to Ruth, who wriggled in her seat, seemingly ready to explore, then to Cain, who appeared to have turned to granite.

"We thought that this kind of thing might be better coming from someone who had a vested emotional interest, such as yourself, ma'am. Right now, they know that they are going to stay with...the...er," the policeman cleared his throat, "donut lady for a while."

"Oh."

Officer Menkin gestured to a paper bag that lay at his feet. "This is all their worldly effects, ma'am. Not much, as you can see. Just an old doll and a few clothing odds and ends. All dirty."

"Nothing more?" Zach was incredulous. "Everything they own is in that bag?"

"Yes. Looks like you have your work cut out for you, sir."

Olivia sighed. That was the second time someone had mistaken Zach for her husband. Oh. Would that it were so. She could certainly use the support about now.

Fishing around in his pocket, Officer Menkin withdrew a business card and handed it to Olivia.

"If you have any questions, call me, or Children's Services Monday morning. A social worker will be calling on you in a few days to interview you."

"I—okay." Woodenly, Olivia took the small bit of paper as feelings of anxiety and panic welled up within. She suddenly had tremendous empathy for Nell. Panic was no fun.

What in heaven's name had she gotten herself into? What was she going to do with three homeless children? Even for a few days. Why, she had nothing to give them. No clothes, no toys, no beds...Good grief.

Ruth, unable to bear sitting still another minute, scooted off the sofa and meandered across the room to explore Hattie's curio cabinet. Her brother opened his mouth but said nothing.

Zach moved around to the front of the sofa and took Ruth's empty seat. A grateful smile tipped Olivia's lips.

Legs spread for balance as he stood, Officer Menkin squared his shoulders, donned his glasses, and began flipping through his notes. Without preamble he proceeded to fill Olivia and Zach in on all he had discovered that after-noon about the children's background.

"Mother's name was Roxanne Grady. She'd been in trouble in other states, had a criminal record—possession, trafficking, prostitution, theft, you name it. She was hardly Mother of the Year. I'm sure the kids suffered because of her choices."

Olivia and Zach exchanged glances filled with trepidation.

Officer Menkin went on to inform them that the chil-dren had been sorely neglected most of their lives, living for stretches with a now deceased grandmother and passed around to various nefarious friends while Mom was in jail.

Luckily, or unluckily, depending on the viewpoint, the children never did spend too much time living with Mom. However, to the best of his knowledge, Mom didn't abuse them physically, and she did the best she could, given her addiction problems.

"I guess you could say she loved 'em, in her own way." Officer Menkin snapped his notebook closed and stuffed it into his breast pocket. His job finished, he turned to go.

"Thank you." Olivia was filled with uncertainty as the officer strode into the foyer. "I guess we'll…" she shrugged, "talk later."

Officer Menkin issued a small grunt of departure before he disappeared into the night.

Beginning to warm up to her surroundings, Esther struggled out of Olivia's embrace and joined Ruth as the child rummaged through Hattie's knickknacks. Not willing to relinquish his position of command, Cain sprang off the sofa and joined them, issuing orders as he went.

"You're not the boss of us, Cain!" Ruth elbowed him out of the way as she struggled to mount and ride Hattie's life-sized Dalmatian fireplace ornament. Esther squealed, wrapping her arms around the spotted metallic neck and kissing the canine chops.

"A doggy!" she cried. "He's mine, mine, mine."

"He's not yours, Esther," Ruth told her. "I saw him first. He's my doggy, and I'm going to call him Rosy Cheeks, because that's the most beautiful name in the whole world for a dog."

"That's a stupid name," Cain muttered, filled with masculine disgust.

"Is not!" Ruth grabbed onto Rosy Cheeks's ears and proceeded to ride over imaginary hill and dale, chattering ninety miles an hour as she went.

Olivia figured they couldn't do any damage to that old iron dog that hadn't been done by generations previous, so she let them explore and take the time to adjust to their surroundings. She watched the children for a long moment, emotions in every color of the rainbow swirling through her muddled brain. Sorrow, gratitude, and fear all warred for top billing.

Unable to contain his curiosity any longer, Zach finally spoke, pulling her from her reverie. "How did you happen to come by these little waifs"—he gestured at the children, his expression tender—"if you don't mind my asking."

"Oh no, no. I don't mind." Olivia smiled up at him, keeping a motherly eye trained on the children as she explained. She told him how she'd come upon them in the convenience store and then tracked them down the next day. She related her conversation with Officer Menkin and how convinced she'd been that she'd never hear from him again.

"But," she sighed, "I was wrong. You could have knocked me over with a feather when I came downstairs just now and saw the kids in here."

"Yeah. I'll bet that did come as a bit of a shock."

Zach's warm chuckle was a soothing balm to Olivia's frayed nerves. Something about his quiet strength made her feel like she could do anything. Although how she was going to manage this three-pronged bundle of energy for the next few days, or even weeks, was beyond her.

"You know," Zach began, leaning forward and propping his elbows on his knees, "I don't have much experience caring for kids, but I hang around Mike and his family all the time, and I'm a pretty swell Sunday school teacher." He lifted his hands from where they dangled between his legs. "I could stay and give you a hand, if you like."

As the kids picked up speed and volume in their explorations, Olivia could think of nothing that she would like better than having Zach stay and lend his support. Being left to her own devices with these three was daunting to say the least. Unfortunately, she couldn't ask that of him; he had his own life to attend to.

The centrifugal force began to build as the kids tore in circles around the sofa with Cain shouting at his giggling and squealing sisters, who were seemingly content in their unfamiliar surroundings. Olivia had to wonder how many nights they'd already spent in unfamiliar surroundings in their short lives. Unnoticed, Hattie moved into the parlor and stood in the corner watching. A look of joy touched her as she murmured a prayer into her tightly clenched fists.

Zach tossed a dubious look at the children and then at Olivia.

She grinned. He seemed to be regretting his hasty offer of help. Ah, well, she would let him off the hook.

"Oh no, Zach. Thank you for your thoughtful offer, but it's late, and I know your wife must be waiting."

His head moved slowly from side to side. "No," he said,

"my wife, AmyBeth, died in an accident about two and a half years ago now. I live alone."

Olivia stopped and stared in amazement at him. They had both been widowed. What were the odds? "Oh, I'm so sorry. I...think I know how you must feel. I lost my husband and daughter in a car accident about five years ago." She heaved a sigh that was filled with sorrow. For him. For herself. For these kids.

"I'm sorry for you too."

"There is something so unfair about an untimely death, isn't there?" Her eyes strayed to the children. Esther, skinny legs pumping, shrieked with laughter as she chased Ruth around the sofa.

Passing a palm over his face, he inclined his head in agreement. "I know what you mean. AmyBeth was killed in a car bombing, of all things. She'd gone overseas to bring home a baby we were adopting and ended up in the wrong place at the wrong time."

Olivia brought her hands to her mouth in horror. "How awful!"

"Mmm. Like you, I not only lost a spouse but a child too."

"Oh...I'm so very sorry."

"Me too."

For a bittersweet moment, they stood, gazes locked, realizing how much they had lost, and the common bond they shared. Only someone who'd been through what they'd been through could even begin to understand. They could sense that about each other and felt a kinship begin in that instant.

The sound of breaking glass roused them from their moment.

• • •

"Good heavens!" Agnes barreled through the kitchen door and shuffled down the hall and into the parlor. The Colonel, Glyniss, and Rahni were hot on her heels. "What on earth is going on out here? And who, might I ask," she screeched, "is in charge of these…hellions?" Rearing her head back, she stared down her pointed nose at Olivia.

The others gawked over her shoulder from the doorway.

Zach stood and helped Olivia to her feet. He allowed his hand to linger at her elbow, an oddly protective feeling sweeping over him toward this tender-hearted woman. He'd only known her for a few days now, but for some uncanny reason he felt as if he'd known her all his life. It was almost as if she had dropped into his path from the heavens. Which was ridiculous. After all, *he* was the one who'd crashed into *her* sunroom. But still. There was something magical happening here. He could feel it deep in his gut.

"I am, Miss Agnes," Olivia confessed. Reaching out, she grabbed the flush-faced Esther as the child shot by and pulled the wriggling three-year-old into her arms. "In fact," she shouted above the hubbub of the still-excited children, "the children will be staying with me for a little while." She cast an apologetic look in Hattie's direction. "If that's okay with you, Hattie. I can explain everything later."

"Of course, my dearie, no need to explain. I wouldn't have it any other way. I knew they'd arrive sooner or later."

"You did?" A perplexed expression crossing her face, Olivia shrugged. "Then you don't mind?"

"Don't be silly. As I'm always fond of saying, 'to feel sorry for the needy is not the mark of a Christian—to help them is.' The pitter-patter of little feet will perk this old place up a tad, to be sure."

Agnes stared at Cain and Ruth as they thundered around the sofa, and then at Hattie as if she'd lost her mind.

Blissfully unaware of this censure, Hattie continued, "After supper, I shall enlist the Colonel's help in cleaning out the storage room next to your suite, Olympia, dear. Perhaps we can fashion some kind of temporary accommodations for the children. In the meantime," the little landlady continued as she reached out and put her hands on Ruth and Cain's shoulders. The two miraculously stilled. "In the meantime, Olympia and Jack, why don't you two get these youngsters washed up for supper? Jack, you will be staying to have a bite with us?"

"Yes ma'am." He wouldn't miss this for the world.

"Good, good. Bonnie, we must set some extra places at the table for our newest boarders."

* * *

"Hey, come back here, you slippery little porpoise!" Zach rubbed the screaming muscles at the back of his neck. Cain had escaped the confines of his arms as he'd been toweling the boy off and completing the postbath finishing touches with ear swabs.

On their way to Olivia's suite, they had decided that a mere hand washing was nowhere near enough, when it came to washing up for supper. These kids had heaven-only-knew-how-many layers of dirt and germs on their skin, and neither Olivia nor Zach dared venture a guess as to what might be crawling in their clothing and hair.

"No!" Cain shouted and scrambled—bare cheeks bouncing—under Olivia's bed. "I don't want you dryin' my ears with those sticks! They might hurt!"

Exasperated, Zach peered under the bed and tried to reason with the little boy. "They won't hurt, I promise. I'll just clean the outside of your ears. C'mon, Cain. You have enough dirt in there to plant a garden."

"No! Never!"

Sighing, Zach decided that if he was ever going to get the upper hand in this relationship, it would have to be now. "Let's go, buddy." He grabbed the recalcitrant boy by the ankle and dragged him out from under the bed.

"No, no, no!" Kicking and screaming, Cain emerged, the random dust bunny clinging to his damp skin.

"Cain!" Wrapping a terry bath sheet around the child, Zach sank down on the bed and pulled him onto his lap. "It's okay, Cain buddy. You're gonna be fine." He hoped. He had no idea if the kid would be fine. It certainly wasn't okay. The kid's mother was in the morgue. And with the exception of Olivia, he had no home. No future. No, it wasn't okay at all. But he couldn't tell that to a five-year-old. Not now anyway.

Cain struggled like a cornered bobcat, and Zach's heart went out to him. Poor kid. In the same circumstances, he'd be freaking too.

"Hey, hey, hey." He whispered into the child's ear and wrapped his arms around the flailing body and held him tight. "Shhh." Going on instinct, Zach rocked the boy and murmured soothing nothings until the fight left his little body and the child sagged against his chest.

"I want my mama." His voice broken and muffled, Cain pressed his face into Zach's neck and twined his little fists into Zach's shirt.

Zach tried to swallow past the lump in his throat. "I know, kiddo. I know just how it feels to be scared and lonely."

Cain nestled deeper into Zach's arms.

As they rocked together, sounds of wildlife filtered to them from the bathroom where Olivia was busy fighting her own battles.

"Look, donut lady! Watch me!" Ruth cavorted in the bathwater like a carefree mermaid, kicking and splashing and swimming in lazy circles around Esther. "Watch, donut lady! Watch this!" Blowing bubbles, she flailed about, oblivious to the discomfort she was causing her younger sister.

Esther started to cry. Then scream. "I got soap in my eye," she blubbered, blindly groping for Olivia's blouse. Locating the cotton placket, Esther grabbed on, pulling Olivia over the edge of the tub and grinding her eyes into her collar. "Get it out! Make it go away! Owww!"

"Uhh—" Olivia grunted, trying to extract Esther's choking grip on her neckline. "Uhh, honey?"

"Look at me, donut lady!" Ruth climbed to the edge of the tub and bombed into the water, sending it spraying in all directions. "Watch! Watch me, donut lady!"

"Uhh, Zach?" Olivia called into the bedroom.

"Donut man!" Ruth scrambled out of the tub and rushed into the bedroom, au naturel. "Come and look what I can do in the tub! Come on!" Cavorting about, Ruth clambered up onto the bed and began to jump. "Watch me, donut lady!"

Carrying a soggy, tear-stained Esther, Olivia sagged in the doorway and watched Ruth thrash about, giggling and crashing into Zach and her brother.

Balefully, Olivia's gaze connected with Zach's, a what-have-I-gotten-myself-into expression on her face.

"You're gonna be fine," Zach assured her. "It's okay. Everything will work out just fine. I'm here," he suddenly heard himself blurting out. "I'll...uh, be glad to give you a hand with these guys."

Cain remained silent, but some of the tension eased from his face.

7

Olivia would never be able to express her gratitude to Zach for deciding to stay and give her a hand with the children. How they ever would have made it through dinner that night without him was beyond her. For not only did he lend some much needed moral support, he was actually quite adept at handling the children. Not to mention Miss Agnes's caustic remarks.

His calming demeanor radiated from the seat next to hers at the dinner table in a nearly palpable way. There was something about Zach that intrigued her. Thrilled her. Filled her with newfound confidence. She couldn't quite place her finger on exactly what it was, but if she had to choose a word, she supposed it would be *peace*. Zach was peaceful. Tranquil. Strong. At ease with himself and the world.

Amazing.

And after everything he'd been through.

It had been twice as long since she lost her family, and she was nowhere near as serene as he was. She was still so angry and bitter, railing against God for the raw deal she'd received. She wondered what Zach's secret was. How had he achieved such inner peace? Making a mental note, she decided that next time she had a minute alone with Zach—and she hoped that would be soon—she would ask him about that.

She peeked up at his strong jaw line and felt a streak of electricity run from the part in her hair to the tips of her light pink toenails. Having him stay for dinner this way was so much fun. She wished he'd eat his evening meal here every night. Beginning to feel as if she were gawking, she tore her gaze away from him and trained it on the kids.

Miraculously the children were all squeaky clean, just in time for supper. Each curly head had been neatly combed, each set of teeth scrubbed—with some new toothbrushes Hattie kept on hand for emergencies such as this—and they were now dressed in some of Olivia's old T-shirts, underwear, and sweatpants. The ill-fitting garments had been pinned and belted and rolled up at the cuffs.

The filthy rags the children had been wearing when they arrived were now out in the Dumpster, awaiting pickup service. Olivia would worry about getting them some decent children's clothes tomorrow. For tonight anyway they were warm and comfortable, and that was all that mattered.

"Shall we pray?" Hattie warbled from the head of the table, bowing her head and grasping the hands to her right and left.

Everyone who lived at the boarding house was at the table that night, along with Zach and the children. It was a tight squeeze, seating thirteen people at a dozen-capacity table. But Hattie could not have looked more pleased.

Everyone murmured consent, and together they bowed their heads.

"Dear heavenly Father, King of kings and Lord of lords," Hattie began in a reverent tone, "I'd like to begin this prayer by thanking you for sending us Payne and Hester and Rose. Your quick answer to our simple prayer is such a joyous reaffirmation of our faith."

"Uh, yes, Lord." Quizzical murmurings came from around the table.

What simple prayer? seemed to be the question hanging in the air. *And who are Payne, Hester, and Rose?* Shrugging, everyone continued to pray in agreement with Hattie.

"Thank you, Jesus," they whispered and buzzed. "Yes, thank you, Lord."

"Look, donut lady! My potatoes are smiling at me!" Ruth stared at her food, and proceeded to poke eyes, nose, and hair into the mash with her fingers.

One eye popping open, Agnes sent scathing darts of annoyance in the youngster's direction. Luckily, Ruth did not notice the bulging eyeball directed at her.

"And, Lord," Hattie went on, "we pray that you will continue the glorious work that you have begun in Olympia."

"Shhh! Ruth, honey, don't play with your food while we are praying," Olivia instructed the child under her breath. Grabbing a linen napkin, she proceeded to swab Ruth's fingers. "Ruth, honey! I said stop!"

Oblivious to the goings-on around her, Hattie continued to speak with her Lord and Master. "I pray that you will bring this plan to its fruition, Jesus, complete with the complimenting man—"

"Yes, Jesus…" Everyone was now more perplexed than ever. Who was this mysterious complimenting man? Several folks darted covert glances of confusion back and forth. Ah, well, if Hattie wanted one, no doubt she would get one.

"No no, Esther." Zach quietly remonstrated, shooting an apologetic look in Ryan's direction. "Don't give the doggy any more of your peas, sweetheart. People food will make him sick. Put your hands together like this." He demonstrated. "We are saying a prayer."

"I don't want to pray," Esther shouted. "I want to give that doggy my peas!"

Everyone at the table, with the exception of Hattie, peered at the situation with an interested eye from behind their clasped hands.

"No, honey. The doggy can't have any more peas."

"But he likes 'em! I don't like these peas!" Esther wailed her vehemence to the praying faction. "They taste yucky!"

This cracked Ruth up. Throwing back her head, she laughed until food sprayed from her mouth like a fountain. "Look at me, donut lady!" She repeated the process. "Watch!" she mumbled, mashed potato flying from her lips.

"Ruth, settle down. And, Esther," Olivia murmured, trying her best to remain unobtrusive. "You heard Zach, honey. Please don't give the dog any more of your peas."

Esther shrugged.

"Thank you," Ryan mouthed on Copper's behalf, holding back a smile as he once again bowed his head for Hattie's prayer.

"Let's finish saying our prayer." Zach gave Esther an encouraging pat on the back.

"Hold me, donut man." Her gaze imploring, Esther lifted her arms.

Olivia's heart swelled as Zach took the small child onto his lap and nestled her against his chest. Together, their heads bent in prayer.

Still unaware of the chaos around her, Hattie continued her prayer, "And Lord, not to bother you, but one last thing would make the answer to my original prayer for Olympia complete. A puppy. Any kind of puppy would be just fine."

As if on cue, Copper staggered out from under the table, mouth open, back hunching in a most distorted manner. He gurgled and gagged and lurched and belched alarmingly for a moment, then proceeded to retch a colorful pile atop Hattie's antique Turkish rug. Peas. Lots of peas. Quite obviously, Esther hadn't been the only one feeding Copper peas.

"So, Lord, it is with a full heart that I thank you for answered prayer and your bounty. I humbly ask that you bless this fine banquet to our bodies—"

His body having rejected the fine banquet, Copper flopped onto the floor and lifted a baleful look up at Ryan.

Sean and Julia stared at the wriggling children and then trained a dubious is-this-what-we-have-to-look-forward-to? glance at Julia's swollen belly.

"—all these things we ask in your precious name," Hattie concluded fervently, "amen."

"Amen." Everyone sighed. Ryan rushed to gather several paper napkins from the dispenser on the sideboard in order to clean the floor. The rest of the gang dug into the sumptuous supper that had been cooling on their plates.

Esther hung over Zach's arm and inspected the mess that Copper had made. "I don't like yucky peas. They're...poopy!" Her rosebud lips began to tremble.

"Then don't eat them, honey." Olivia sighed. "But leave them on your plate."

"I don't like poo-poo on my plate."

"Child, we do not use such despicable language at this table," Miss Agnes informed Esther. "Sit up and use your fork. And the rest of you, puleeze, chew with your mouths closed. This disgusting noise is enough to send me to my sickbed."

Lips smacking in symphonic stereo, the children all looked dully at Miss Agnes, wondering if she'd been addressing them or was simply complaining again.

"Olivia," Agnes throbbed, piercing her with a hawkish stare, "why don't you fill me—and everyone else here at the table—in on why your children refer to you as the...er, 'donut lady.' Is this," she paused, revving up her engines for a grand inquisition, "some kind of new trend for today's parent? Because if it is, I have to warn—"

"Miss Agnes, the children call me donut lady because I brought them some donuts yesterday."

"How unusual. I've known of many mothers in my time who have provided the occasional donut for their offspring. However, I'm hard-pressed to recall any child referring to his mother as...ahem...'donut lady.'" Agnes dabbed daintily at her prunish lips, as if mentally chalking up her debate points.

Olivia looked around the table, flustered to find all eyes riveted on her. What was Agnes trying to say about the children's mother? She hated to bring the subject up before she had a chance to discuss it with the children. Did the older woman know that Olivia would be acting as their guardian for a time? Why was Agnes acting so mysterious? "I, hmm, well, I guess the kids don't know what else to call me."

"Could that be," Agnes wondered, ready to drive home her point about today's lackadaisical parent, "because you never spend any time with them?"

Shrugging, Olivia smiled warily at Agnes. "Probably."

"Aha!"

"I don't want this yucky stuff on my plate!" Esther shouted.

"There!" Agnes pointed a shaking finger at the child. "That would also explain your children's complete lack of manners and social skills?"

"I guess so..." Olivia looked at Zach and was pleased to see that he looked as befuddled as she felt.

Huffing, Glyniss glared at Agnes. "Give the kids a break, Aggie. I seem to remember you disliked peas as a youngster yourself."

"That's not true!"

"Yes it is. In fact," Glyniss confided to the rest of the boarders that crowded around the dinner table that evening, "Agnes hated peas so much, she hid them in her nose. As you can see," she proceeded with glee, gesturing to Agnes's sizable beak, "she could put away more than a few peas. Had to call the doctor to come and get them out more than once."

Laughter rumbled round the table as grownups and kids alike found this image hilarious. The Colonel wheezed for a solid minute. Ruth looked at Agnes with a new respect.

Scandalized, Miss Agnes clucked like an outraged hen. "Why, that's the most ridiculous thing I ever heard. And certainly not true! The doctor was summoned because I had croup, and you know it, Glyniss!"

Glyniss rolled her eyes. *"Peas,"* she mouthed to the children.

The girls giggled.

Even Cain's stony expression was cracked by a glimmer of humor.

• • •

After everyone had polished off the last of Rahni's pecan pie and was stuffed to the gills, the entire household retired to the parlor. The Colonel took his usual spot on the recliner and, after pretending to read the paper for a minute, fell fast asleep. His nasal rumblings could most likely be heard in the next county, but nobody seemed to mind or even notice.

Glyniss and Agnes sat in the matching wing chairs next to the crackling fireplace and, when they weren't squabbling, worked on some needlepoint. Hattie, cozy with a cup of tea and an afghan, sat on the delicate love seat and studied the well-worn pages of her Bible, every so often pausing to communicate with the Lord.

Sean, Julia, Rahni, Ryan—and of course, the now recovered Copper—entertained the kids with a rousing game of Old Maid around the giant old oak coffee table. Cain was sullen, but Olivia was relieved to see that he at least was playing.

Propping their feet up on a shared ottoman, Olivia and Zach settled onto the sofa and used this time to get to know each other a little better and try to brainstorm a plan of action for the children. As they discussed the myriad ins and outs of the situation, now and again Ruth would leap to her feet and perform some gyration that would require the attention of the donut lady.

"Look at me, donut lady!" she would cry and clumsily pirouette around the area rug. Another time she would shout, "Watch, donut lady!" then somersault into her sister or brother, who would retaliate as the situation warranted. But it was when she cartwheeled into Agnes that everyone froze and held their breath. For a moment, the old lady rubbed the side of her arm that had been battered and studied Ruth's terror-stricken face.

"Child," Agnes huffed, arching a forbidding brow, "puleeze watch where you are going." Somewhere in the depths of her baggy, watery eyes, a twinkle lurked, belying the harshness of her words.

Ruth scurried away, the card game resumed, and Agnes went back to her needlework.

"Well..." Zach sighed, stretching. A contented yawn overcame him, and he cast a sheepish glance at Olivia as she sat close to him on the small sofa. "I suppose it's time I should be on my way."

Olivia's heart sank. She didn't want him to go. How was

she going to get three rambunctious kids into strange beds all by herself? The very idea left her exhausted, deflated, and lonely.

"Oh," was all she could manage. A halfhearted smile pushed at the corners of her mouth.

As if reading her thoughts, he back-pedaled a little. "Unless you...I mean, I suppose I could stay awhile longer and help you get them into bed."

"Oh, would you?" She hated how breathless she sounded, but she couldn't help it. She really wanted him to stay. "That would be great."

"Probably should get to it pretty soon. Tomorrow's a workday."

"Don't remind me." Olivia grimaced, her head flopping back on the sofa. The headaches hadn't even begun.

"You have to work tomorrow?"

"Mm-hmm."

"What are you going to do about the kids?"

"I haven't got a clue." Lifting and dropping a shoulder, she watched her three little charges play cards with her friends. "I don't suppose you need a hand remodeling the sunroom?" she teased, her head lolling against the back of the sofa so that she could better see him.

"Hmm. I don't know. S'pose Esther can handle a saw?"

"Ruth could talk her through it," Olivia deadpanned.

Zach chuckled. "Maybe you oughta call in sick."

"Maybe. But that won't work forever."

"True."

"I'm gonna have to figure something out."

"You probably won't have 'em forever."

"Probably not. But how long will it take to find a family that can take them? Three little homeless kids must be kind of hard to place."

"It would take a special person."

Olivia nodded.

"They're sure cute. I had no idea they were all so blond until we got them out of the tub."

"Mmm. Me either. I like how they all have freckles right here." Olivia trailed her forefinger lightly across the bridge of his nose and then drew back, feeling suddenly goosey and out of sorts. It had been a long time since she'd felt such freedom to touch a man like that.

Lazily allowing his head to slide toward hers on the back of the sofa, Zach lowered his voice and whispered in her ear, "Why do you suppose they have such strange names?"

"Strange?"

"Well, not strange really, but hardly the Tiffanys and Ashleys and Tylers that are all the rage today."

"True, but that's why I like them. They're different." Olivia smiled up at Zach and pulled the quilt she shared with him a little higher under her chin. She hadn't felt this wonderful sense of male-female camaraderie since John was alive. Did Zach feel it too? Her mouth was suddenly dry. With the tip of her tongue, she moistened her lips. "Yesterday, Ruth and Cain told me where they got their names. Actually, Ruth told me where everyone in the neighborhood got their names, but I'll try to stick to the pertinent facts in the interest of time." She grinned.

"Please." Zach returned her grin.

"Ruth says her mother picked names out of the family Bible. Cain had a twin brother, who died at birth. That's why his mother chose Cain for him. I gather she figured it symbolized the brother that lived."

"Wow." Zach stared at her with fascination. "That's quite a handle to live up to. Or down to, I guess, depending how you look at it."

"No kidding. But I like the name. I think it works for him."

Zach's gaze traveled to the boy with the haunted face who sat protectively between his sisters. The child seemed to carry the weight of the world on his shoulders. "Yeah. The name fits, all right."

"Mm-hmm. Anyway, for the girls, she wanted them to have strong names, so that they might turn out stronger than she did."

"Well, let's hope it works."

"No kidding."

They shared a poignant moment of silence, each thinking their own private thoughts about Roxanne Grady and her untimely death.

Finally, with great reluctance, Zach sat up and pulled his half of the quilt they shared off his legs. "As much as I hate to break up this little party, it's getting late, and we should probably figure out what we're going to do about putting these rascals to bed."

"I'm not tired," Ruth proclaimed, her bedtime radar zeroing in on his comments. "We never go to bed before midnight anyway."

"Well I do and, for tonight anyway, you are too."

Ruth's mouth dropped open, but Zach's firm, parental tone brooked no argument. Leaning forward on his elbows, he pushed himself to a standing position.

Olivia nudged the quilt off her own legs and, taking his offered assistance, came to a stand beside him. She tried to ignore the way his hand lingered at her elbow.

"Finish up your game, kids, while Zach and I go upstairs and fix a place for you to stay." She turned to Julia and Sean. "Would you mind looking after the kids for a few minutes?"

Engrossed in the card game, Julia and Sean gave them the high sign and motioned for them to move along.

Hattie's birdlike gaze landed on Olivia and Zach as they prepared to leave the parlor and, grasping her cane, she struggled to her feet.

"Olympia, darling, I have some extra cots in the closet of the storage room next to yours. The Colonel and I can fish those out for you while you and Jack clear a spot in your suite."

Zach cast a dubious glance in the snoring Colonel's direction, then gently squeezed Olivia's arm.

Moving near to the little landlady, Olivia bent to shout in her ear. "Oh no. Thank you so much, Hattie, but Zach and I can find them ourselves, isn't that right, Zach?

Zach bobbed his head and flexed his muscles, causing Hattie to giggle girlishly.

"Oh, you!" Waving them off, she sank back down into her seat. "There are extra single-bed linens in the closet at the end of the hall," she called after them. "Pillows too!"

"Thank you, Hattie."

"We're stayin' here?" Cain asked, his expression morose and fearful as he watched the donut lady and man move to the door. "What about our mom? She'll wonder where we are."

Olivia swallowed, her brain racing for the proper wording. Breaking the news to these three was going to be one of the hardest things she'd ever had to do. She dreaded their reactions. How would she begin to handle their emotional outpourings when she was not even capable of handling her own?

Taking a deep breath, she decided she would do it later. Right now, she'd work on getting them settled in.

"You guys are staying here with me for now, kiddo,"

Olivia responded, injecting what she hoped was the right mixture of compassion and enthusiasm. Her eyes darted to Zach. Perhaps she could prevail upon him to stay and help her break the news. Maybe between the two of them, both having been there before and all, they could figure out some way to help the kids understand and accept their mother's death. "I'll fix toast with jelly and a big glass of milk for breakfast. Won't that be...nice?"

"Mom won't let you keep us. Even if that cop says so. She always comes and gets us." That said, Cain withdrew into himself, his surly expression dropping into place as if to shutter the window to his wounded soul.

"Yea!" Ruth shouted. "I will love to stay here. I want to stay here forever. I like it here, donut lady! I want to go swimming in the tub again!" Springing to her feet, she began to dance around and sing at the top of her voice. "I'm gonna live with donut lady! I'm gonna live with donut lady!"

Wincing, Agnes shook her head and rolled her eyes.

8

Muscles screaming, Zach lifted the gigantic old cot over his head and stumbled through the obstacle course that made up the storage room next to Olivia's suite. The wretched frame of this prehistoric bed had to have been made of lead. With the mattress flopping over his face in a most disorganized manner, Zach struggled to keep his balance and, at the same time, maintain his bearings in the dim light. There were so many pieces of furniture in his way—not to mention boxes, crates, and trunks—he was certain Hattie could pronounce this haphazard clutter a maze and charge admission. Unfortunately, most folks would probably never make it out alive.

To make matters worse, there were still two more of these man-eating cots in the closet that he had yet to heft into Olivia's room that night.

"You're doing really well. Just inch it a little this way." Olivia instructed him from somewhere just beyond his field of vision.

"Which way?" Grunting, he relied on her not only for directions but to catch the other end of this musty old toad before he broke his neck. He was still very battered and sore from his slide down the hill in his pickup truck. No doubt he should be in traction in some nice, cozy hospital room about now instead of trying to show off for Olivia. Although showing off for Olivia was a lot more fun.

"To the right. My right. No, not your right. That would be my left. Go to my right. Right. That's right. You're fine…"

"That's debatable."

"No, no, no! Not that way! The other right!"

"Which way?" Zach ground out through his tightly clenched teeth. "I thought you said right!"

"Right! I mean *correct*. Keep going."

"Where?"

"The way you're going!"

"I'm not going anywhere."

"Yes, you are."

"I'm not meaning to."

"Just watch it on the left."

"Whose left?"

"Yours. Oof."

"What'd I hit?"

"Doorframe." Olivia grunted. "And my fingers." Air hissed though her teeth as she inhaled in pain.

"Sorry."

"That's…okay."

"Can you grab the bottom there on your end and help me twist it on its side?"

"Sure. Give me a second while I locate my fingers. I think some of them may be on the floor."

Zach groaned. "Don't go and make me laugh. As it is, something in my head is on the verge of an aneurysm."

"Good thing you're already wearing a bandage," she joked.

"Very funny." He shifted his aching hands to better wrangle the bed. "You ready?"

"Ready."

"Good. Because I'm about to pop a neck vein or an eyeball or something."

Olivia's giddy giggles reached him. "Can you imagine the Colonel and Hattie digging this stuff out for us?"

Zach's guffaw was muffled by the mattress. "Finding the closet alone would take the average person a week." He could feel her lifting and twisting her edge of the bed. She was strong for a woman.

"Lucky thing you're not average." She teased him, a flirtatious edge to her voice. Her lilting laughter wafted back to where he stood.

As Olivia's words penetrated his muzzy brain, Zach suddenly felt as if—like the mythical Atlas before him—he could shoulder the world, her compelling voice affected him so.

"Look out!" He leveraged the unwieldy tonnage a bit higher. He would worry about his broken sacroiliac another time. "Comin' through."

Staggering like a drunken sailor, Zach wrested the bed out of her hands and barreled into the hallway. "Where am I?"

"Eastbound lane, picking up speed."

"Which way now?" He began to chase the massive bundle he so precariously balanced on his head.

Or was it balancing him?

"First exit on your left!" Olivia ran after him. "Slow down!"

"I'm trying!"

"You've passed my door!"

"Well, doggone it, now you tell me!"

"Zach!"

"What?" He was becoming irritated at the small talk. He had a job to do, and he was trying to do it.

"Stairs!"

"Uhh, uhh, ohh, ohhh!"

Fortunately, Olivia lunged after him and reached his belt just before he went over the falls, barrel first. Unfortunately, the cot had other ideas and—as it hurtled down the giant mahogany staircase—it took Zach and Olivia down with it. Fortunately, they landed on the mattress and rode it down. Unfortunately, the cot punched a watermelon-sized hole in the hand-carved, imported European mahogany wainscoting. Fortunately, Zach had insurance.

"Man, Hattie's gonna kill me for sure this time." He moaned in agony, once he'd deduced that both he and Olivia were still alive and relatively unharmed.

"You do have a way of shooting the rapids around this place," Olivia agreed, somewhat breathlessly, rubbing what would surely become a colorful bruise on her arm.

Though they had landed in a most uncomfortable heap—tenaciously clinging to the mattress as it threatened to round the landing corner and continue the trip south—they were each able to find the humor in the situation.

"I'm afraid to set up the rest of the cots."

"Why?" Olivia giggled.

"Because I'm afraid the house might not be standing when I'm done." He started to laugh.

"I'm afraid you might be right."

For a long time they lay there, howling at the chandelier that glowed directly above their heads. Tears streamed down their faces, and they laughed until their bellies ached.

Sniffing and dabbing her eyes on the sleeve of her blouse, Olivia tried to sit up. "Excuse me," she gestured to his elbow, "my hair seems to be caught...ouch..."

"Oh sorry!"

"...oh, that's okay."

"Sorry. Oh, sorry." Zach apologized again, scrambling away from her as they attempted to sort themselves out.

"Could you...?" She winced as his watchband snagged her hair.

"Oh sure. Sorry about that!" He reiterated his profuse apology while trying to extract his watch from her locks. "I guess I just like your hair so much, I'm trying to take some with me."

"That's fine with me." Olivia smiled. "But I know there has to be an easier way."

Their gazes collided for a spine-zinging moment, and they stared idiotically at each other, two adults in the process of developing a crush.

Finally, they were able to stand and drag the cot back up to the top of the steps. Then, once again, Zach muscled the cumbersome bed up onto his shoulders.

"Okay." His grin peeked out from under the lumpy mattress. "Where to?"

"This way." Mirth bubbling past her lips, Olivia put her hands on his waist, lightly guiding him down the hall and through the doorway to her suite of rooms.

Zach took a deep breath. Her hands branded every place they touched with an electric current. Though his muscles shrieked for mercy, Zach could think of nothing else but her delicate touch. He stumbled and nearly ended up on his knees. What was it about this woman that always had him acting like such a complete doofus whenever he was within fifty feet of her?

"Watch out for the...uh-oh." Olivia's hilarity filled the air. He loved the sound of her laughter. "That's okay," she assured him, "we can fix that. You're doing good...just a little to the...uh-oh. No problem. I didn't want that anyway. Okay. Straight ahead. Look out for the...uh-oh. Never mind, that was old. Good job! Right here, then. Put it down."

Feeling as if he were sweating blood, Zach paused and studied the situation. "How?"

"Hmm. Good question."

"Well, we can't stand here debating all night."

"Should I go get the Colonel?"

In spite of his extreme pain, Zach laughed. "Ah, no. He already thinks I'm out to get him. This would only cement that assumption. Anyway, whatever we do, let's do it soon."

"Of course, of course." Wringing her hands, Olivia hopped from foot to foot. "How about if I grab this end over here, and we both lower the whole thing to our knees, then we'll grab on to those bars there, and then we can lower the rest to the floor."

"Sounds…like…a plan."

Hurrying into position Olivia grasped her end, and soon they had cot number one in place. Barely half an hour later, number two followed, and finally, after much exertion, cot number three fell into line against the far wall, just like the bedroom Goldilocks stumbled upon in the three bears' cottage. Thrilled that they had finished the task with a modicum of damage to the house and their persons, Olivia squealed with joy. Grinning, Zach held up his hand, and she rushed forward to give him a high-five. Then a low-five, another high-five and then, after dancing a little jig, a hug.

They held each other for a few victorious moments, until they felt awkward and—eyes darting about—took a step back. Olivia gestured to the hallway beyond.

"I'll just go see about…uh…" Her eyes were glazed, her tone dazed. "I'll see about getting some linens for…the children." A goofy smile graced her lips as she backed into the wall. "Oops," she giggled, her cheeks flaring with mortification. "I'll, just, uh"—she waved her hand behind her—"go through the door."

"Easier than the wall. Take it from me."

Her laughter echoed down the corridor. As he stood watching her walk away, Zach thought he'd never seen a lovelier woman than Olivia. Both inside and out.

• • •

"What are you going to say to them about their mother?" Zach asked as they tucked and smoothed the last of the sheets and blankets into place.

"I have no clue. Any ideas?" Olivia slowly straightened and, facing him, dragged a tired hand through her hair.

"No. Not really." Folding his arms across his chest, Zach leaned against the wall and regarded Olivia. She looked exhausted, and this was only the beginning. His heart went out to her. "I think the best thing to do would be to start with prayer."

"I think that's what got me into this mess." Olivia sighed, her tone filled with irony. She sank down onto the edge of the middle cot.

"How do you mean?"

Olivia proceeded to tell Zach that she'd asked Hattie to pray for her and feared that the children's coming to stay with her were part of the answer.

Not sure he followed, Zach inclined his head in her direction. "Oh?"

Olivia smiled that sweet, haunted smile that ignited a flame of something long forgotten in his gut. He studied her lovely face as she backed up and began at the beginning of her story. In a halting, emotional way she told him quite candidly of her bitterness since John and Lillah's deaths. She told him how she'd blamed God for her un-happiness and the unproductive turn her life had taken. She told him how she'd cut herself off emotionally from the world for the last five years and how useless she felt without her husband and child. Tears trickled down her cheeks as she explained how she'd finally become so bored and lonely, she'd gone to Hattie and asked the elderly woman to pray for her.

Zach listened to her and longed to join her at the edge of the cot. He wanted to take her in his arms and rock her. To stroke her hair and dry her eyes. To kiss the blotchy red patches that stained her porcelain cheeks. But he couldn't do that. It was too soon. So he nodded and murmured sym-pathetically until she finally ran out of steam and sagged, hands clasped tightly together on her lap.

Finally he could resist no longer and slowly approached the cot next to hers and lowered his lanky frame to the edge of the mattress.

"Would you like me to pray for you?" he asked, feeling fearful that she would find this question offensive. He knew she needed desperately to connect with God, and he wasn't sure how to help.

"Oh...I..." Her face brightened, then she grew embar-rassed. "Oh, no thanks. You don't have to do that." Looking up at him as he settled across from her, Olivia smiled a wa-tery smile and swiped at her tears with the back of her hand. "As you can see, Hattie has already prayed for me." She patted the bed. "My cup overfloweth."

Zach smiled in empathy. "You're still pretty ticked at God, aren't you?"

A muscle jumped in Olivia's delicate jaw, and she be-came immediately defensive. "Aren't you?"

Taking a deep breath, Zach held it for a long moment

then slowly exhaled. "I was." He scratched at the five o'clock shadow at his jaw. "But then someone asked me a question I had no answer to."

"What question?" Her long lashes sparkling with tears, Olivia peered up at him with curiosity.

"Well, a good buddy of mine must have gotten sick of my blaming God for everything after AmyBeth died, because he finally asked me, 'Why is it, when everything goes bad, we blame God. But when good things happen, we take the credit?' I had no answer for that."

Olivia stared at her hands.

Taking this as a cue to continue, Zach went on. "I eventually came to the conclusion that God didn't kill AmyBeth. Some misguided people with a political agenda killed AmyBeth. I needed God to help me forgive those people and to give me strength to carry on."

"But if God really loved you, why didn't he stop those people?" Olivia wondered, her voice barely audible.

"I don't know for sure. I believe that God allows us to control our destinies. I believe if we ask him to take control, he will. I believe that we are all here on this earth for a reason. And I believe that God knows the number of our hours here on this earth, and that our job is to put those hours to the best use possible. I guess I think it's his way of testing us. Seeing how we rise to the challenge. Seeing what we're made of so that he knows where and how to use us in his army." Zach shrugged. "Life isn't always supposed to be easy. I don't claim to understand everything, and I won't try to diminish your pain with trite platitudes, such as they're better off in heaven anyway."

A smile tinged the corners of Olivia's mouth. "You *have* been there."

"Yep." Zach grinned. "It's the pits for sure. But I do

know this, Olivia Harmon. God has a plan for your life. And when you make yourself available to him, he will reward you in more wonderful ways than you ever thought possible."

Olivia's gaze swept her disheveled room. "Oh, I can see that," she said dryly. "This"—she motioned to the cots that they'd nearly killed themselves lugging into position—"is just a little bit of heaven."

• • •

Zach stayed just long enough to help the children brush their teeth and help Olivia hustle them into their new beds. Of course, during the process of these preparations, everyone had to come up to view the new sleeping arrangements and offer sage bits of advice and a few gifts for the children.

The Colonel was the first to arrive, frosty and wheezing from his nightly forages through the Dumpster outside the kitchen door. His snow white hair stuck out at crazy angles created by the mist, and his thick, bottle-bottom glasses were fogged from his outdoor exertions.

"Hehh," he wheezed, holding up a handful of filthy children's clothing. "Found these duds in the trash, if you can imagine that. I figure a good washing should do the trick. As luck would have it, there were just enough clothes for the whole crew." Without ceremony, he deposited the entire mess—now worse for its evening spent with the yard clippings—on the floor next to Olivia's bed.

"Hey, donut lady," Ruth cried, "those are my pants!" Dismayed, she pointed to the stinky heap. "How come they were in the trash?"

"Why, that's a very good question." Olivia neatly evaded the issue. "And, Colonel, I...I...don't know what to say!"

Eyes wide, she peeked over at Zach, who was biting his lip to keep from laughing.

"Don't thank me," the Colonel rasped. "I was out there anyway. Well"—he blinked at the three little towheads as they sat in their beds—"nearly twenty-one hundred hours. Lights out soon."

"Glyniss," Agnes shrieked, slowly rounding the corner and coming to a stop behind the Colonel. "I'm in here!"

"I know where you are, Agnes," Glyniss grumbled from just over her shoulder. "Everyone knows where you are."

"Good heavens!" Agnes's throbbing voice threatened to rattle the windows. "What happened here? Why, this place looks like a disaster area! It's nearly worse than the sunroom." Her accusing gaze swung to Zach. "I don't suppose you had anything to do with that new hole in the stairwell wall?"

"I...uh..." Zach's face grew hot.

Olivia hid her smile behind her hand.

"I might have known!"

Agnes turned to the Colonel and Glyniss, and soon the three of them were in a heated debate about the wisdom of allowing Zach to visit. As they argued, Copper bounded into the room and jumped up on Cain's cot and began licking the child's face. Though he tried not to show it, the little boy was greatly amused, and soon his sisters were green with envy. Using every gymnastic at her disposal, Ruth tried to coax the pup away, but to no avail.

Copper was a one-boy dog, it seemed.

Soon Ryan arrived, looking for his charge, and Julia and Sean came to see what all the fuss was about. Rahni brought up the rear with a tray of cocoa for everyone. Olivia's place was suddenly party central.

"Look, donut lady!" Ruth jumped from cot to cot. "Watch this!"

Copper's shrill bark nearly drowned out Agnes as she veered off on another rabbit trail and began hotly debating the role of the modern woman as both parent and provider.

Rubbing her temples, Olivia surveyed the chaos taking place in her once serene hideaway and wondered if she didn't prefer solitude to this three-cot circus. When had her life as a hermit become so out of control? A still, small voice rose above the hubbub in her mind and gently informed her, *When you gave control to God.*

Casting a look of mute appeal at the ceiling, Olivia shook her head and sighed. She backed a few steps toward the door to her suite for a moment of blessed peace and quiet that filtered from the hall. "Why me?" she whispered, feeling dazed and confused and thoroughly afraid of the future.

"You know," Hattie's comforting voice came from the corridor, just over her shoulder, "I think it's a wonderful thing you've done, Olympia, dearest."

Olivia turned and stared at the little old lady who stood behind her. "You do?"

"Oh yes. You know, it says in the Good Book, somewhere in Psalms, I believe, 'You who have shown me great and severe troubles, shall revive me again and bring me up again from the depths of the earth.' Isn't that wonderful?" Hattie patted her arm and peered up into Olivia's face. "You know it is said that the ground in the valley is most fertile for growth. I'm beginning to think, my dear, that the good Lord believes you just may be ready."

"Ready?" A small frown tugged at her brow. That was the second time she'd been told that tonight. Could it be true? But ready for what? To come out of the valley?

Slowly, she inclined her head, peering through the doorway to the three little children cavorting with a dog on their beds. How, she wondered dismally, could she be coming out of the valley? It felt as if she'd just gone in.

• • •

"Good night," Olivia whispered, stepping with Zach just outside the door to her suite. "And thank you so much for staying and helping me with the kids." She wished he'd stay forever, but she knew that was impossible. Besides it was late and these kids were her problem now. She'd imposed enough. For one day anyway.

"Good night." He took her hands in his and gave them a gentle squeeze. "Try to get some sleep tonight."

"I will."

"Good luck telling the kids..." His voice trailed off, and they listened to the children play with Copper, the lone leftover from the impromptu party. Much to Ryan's chagrin, the puppy refused to leave Cain's bed. So, taking pity on boy and dog, he had let the lessons slide for that night.

"Thanks. I need all the luck I can get."

"I'll pray for you tonight."

"That would be nice," Olivia said, surprised to find she meant it.

"I'll see you in the morning?" He traced the backs of her hands with the pads of his thumbs.

"Uh, yes. I guess you will." A current of joy shot up and down her spine. She looked into his clear, hazel brown eyes and felt herself begin to melt.

"You decided what you're going to do about work tomorrow?"

"I guess I'll call in and explain everything and see what they want to do."

"Good idea." Slowly, Zach released her hands.

They stood for a long time gazing at each other, the

protocol of a good-night kiss hanging over their heads. It was too early, they both knew. But that didn't stop them from imagining.

"Well," Zach said.

"Well," Olivia echoed.

"I gotta get going."

"Me too."

"Right." Finally, Zach leaned forward, planted a quick kiss at her temple. "'Night." He backed down the hallway, nearly colliding with Agnes as her door popped open.

"Please, keep it down out here," she huffed, her nightcap askew. "Some of us are trying to sleep."

Glyniss's door swung open, and she glared accusingly at her sister. "Give me a break, Agnes. You weren't trying to sleep. You were trying to hear, and you know it."

"I most certainly was not!"

Zach waved good-bye to Olivia as the two women bickered, then bounded down the stairs and into the night.

• • •

Reluctantly, Olivia nudged open her door and peered in. The children were deep in conversation and didn't notice that she was watching them. Their childish voices filtered through the crack in the door, and what she heard filled her with trepidation.

"Mom's gonna come and get us," Cain was insisting.

"But sometimes she doesn't," Ruth protested. "Sometimes she forgets all about us. What if she forgot again?"

"She didn't forget, Ruth, you pinhead. She's comin' back, so we're not stayin'."

"I want to stay here." Esther offered her opinion. "I like it here. I like the donut lady."

"So? You think she's gonna keep us? No way. I don't

know when, but pretty soon the donut lady is gonna get mad at us and kick us out."

"She will not."

"Shut up, Ruth. You don't know anything. If we lived here, someday, the donut lady would start yelling at us and hitting us, and then she'd throw us out."

"She will not."

"She will too."

Taking a resigned breath, Olivia stepped into her room and shut the door behind her. She smiled at the children who'd suddenly become silent. Leaning against the door's cold surface, she wondered what to do next. She dreaded facing the music, but seeing these three babies staring with such expectation at her, she knew the time was now.

Feeling awkward and inadequate, she stepped over to their cots and sat down on the edge of Esther's bed, which was between Cain's and Ruth's. Esther threw back her covers and scrambled into Olivia's lap, and in a flash, Ruth had leapt from her cot and snuggled up next to her sister.

Cain remained silent, clutching Copper for dear life. The dog explored his ear and nose with a sloppy tongue.

Since there was no time like the present, Olivia dove in, headfirst. "So, I suppose you kids are wondering why you are here with me." She looked at Cain, who pretended preoccupation with the puppy.

"Are we gonna live here with you, donut lady?" Ruth wanted to know. Esther gazed at her, curious.

"Well, I don't know for sure, but I hope so. I—"

"We live with our mom." Cain masked his lost expression with a curling upper lip.

Olivia felt the familiar coil of grief wend its way through her stomach. Cain would be hit hardest by this news.

"Yes, honey," she began, remembering the officer who'd

had to tell her about John and Lillah. Suddenly her heart went out to him. "That's true, you have been living with your mom"—she had no idea what to say next—"but your mom…"

"Where is our mom?" Ruth queried, getting to the crux of the matter far earlier than Olivia preferred.

She'd hoped to give them a sense of security first. Then she hoped to paint a lovely picture of the hereafter. After that, she wanted to assure them of a bright future, here at the boarding house with her and the rest of this rather eclectic family. But that was not to be. The children wanted the facts now.

"Is our mom coming to get us?" Esther wanted to know.

"No, sweetie."

"Why?" Cain demanded.

"Because she can't. You see, I'm sure your mama really wishes she could be here to take care of you. But she got really sick. That's why she's been gone for a while now."

The three children looked at her, waiting for the explanation that she dreaded giving.

"Is she coming back?" Ruth asked.

"No, honey."

"Why?" Ruth's freckled nose wrinkled as she thought.

"Because she's dead," Cain guessed, his face pale and devoid of emotion.

9

The room was silent.

Ruth and Esther stared at their brother, trying to digest this unusual announcement. Cain glared at Olivia, daring her to disagree. Finally, Ruth could stand the silence no longer.

"Is that true, donut lady?"

Slowly, Olivia nodded.

"What means *dead*?" Reaching up, Esther patted Olivia's cheek, then explored her features with curious fingers.

Olivia attempted to swallow past the wad of cotton suddenly lodged in her throat. *O Lord*, she prayed, *what should I say?* This was too hard. Blinking rapidly, she nuzzled Esther's soft cheek and spoke low, comforting tones.

"Well, sweetheart, *dead* means…going to live in heaven with Jesus." Olivia knew it also meant several other things, but she was prepared to give Roxanne Grady the benefit of the doubt tonight. The fact that the young mother consulted her Bible before naming her children said something vaguely comforting to Olivia.

"Who is Jessie's?" Ruth asked.

Since her own relationship with Jesus had been less than perfect on her part since John and Lillah died, she wondered how qualified she was to answer this question.

"Uh, well, Jesus is our friend. He is everybody's friend.

He loved your mommy." She was surprised at how easily these core beliefs flowed past her lips.

"Like George?" A sour expression crossed Ruth's childish features. "Does Jessie's have baaad breath, like George?"

"No no, honey. Jesus is not that kind of friend."

Cain snorted.

"Mommy went to live at Jessie's and she's not comin' back?" Esther's lower lip began to tremble as this stark realization dawned.

"No, honey," Olivia whispered.

"Never?" Ruth probed.

"No."

"Never ever?"

Olivia shook her head. "I'm sorry, sweetie."

The child stared at her for a long moment, speechless.

Gathering the little girl against her breast with her free arm, Olivia stroked Ruth's fine, blond hair. The child burrowed close, clutching Olivia's blouse in her small fists.

"Why?" Ruth bawled, finally catching on to what her sister and brother already knew. "Why isn't our mom coming back?" Tears flowed down her freckled cheeks, and her face twisted with grief. Her sobs sparked Esther's, and soon both girls were weeping inconsolably.

His expression hard and impenetrable, Cain stared unseeing at the wall. His fingers worked the soft fur at Copper's neck. One lone tear streaked down his cheek, the only sign that he had connected emotionally to his mother's death.

"Oh, honey." Olivia sighed. Throat tight, eyes stinging, she fought for composure. It wouldn't do to fall apart in front of the kids. "I think she really, really wanted to live with you guys and take care of you and be your mom. I know she truly loved you with all her heart."

"Then how come...she went to live...at Jessie's?" Esther

demanded haltingly. Her ragged sobs racked her small body. "How come she's not comin' back?"

Knowing no other way to say it, Olivia forged ahead. "Because, doll baby"—she wrapped her other arm around Esther's little body and gave in to the tears that had threatened the backs of her eyes since she'd stepped back into the room—"when people die, they can't come back."

"I don't like Jessie!" Esther shouted. "He took my mom away. He's bad and mean."

Olivia knew just how the child felt. But she was also learning that these feelings weren't true. Zach's words echoed in her mind. *Why is it that when something bad happens, we blame God?* It was easy to blame God for Roxanne's death, but when Olivia looked at the situation objectively, the children's mother was dead because of choices she'd made. Not because God didn't care about these children.

Rocking slowly back and forth, Olivia, her tears mingling with theirs, let the children sob—from confusion, exhaustion, and grief. Cain continued to sit on his own bed, huddled with the dog, struggling desperately to be brave. His head dropped into the puppy's ruff, and Copper, seeming to sense his distress, whined and licked his cheeks.

Deciding it best, Olivia let him be for now. Eventually, he would come around. She hoped.

After a long, heart-wrenching cry, the tears began to ebb, and a sense of normalcy began to return to the room. The girls were vocal about their fears and seemed more concerned about themselves and the future of their living situation than about their mom. Truth be told, they hadn't spent all that much time with her. They'd been passed around so much already in their young lives, and Olivia could only imagine that most of the places they'd lived had been anything but secure. Cain, as firstborn, seemed to have bonded more firmly to his mother than the girls. And though his mother was really no mother at all, she was all they had. His pain, although quiet, was palpable.

"Do you think Mom is happy with Jessie's?" Ruth wondered, scrubbing her face with the hem of her T-shirt. "Do you think he yells at her and makes her sad like George?" Her lip quivered, and her eyes were red rimmed and watering.

"No no, honey. Jesus lives in heaven. He is our wonderful savior, and he loves your mommy and would never ever yell at her. I think maybe your mommy is in heaven with Jesus and the angels now. I think she is not sad anymore." With comforting motions, Olivia soothingly stroked the girl's hair. "I think your mommy feels good and happy and, though I'm sure she misses you, she is glad that she will see you again, when you go to live with Jesus someday."

"I don't want to go live with Jessie's," Esther wailed.

"No no. You will stay here with me for now," Olivia assured her.

"Okay." Esther seemed appeased by that.

"I like it here," Ruth said.

"Me too." Her sister agreed.

Cain was silent.

"Are you gonna go live with Jessie's too?" A fearful knot crept into Ruth's voice as she stared at Olivia.

"Not yet, honey. But someday. I hope to someday, when I'm very old." Though she'd gone forward and been baptized as a young girl, Olivia knew that if she was going to enter the pearly gates when her number was up, she was going to have to make amends with her maker. Zach had done it. Surely she could too.

Oh, how she longed for the sweet relationship Hattie had with Jesus. She wanted so badly for the bitterness to end. It had been so long. She was so very tired of fighting.

Absently, her eyes strayed around the room and landed on the calendar hanging over her desk. John and Lillah had been gone for five years now. Her eyes scanned the blocks for today's date. October. Today was Tuesday. Was it really only Tuesday? It seemed like this week had gone on forev—

Olivia froze.

This day, five years ago, had been the last time she'd held her little girl.

• • •

By the time Olivia had all three children tucked into their respective beds and dead to the world from exhaustion, it was nearly midnight. Her back ached, her head pounded, her feet hurt, and she could feel the bruise—which she'd acquired from her slide down the stairs with Zach—throbbing on her upper arm.

Slowly standing upright, she studied the sleeping children in the dim glow of the night-light. They were all so precious in repose. The poignancy of the sight crowded her throat, making it difficult to swallow.

The girls' golden curls fanned out on their pillows, and their smooth, softly rounded cheeks gave them such an angelic look. Cain slept, his face relaxed, his rosy lips slack, his arms wrapped solidly around Copper. The pup snoozed in contentment within his embrace. For a long moment, she stood and watched the children and wondered what evil had such a grasp on Roxanne that she could virtually abandon her babies.

With a heartfelt sigh, Olivia knew she couldn't judge the young mother. Many times, she'd been so depressed herself that she hadn't cared whether she'd lived or died.

"There, but for the grace of God, go I," she murmured, feeling an overwhelming need to pray and pray hard.

Shuffling to her bed, she snagged her sweater, then moved to the large French doors in the alcove near her bathroom. The crisp night air chilled her cheeks as she stepped onto her balcony. She loved this secluded area. It was the perfect little hideaway. From the springtime, when the trees were leafing out, to the fall, when they were a riot of color, this perch was a haven. A tree house, of sorts.

The railing was ornate, the balusters hand carved and painted in the multitude of colors that were popular in the Victorian era. The posts sported fancy bric-a-brac at the top, corbels, and spindles, and the gable that covered this oasis was a stunning work of art. Fish-scale shingles cut into an intricate diamond design surrounded a stained-glass window imported from Italy over a hundred years ago.

A wicker grouping, consisting of a table and two padded chairs, welcomed Olivia in all seasons but the very coldest of days in winter. Tightening her sweater around her waist, she sank onto one of the cushioned chairs.

"Dear God." Olivia's gaze searched the sky, afraid and weary to the core. "It's me again. Olivia Harmon. The one who's been sort of hounding you lately. Forgive me, Father, but I don't really know how to pray that well anymore, so I hope you're there, listening to me." She paused, huddling farther into her seat. "I think you are. I hope you are."

"Anyway," she clasped her hands to her lips and murmured against her fingers, "I've only had these children for a few hours, and already I know I'm in way over my head. Surely you can't mean for this to be my entrance into the world of volunteer work, Lord. You say you won't give us more than we can handle, but this...forgive me here, but this is too much!"

Her thoughts strayed for a moment. She contemplated the children, especially Cain. He was so guarded. So unreachable. And he was a boy. She had no experience with little boys. She didn't even know what to do with him.

"What if I can't do this, Lord? I...I...don't want another family! I thought I made that clear! Yes, I know I told the officer that I would take them, but I don't know what made me say that! I was out of control. I was out of my mind. I was...feeling sorry for them, I guess. That's no reason to jump into something like this, Lord.

"I mean, I have a job! What about that? Who will take care of them when I'm at work? Who will buy their clothes? They can't go around wearing my pinned-up underwear and T-shirts forever, and I can't afford to buy them all new clothes. And it's not like I'm married or anything. These kids need a father figure. What should we do about that?"

The more Olivia prayed, the more worked up she got.

"I'm scared, God! I can't do this! Can you hear me? Are you listening?"

She was quiet for a moment.

Silence.

She waited some more, and slowly, a warm, comfortable feeling began to build in her belly and spread throughout her body.

Images of the three slumbering ragamuffins in the next room filled her head. They looked so funny in their im-promptu nightclothes. Especially Esther. She hadn't real-ized, until Esther had whispered in her ear, that the child would need a night diaper, so Olivia had pinned a guest towel into her panties, then duct-taped a plastic bag over the whole affair. Tomorrow, she would add a pack of dis-posables to her shopping list.

She shook her head and—smiling in spite of her current predicament—looked into the miraculously cloudless night sky. Stars twinkled overhead like diamonds on black velvet.

Feeling small and insignificant, she sat for a long moment and simply stared into the heavens.

And, as she sat, a realization began to dawn.

"I'm not supposed to know what to do, right?"

It was as if a light bulb had suddenly clicked on in the darkness of her soul, shedding light into musty corners for the first time in five long years. "I'm supposed to be leaning on you!" Squinting, Olivia turned this new idea over in her head. "I know, I haven't been doing that much lately." She listened for God's voice.

More silence.

"Okay," she admitted, "I haven't been doing that at all. But, Lord, I've been in pain." Again she paused. "All right, I've *been* a pain. But, Lord God, as you well know, it's"— Olivia swallowed against a sudden flood of emotion as she thought of Jesus on the cross—"it's tough to lose a child."

Her thoughts strayed back to the three asleep in her room. "Just as it must be tough to lose a mother."

As Olivia sat in the darkness, goose flesh, starting at the tips of her toes, rippled up her entire body and tingled her scalp. Funny thing was, she was not cold.

"Help me, O Lord," she prayed, as another wave engulfed her. And, suddenly, Olivia felt as if she just might be able to face the morning.

• • •

Something was different. Groggily, Olivia tried to put her finger on the problem, but it evaded her conscious mind. It almost felt as if...no, that couldn't be right. Drowsy and content, her mind mulled over the funny dream she was having. Something, or someone, was pressed against her belly. The feeling was warm and delicious, like something out of a distant memory. Hairs, like gossamer angel wings, tickled her nose. Instinctively, she snuggled closer to the warmth and nestled her cheek against the silky nest.

The warmth at her back wriggled after her, then stilled. How wonderful. She hadn't been this delightfully comfortable in ages. Even her feet were toasty, like two hot potatoes wrapped in a warm blanket. Movement, down at the end of the bed, roused her just enough to realize that she was surrounded by love.

John? Lillah?

They were here. She could feel them. Just like before. Perfect. Heavenly. She never wanted this dream to end.

● ● ●

Good grief. *What kind of a nightmare is this?* Olivia sat bolt upright in bed and tossed her tangled hair out of her face. One crying child was clinging to her neck. And one jabbering child was clinging to her arm. A dog, for pity's sake, was barking wildly at the end of her bed at some idiot who was pounding on her door and calling her name.

"Olivia?"

"Uh...just a minute!" She pawed through her blankets, trying to locate her robe. It was a horrendously early hour, she guessed, judging by the predawn light that filtered in through her French doors. Who would be here, dropping in unannounced, so early this way? How had they gotten through the front door? Finally locating her robe, she began to pry Esther off her neck.

"Honey?" Wow, the kid was a lot stronger than she looked. "I, uh, need to put my robe on."

"Olivia?" More knocking.

"Coming!"

Cain and Copper leapt off the end of the bed and padded to the door.

"No, Cain!" Olivia hissed. Wait till I get my robe—"

It was too late.

Flipping the overhead light on, Cain pulled open the door and invited their guest inside. Then he hopped back up on the end of Olivia's bed with the dog.

"Donut man!" Ruth squealed and began jumping on the bed.

Ohmygosh. Frantically, Olivia tried to wrestle Esther off her neck. The frumpy T-shirt she'd worn to bed was not exactly the outfit she wanted Zach to see her in first thing that morning. Her gaze darted to the giant mirror that hung above her vanity. What was with her hair? Good heavens. It was, for some odd reason, filled with static electricity. From where she sat, she could see it literally standing on end.

And the pièce de résistance?

She'd been so tired she hadn't bothered to wash her face last night. Her eyes were smudged coal black with smeared mascara, and she looked like Zorro staring out from under the crackling pile of straw on her head. Oh, for a shower and a toothbrush and some minty mouthwash. She wanted the bed to open up and swallow her whole. Pulling Esther around front, she only hoped the clinging child would hide most of the damage. Her lap was suddenly damp.

Esther's makeshift diaper was leaking. Great. Just great.

"Good morning." Zach's cheery voice resonated around the room, making her feel more disheveled than ever. Striking a comfortable pose, he leaned against the doorframe, crossed his arms over his broad chest, and smiled a pearly-toothed smile at the motley group on the bed. Why did he have to look so calm, cool, and collected first thing in the morning? Olivia wondered churlishly. Even the bandage he still wore on his forehead looked jaunty.

"Good morning." Her face grew so hot she was sure an egg would fry on its surface.

"Sorry to disturb you, but I wanted to talk to you, before I had to go to work."

"That's okay," she chirped, hoping she sounded much more magnanimous than she felt. "I had to get up and call my boss anyway." But not for another hour. Had she really only slept five hours last night?

"Looks like we labored in vain." He gestured good-naturedly at the three cots.

Her smile wan, Olivia nodded. "I guess it was warmer over here in my neck of the woods."

"I can imagine."

Something flirtatious in his voice made her feel even more rumpled than she was. She peeked up at him. A broad smile split his face from ear to ear, and a twinkle of interest was in his eyes. Olivia ducked her head.

"Donut man," Esther piped up from under her chin, "my mom died and went to live at Jessie's."

"Is that right?" Zach was clearly taken aback.

"Yes!" Esther wailed, then sniffed and ground her fists into her eyes. Olivia patted the child on the back, and Esther forgot her troubles as suddenly as she had remembered them.

He glanced at Olivia. "Well, that answered my first question."

"Oh yes." Fishing a tissue out of her bathrobe pocket, she attempted to scrub away some of the black streaks on her face. "We had quite the talk last night."

"Yeah, and my mom is in heaven, where Jessie's lives with the angels, and she is happy there." Ruth bounded on the bed as if it were a trampoline. "Watch, donut man." She flounced and twirled and kicked her feet like a young colt.

"Very good," Zach praised.

Ruth beamed. "My mom's never coming back." Abruptly,

she sobered. "She likes it at Jessie's. So we're stayin' here. Forever."

Cain looked skeptical, but didn't offer an opinion. Copper chewed on the boy's fingers and slobbered on his hands, diverting him from the painful subject of his mother.

Jessie's? Zach mouthed.

"Jesus."

"Ah." He winked solemnly at Olivia. "Must have been some talk. Looks like you survived."

Olivia smiled. "I'm a survivor."

"That's what I like about you."

Again, Olivia felt her face flare.

"But," he continued, maintaining his casual pose against the doorframe, "that's not why I stopped by this morning."

"Oh?"

"Actually, I wanted to invite you and the kids to church tonight."

Puzzled, Olivia frowned and squinted at the calendar. "But it's Wednesday."

"True, but we have a children's program we call Jungle Jam every Wednesday night. It's a lot of fun for the kids, arts and crafts and candy and cookies and singing songs about Jesus."

"Will Jessie's be there?" Esther wanted to know.

The kids all stared at Zach, eager to know how much he knew about this mysterious Jessie's fellow.

Stymied, Zach thoughtfully stroked his chin and darted a glance at Olivia.

Her eyes widened, and she shrugged. He was on his own here.

"Well now," Zach mused, "I imagine he will. But not the way you think. Why don't you come with me tonight, and we'll see if we can't find him?"

All three children shot dubious looks at one another, then nodded. Candy and cookies were always a good incentive.

"But what about their clothes?" Olivia wondered. "They don't have anything suitable to wear.

"Well, if you can rustle up some pants and shoes, I can do the T-shirts. The kids all wear purple Jungle Jam shirts, so everyone fits in. Of course, you'll want to come along. Parents are welcome."

Olivia hadn't attended anything in the parental capacity for a long time. The idea was as exciting as it was daunting.

"Okay. Somehow or another, we'll be there. Count us in."

"Great!" Zach whooped, his enthusiasm getting the better of him. Darting a look over his shoulder, he lowered his voice. "Great."

"Great!" Ruth rejoined, climbing off the bed and bounding from cot to cot like Tigger on a sugar high.

"Will you puleeze *try* to keep it down in here? There are people here who like to sleep in till at least six," Agnes groused, pushing past Zach and into the room.

Rolling her eyes, Olivia dove under the covers. Who had declared these insane visiting hours?

Taking a hundred tiny steps, Agnes turned and stared up at Zach's chin. "Don't you have something that you have destroyed that you could be fixing?"

Backing out into the hall, Zach grinned his charming grin. "Yes ma'am."

From under her blankets, Olivia peered out and laughed.

Agnes wobbled, beckoning the children with a bony arm. "Come on, children. Let's go downstairs and get a cinnamon roll. I made some fresh this morning, with lots of frosting and no nutritional value, the way parents like to feed their youngsters today. But," she harrumphed, shuffling back out the door, "I must insist that you all drink some milk. And juice. Lots of fresh-squeezed orange juice. It's good for your bones. I have some educational materials you might be interested in..." Agnes's voice grew dim as she moved toward the stairs.

The kids all looked to Olivia for guidance.

She smiled and sighed. Would wonders never cease? "You may all go, after a quick trip to the bathroom," she encouraged. "She doesn't bite till afternoon."

Esther blanched.

"C'mon, Esther," Ruth chided, grabbing her sister's hand. "She's just teasin'." She stopped on her way to the bathroom and frowned. "Aren't ya?"

Olivia smiled. "Yep. I'm just teasin'."

• • •

"You *what?*" Nell's flabbergasted voice buzzed across town from their office at the Department of Tourism and into Olivia's bedroom.

"I ended up with the kids."

"How? When? Why? What in heaven's name are you going to do now? I mean, how are you going to work? You can't take care of three kids! You have a full-time job!"

Nell fired questions so fast Olivia had no idea where to begin. So she addressed the last comment.

"You do it, Nell," Olivia gently reminded her friend.

"But that's different. My kids are older. And I have a husband. Tell me what happened!"

"Long story. But anyway, I need to talk to Lorna about what's going on. Is she there?"

"Yeah, I'll transfer you in just a minute, but first, I'm gonna pop over to your place on my lunch hour, okay?"

Olivia sighed. More company. Just what she needed. "Okay." Her life wasn't her own anymore. "Now transfer me."

10

"Would you like to join us for a tuna melt?" Olivia tossed out the invitation as she spread mayonnaise over the bread she'd sliced for the kids' sandwiches. Without turning around, she could feel Zach hovering over her shoulder, hungrily watching as she worked. Nerves, like little fireflies, performed acrobatics in her stomach at his nearness.

It was almost lunchtime, that Wednesday afternoon. The cheerful kitchen was beginning to fill with children and boarders looking for their midday meal. The kids sat in chairs at the kitchen table, swinging their feet and playing with Copper. Rahni, humming happily, worked across the giant old room at the industrial-sized stove. She was preparing soup and salad for Julia, Glyniss, Hattie, and the Colonel, who were—one by one—all settling in at the table to visit with the kids. Agnes was visiting her friend Bea several blocks away.

"I can make one for you too." There was a goofy, breathless tremor in her voice, so she shrugged airily and donned a mask of studied indifference to counterbalance it.

"Oh, no thanks. I brought my own." Zach held up the paper bag in his hand. "Leftovers."

Nose wrinkling, Olivia peered into the bachelor lunch

bag he extended for her inspection. "Is that pizza or mashed potatoes?"

Zach's shrug was good-natured. "Beats me."

"How old is it?"

He favored her with that pearly grin that could make butter melt in even crotchety old Agnes's mouth. "Can't remember."

"Give me that." Eyes darting to the ceiling, Olivia shook her head and tossed his lunch bag into the garbage. Then she grabbed four pieces of freshly baked bread and added them to the ones she was working on for the children and herself. Feeling suddenly abashed for her boldness, she lifted her gaze to his and tried to explain. "We, uh, can't have you getting food poisoning. I mean, what would happen to the sunroom repairs?"

"Don't worry. Mike's in there, slaving away as we speak." Feigning a wounded expression, Zach hung his head. "And here I thought you were cooking for me because you cared. Now I can see you just love me for my building talents." He slapped the tool belt that he wore slung at his narrow hips and bestowed on her a wolfish wink.

Flustered and blushing madly, Olivia's gaze darted from his tool belt to his broad, plaid-flannel chest and then up to his eyes. He was teasing her.

Flirting.

For the life of her, she couldn't remember how to react, so she nudged his rock-hard body out of her way and nodded at the faucet. "Go ahead and put your tool belt away and wash up. And then get the milk out of the fridge, will you? And five glasses from the dishwasher."

At this point, it was easier to order him around than to look into those velvety brown eyes that seemed to see past her defenses and into her soul.

As she bid, he scrubbed up, then fished the glasses out of the dishwasher and proceeded to fill them all with milk. "So how's it going today?" He glanced in her direction.

Olivia drew a weary breath, feeling as tired as if she'd already worked a double shift down at the office. And it was only lunchtime. "Pretty well, I guess." Tearing open a bag of potato chips, she piled a handful on each plate. "By the time I got them all finished with breakfast, dressed, and teeth brushed and then got my room semistraight, it was time to eat again."

"I hear ya." Zach's comforting laughter resonated pleasantly around the room. "I think wrestling Cain into the tub is an all-day chore." The little lines at the corners of his eyes forked as he glanced at the young lad who lolled on the floor, tenaciously clinging to his pup.

"True."

Olivia opened the top door of the double oven and slid the tuna melts under the broiler. "But," she boasted, "I did manage to accomplish one thing that I'm rather proud of."

"What's that?"

"I finally convinced them that my name is not donut lady."

Zach chuckled. "What are you going to have them call you?"

"Olivia."

"Good choice. That's a beautiful name."

A smile pushed at her cheeks, and a warm, bashful, liquidy feeling coursed through her stomach. "Of course. That's why I picked it." Bantering with him was fun. Moving to the fruit bowl, Olivia grabbed a bunch of bananas and, pulling them apart, put one on each plate.

"I spoke with Officer Menkin this morning." She spoke

in low tones, glancing over her shoulder to make sure the children were still occupied.

"Yeah? What did he have to say?"

She peeked into the oven. The cheese was just beginning to melt. "Not much. Just that he'd tried to get a social worker lined up, but they were too busy at Children's Services this week. He said the soonest anyone could call would be sometime next week." Cocking a hip against the counter, Olivia plowed a hand through her hair. "I tried to get some more information out of him, but talking to Officer Menkin on the phone is even worse than talking to him in person."

"You're kidding." Leaning back against the counter with her, Zach laughed. Arms crossed over his chest, he studied her and stroked his jaw with his thumb. "What are you going to do about the kids while you are at work?"

"I don't have a clue. So far, my boss has been really understanding. I said I'd probably be out for the rest of the week, till I figure out what to do." Stepping around Zach, she turned the broiler off and cracked the oven door. "I called a couple of day-care places this morning. They want a small fortune. Especially for three. It would eat an entire paycheck every month. I don't know if the government will help or not. I don't know anything about foster parenting. And Cain is going to need to start kindergarten in the mornings. I have no idea how I'm going to arrange that."

"Sounds like we need to pray for a ram in the thicket," Zach murmured.

"Pardon?"

"Abraham? Isaac? The sacrifice? No?" Zach grinned. "I'll explain later."

"Please do." She was becoming aware of a sudden thirst to get back into the Word of God. Who better to teach her than the extremely easy-to-listen-to Zach Springer? "The sooner the better."

With a slow hand, she dragged her hair out of her eyes and over her shoulder, then peeked behind her, checking on the kids. They were giggling. Rahni was putting on a puppet show with oven mitts while her pot of soup heated. The little fable, native to her country, delighted the kids and miraculously kept them in their seats. Although now and again Ruth, unable to contain herself, would leap from her seat and demand that everyone watch as she performed bits of Rahni's story as an interpretive dance.

The adults, on the other hand, were clearly eavesdropping on Zach and Olivia's conversation.

"Olympia, dearie," Hattie warbled, holding up an arthritic finger, "forgive me, but I couldn't help but overhear you and Jack discussing your dilemma."

Olivia and Zach exchanged amused glances. Just exactly what Hattie heard would probably always be a mystery.

"My dilemma?"

Adjusting her specs higher on her nose, Hattie pondered Olivia's words. "No no, dear, the antenna is fine. TV picture is clear as a bell. But thank you for asking. No no. I'm thinking more along the lines of what you will do with these three little chicks while you are at work every day. The Colonel and Glyniss and I have put our heads together this morning, and I think we may be able to help."

"Really?" Olivia's brows shot up. The Colonel was in on this? Yikes. Oh well. Ready to hear any ideas, no matter how far-fetched, she nodded and waved for Hattie to continue as she, with Zach's able assistance, unloaded the oven and piled the plates with piping hot tuna-melt sandwiches.

"Offering good advice may be noble and grand," Hattie quoted sagely, "but it's not the same as a helping hand. So,

Glyniss and I have decided that we will be more than happy to look after Hester and Rose during the day. Agnes has expressed interest in some afternoon tutoring and so forth. And the Colonel will keep an eye on Payne."

"Make a soldier out of him!" The Colonel's shriek startled them as he jumped into the conversation, dentures clicking. "Teach him conservation."

"Conversation?" Hattie asked, puzzled.

"That too!" the Colonel cried. "Why, we'll converse up a storm about conservation! I'll teach him everything I know about fiscal responsibility and recycling." As an afterthought he added, "And the war!"

"Can we get stuff out of the Dumpster?" Cain wanted to know. He'd only lived at the boarding house for less than a day, but already he was familiar with the Colonel's miserly habits.

"Can we get stuff out of the Dumpster, *sir*," the Colonel shouted. "Yes!"

A glimmer of interest flirted with the corners of the boy's mouth.

Hattie prattled on, oblivious to the Colonel's rantings. "Beulah said she'd be glad to help us all."

Julia winked reassuringly at Olivia. "I'd love to help. I figure," she lamented, patting her burgeoning belly, "I could use all the practice I can get."

A lump the size of a cantaloupe suddenly lodged in Olivia's throat. These people were so incredible. How very lucky she was to be surrounded by such concern and generosity.

The back door opened, bringing with it a sudden gust of frigid air. And Nell.

"Yoo-hoo!" Her yodel reverberated around the room, "I come bearing gifts for the kiddies. Rummaged around in the attic on my way over here and found some clothes that still have a lot of life left in them." Dropping the filled-to-bursting plastic trash bags she had dragged from the car, she loosened her scarf and slammed the door.

"Hi, hi, hi, everyone." Her nervous giggles echoed off the cathedral ceiling. "Stay out of that weather! Why, the wind is howling something fierce. You don't think a branch will hit my car, do you? Or a tree? Or a spinning farmhouse?" Fluttering at the back window, she peered out. "Never mind. My counselor tells me I need wings of faith. God has not given us a spirit of fear," she chanted. "If the car blows away, so be it. I guess we'll just have to pray that it doesn't hit us here in the kitchen..." She wrung her hands in consternation, jabbering a mile a minute, as if verbally working out her fears. "The car won't hit us, why that's ridiculous. Lord," she glanced at the ceiling, "I take these foolish thoughts captive to your obedience.

"Thank heavens for counseling, that's all I can say. Why, without it, and the good Lord standing by my side, I fear I'd be a complete basket case. My blood pressure only spiked once on the way over, and it's a virtual tornado out there. But I did it, praise God. Jesus is my copilot, which is good since I drove most of the way with my eyes closed.

"I think I'm getting better. A little stronger each day. I'm here, aren't I?" She flashed a hundred-watt smile at her audience. "So. What's going on?"

"Hi, Nell." Smiling, Olivia ushered her friend to the table and pulled out a chair for her. Nell was such a dear. Just coming over here was an ordeal—it was obvious how much she cared. "We were just discussing how we were going to provide day care for the kids while I'm at work."

"Oh. Perfect timing then," Nell twittered, waving at the chair. "I can't stay. Anyway, I just spoke with my daughter during her lunch break at school, and she says she would love to baby-sit for you after school and on weekends. She works cheap."

"You know," Zach volunteered, as he helped to serve the kids their plates of food, "I could pick Cain up from kindergarten on my lunch hours. I could use a boy and his dog as a helper on the job now and again."

Olivia's vision became blurry as she stared at these thoughtful, giving people through tears that pooled in her eyes. How could she ever have believed that she had no surviving family? She had a big, wonderful, wacky family, and they were all right here, under her very nose. How blessed she was, and she'd never bothered to notice before now. Tears sprang from her lashes and streamed down her cheeks.

She lifted her watery gaze to Zach. "Thank you," she murmured, her throat tight with emotion. "Thank you all." Gripping Nell's hand, she gave a squeeze, and smiled a lopsided smile at the endearing faces that surrounded the table. "You are all an answer to"—that warm, tingly feeling enveloped her again—"prayer."

• • •

After the lunch dishes had been cleared, the day-care routine began. Hattie, Julia, and Glyniss swept the girls out of the room for a sewing lesson, and the Colonel mustered Cain and the dog to action in the Dumpster. Rahni had class, and Nell had to go back to work. This left a very peaceful kitchen within which to enjoy an after-meal cup of coffee for Zach and Olivia.

Zach knew he should be getting back into the sunroom to give Mike a hand, but something about the angel-faced woman sitting across from him kept him locked in place. Absently, he wondered if she was as aware of him as he was of her. Did she notice his every movement the way he noticed hers? Was her stomach bound in knots every time they were in the room together? Did she consider each word before she spoke, wondering what he would think?

Nah. She had far too much on her mind right now to be bothered with such juvenile thoughts. His eyes followed her lips as they touched the rim of her cup and blew on the coffee. He shifted uncomfortably. Man, he had to get a handle on his thoughts before he gave in to his urge to climb over the table and kiss her senseless.

She smiled that beatific smile that had the blood roaring in his ears. "I can't believe how sweet everyone is to jump in and help out with the kids this way."

"Looks like you've found your ram in the thicket."

"Would you mind explaining that to me?" Setting her cup down, she ran her finger around the rim and leaned toward him with interest.

"Sure." Explaining the Bible story would certainly help keep his mind on the straight and narrow. And right now, he needed all the help he could get. "Well, now, let's see. The Lord commanded that Abraham take his beloved son Isaac to Moriah to be sacrificed on an altar."

Olivia grimaced.

Realizing that she was probably remembering her own daughter, Zach nodded. "Yeah, I know. That would be a tough job. So, though he didn't know how he would possibly be able to do what he'd been called to do, he stepped out in faith. He packed up his son, some wood for the fire—"

Olivia winced again.

Head tipped, Zach slanted a glance at her and grinned. "Yeah, I know. Gruesome, huh? Anyway, he brought a donkey and a couple of guys to give him a hand. He even had to bring the fire. He carried that, and the kid carried the wood."

"For his own barbecue?" Olivia stared, aghast.

"Yep, but luckily, he didn't know it at the time."

"Lucky kid." Her tone was sardonic.

"Yeah, well, he must have figured something was up, because he asked his dad, 'Dad, the fire and the wood are here, but where is the lamb for the offering?' and his dad said, 'God himself will provide the lamb.' So, when they got to the place that God had shown them, Abraham built an altar, laid the wood, tied up the boy, and took out the knife."

Completely engrossed, Olivia's eyes were nearly popping out of her skull. "You're kidding!"

"Nope."

"Funny, I don't remember this one from Sunday school. Musta blocked it out."

"Probably. You do seem a little queasy."

"I'll be okay. Go on."

"Well, just as Dad was about to kill the kid with the knife, God said, 'Don't kill the boy, because now I know you fear God.' God was testing Abraham. He wanted it to be clear that Abraham loved God more than anything and that he was willing to trust in him to provide. And that's when Abraham looked up and saw a ram, caught by the horns in a thicket. He sacrificed the ram instead of his son."

Cradling her cheeks in her hands, Olivia wore a bemused expression. "So the moral of the story is," she murmured more to herself than to Zach, "even though you don't know how you are going to do something, go ahead and step out in faith. God will provide what you need."

"Bingo." Zach beamed. She was pretty astute. He liked that about her. He liked everything about her.

"You know"—she spread her elbows on the table, angling her face to his—"I think God's been doing that for me. Testing me. I don't know why, exactly, but I feel just like Abraham today." She grinned. "After the sacrifice."

Zach chuckled.

"Let's see some of the stuff that Nell brought." Standing, she moved to the corner and retrieved the plastic bags that Nell had left for the children. The plastic crackled as she rummaged around, gleefully sharing her treasures with Zach. "Some of this stuff looks brand-new."

Her smile kindled a fire in his belly. Obviously, a great work was being done in this woman. He was happy for her. He was happy for himself, that he was in some small way a part of this awesome picture.

"Nell's kids are teenagers now. I'm surprised she kept these clothes. Look at these cute little ski jackets. And these jeans. I can really use all of these things. What a sweetie she is. Everyone is being so"—she blinked rapidly to stem the tide—"so wonderful." Chin quivering, she smiled at him. "You too." Her voice was rough with emotion as she moved back to the table and took her seat. "I don't know how I can ever thank you enough for everything you've done."

"Nah. I haven't done anything."

Olivia shook her head in mute disagreement.

Sliding his arms across the table, Zach took her hands in his. Her hands were so soft and delicate in his large, work-callused hands. He traced the contours of her knuckles with the pads of his thumbs. He wondered if she had any idea how fast his heart was beating at that moment. The way she was looking into his eyes communicated that there was something there. Just the tiniest hint of things to come.

For a moment of suspended time, they sat, smiling at

each other. Silly smiles, that they didn't yet fully understand, graced their faces. Finally, the hall clock chimed one, pulling Zach from his starry-eyed ruminations.

Mike would be needing a break about now. It was time to get back to work.

• • •

And, thus, the daily routine began.

That Wednesday night, the kids put on the jeans and ski jackets that Nell had brought, the new underwear and shoes that Olivia had gone shopping for that afternoon, and the purple Jungle Jam T-shirts that Zach had provided from the church.

Though there was some concern and tears on Esther's part about running into "Jessie's" at church, for the most part, the kids had a ball. Bible stories, crafts, other kids their age, a bag full of cavities in the form of cookies and candies, and the kids were sold.

Jessie's—they found—wasn't such a bad guy after all.

Some of the songs and stories even convinced Esther and Ruth that he liked little kids. All colors. Even purple ones, Esther had confided in Olivia that night, as she was being tucked into bed.

Olivia had stroked the child's golden hair as it lay on the pillow, and assured the little girl that it was true. Jesus loved the little children. All the little children. The burning lump in her throat was becoming a permanent fixture as she became more attached by the minute to each of these precious cherubs that God had dropped into her lap.

Though he and Mike didn't work on the weekends, Zach arrived at the boarding house bright and early each day to lend a hand with the kids. By Sunday morning, he was a bit of an expert at combing tangled locks and finding lost shoes. Again, there was some trepidation about visiting Sunday school, but that melted when the kids discovered that Zach co-taught the preschool set. Soon, Ruth was demonstrating a somersault dismount from the craft table-top, and Esther was in there throwing her weight around, fighting over the plastic cash register with the best of them. Cain took a lot longer to warm up, but under Zach's caring tutelage, he was soon cutting and pasting and singing when he thought no one was looking.

The subject of Mom was brought up intermittently by the girls.

"Olivia," Esther wondered, "can my mom see us?"

"Does she have wings?" Ruth asked.

"Is she ever coming back?" they both wanted to know.

Olivia fielded their questions the best she could and comforted their occasional outbursts of emotion.

As usual, when it came to discussing his mother, Cain was silent.

* * *

In the days that followed, everyone pitched in to help, just as they had promised. Monday, Olivia had to return to work, so Zach volunteered to enroll Cain in kindergarten.

Like a lamb being led to slaughter, Cain had docilely followed Zach into the schoolroom. The poor kid didn't like at all the idea of being so far away from his sisters. Sensing that the child was on the verge of tears but too stubborn to ask for help, Zach stayed until Cain seemed comfortable in his surroundings. By the time Zach was ready to leave to join Mike at work, he was able to coax a wobbly smile out of the little boy.

When Zach had returned to pick Cain up from school, he brought Copper with him. The joyful reunion between boy and dog had Zach misty with strong, very protective emotions that took him by surprise. Is this what it would have been like had AmyBeth lived and they'd adopted their child? The feelings of love for these helpless kids were fiercer than anything he could ever have anticipated.

What would he do when his stint at Hattie's place was done? When the kids were assigned a permanent home? When Copper went to work full-time for the police department? These thoughts swirled depressingly in Zach's head the entire way back to Hattie's place. He was getting too attached here. Way too attached. He was going to have to pray for the safety of his puny little heart before it was pulverized again. He didn't think it could take another fracture. Not after losing AmyBeth.

11

Early Tuesday morning, about an hour before she usually left the boarding house for work, Olivia ran into Zach in the front hall. They were alone, as Cain and his sisters were still upstairs in the land of Nod. Kindergarten wouldn't start for another hour and a half, so there was plenty of time for them to have a nutritious breakfast and bath, once Olivia roused them.

Elderly voices could be heard in the dining room, along with the clinking of silver against china.

"Can I talk with you for a minute?" Olivia knew her whisper bordered on urgent. She clutched the sleeve of Zach's flannel jacket as he walked by.

Zach looked over his shoulder toward the dining room, as if to discover the source of her secrecy. "Sure," he agreed easily and bestowed on her a thousand-watt grin that had her blinking.

How could anyone look so put together and awake at this hour of the morning? She couldn't even focus until she'd had her first cup of coffee. Doing her best to feign indifference at his incredibly handsome mug, she forged ahead. "Officer Menkin called."

"Again? I'm beginning to think he may be sweet on

you." His teasing gaze dropped to her pinkening cheeks. "You're blushing! Should I be jealous?"

"Oh, stop!" Tugging him by the front of his jacket, she pulled him into the nook under the stairs and tried to ignore how, in this close proximity, her legs felt as if they were made of bread dough.

"Should I challenge him to a duel? Donuts at fifty paces?" Zach murmured, his face now inches from hers. His gaze traveled about the confining space where they stood. "This is cozy. I like this. We should meet here every morning." He tugged a lock of her hair. "Just promise we don't have to discuss Officer Menkin." His noisy, snorting whisper was silly. Playful. Flirtatious.

Laughing, Olivia pushed at his chest. "Will you be serious? We're hiding back here because I don't want the kids to hear. Just in case they should wake up and come looking for me."

"Ah, too bad. I was hoping you had designs on me." His warm, minty breath fanned her cheeks.

Olivia filled her lungs. If he only knew. Slowly, she exhaled and wondered how to begin. It would be much more fun to stand here and banter with Zach than to discuss the subject that haunted her. But she couldn't do that. She had to think of the kids first. For now, anyway. "It's about Roxanne. The kids' mother?"

Zach nodded.

"Well, the medical examiner's office has finished with its investigation into her death. They have found no living relatives, other than her three children. So Officer Menkin told me the medical examiner wants to know if I had any ideas how they should proceed with the... er...burial."

A pained expression crossed Zach's face. Lifting his

arm, he ran a hand over the back of his neck and rubbed. "Oh, man. This is my least favorite subject. I'm sure it's yours too."

"Uh-huh." She nodded and looked up into his eyes. Beautiful, soulful brown eyes, filled with compassion. "I could easily wash my hands of the whole thing. You know, let the funeral home handle everything and just stay out of it. But for the sake of the kids, I think we should do something." She sighed, unconscious of the fact that she was starting to include Zach in her plans.

Tilting his head, he encouraged her to continue.

"Officer Menkin says that if Roxanne had no one—no family or friends—she would be buried by the indigent burial fund. But since she has family, and since I am in charge of the 'family,' for the moment anyway, I can have a say in the...uh, well, the arrangements. If I want. Or, since the kids are minors, we could let the indigent fund handle the responsibility."

"Boy. Lucky you." Zach's grin was sardonic.

"Tell me about it." Gathering her hair—still damp from her shower—in one hand, she pushed it over her shoulder and away from her face. "Anyway," she sighed, "the body has been moved to the McLaughlin Chapel of the Hills Funeral Home. I've been thinking that a little memorial service might be nice. Something simple for the kids. But I'm not so sure we should have it at the funeral home. I was thinking that might be too upsetting for them..." Her voice trailed off, and she lifted her shoulders.

"Maybe Hattie would let us have a small service here, in the parlor," Zach mused aloud. "I could talk to Pastor Wythe at my church. I'm sure he could spare an hour to come help us pay our respects."

"Good idea." Her shoulders dropped, and her energy

flagged a little. "Do you think we should request earth burial or cremation?"

Zach thought for a moment. "Well, the kids might like to be able to visit her grave later, when they are old enough to understand this kind of thing. So, I think maybe in this case an earth burial? Gee. I don't know."

"No, you have a very good point. Earth burial it is. According to what I've been told, the indigent fund will cover the costs of that, considering the circumstances. Okay. Good. I'll call the funeral home and have them go ahead with the burial before we have the memorial service. I don't think the kids should necessarily attend that, but…maybe you and I could run over and, you know, be there?" She didn't want to go by herself.

He nodded. "Sounds good."

"Uh…when do you think we should have the memorial service?"

"Well, hmm. The sooner the better. We've already waited far too long. Why don't we talk to Hattie and shoot for Friday afternoon? I know that Pastor Wythe leaves that time open for that kind of thing. That's"—Zach faltered for a moment—"when he conducted AmyBeth's memorial."

Reaching out, Olivia lightly cupped Zach's freshly shaven cheek in her hand. "Thank you." She could hear the distant pain in his voice. The same pain that she was only learning to deal with so recently. "You have been such a rock for me."

Zach flexed his biceps, then, looping an arm around her waist, muscled her out of the alcove and into the hall proper. "Anytime, little lady." His deep, basso profundo was meant to make her laugh. He had such a delightful way of pulling her out of a funk.

Her giggles were as nervous as Nell's.

"I'll go get my cell phone and call Pastor Wythe." He slowly let his arm slide from her waist.

Her glance darting about, Olivia took a step back and waved toward the parlor. She wished fervently at times like this that she was cool and sophisticated, with an endless repertoire of witty repartee. Unfortunately, at the moment, she was tongue-tied and feeling about as sophisticated as an ox. "Okay, good. I'll...uh, I'll just go call Officer Menkin."

"I'm tellin' ya, I'm startin' to get more than a little jealous."

"Would you stop?" Olivia's giddy mirth trailed behind her as she rushed down the hall, slippers slapping, and disappeared into the parlor.

• • •

Everyone thought the memorial service was a grand idea. Especially once they got over the initial shock that the children's mother was not Olivia but, instead, some poor soul who went by the name of Roxanne Grady. So Wednesday evening, after Jungle Jam was over and the children had been put to bed, Hattie—in her usual take-charge manner when it came to organizing social events—took charge. Electricity fairly crackled in the air around the dining table as the entire boarding house population brimmed with plans, adding to Hattie's ideas and offering some of their own.

"I'm so very glad we've decided to have a memorial service in the parlor for Rosanne!" Hattie's declaration burbled with enthusiasm. "Everyone deserves a proper send-off. Why, when my sweet Ernie—God rest his soul—went to be with the Lord, the party we threw here at the house! Oh my! Just what he would have wanted, I tell you. Except for the sweet-and-sour meatballs. No no. Those tended to repeat on him, poor man. But I figured his having moved in with the good Lord and all, he was beyond that…"

Touching her pencil to her tongue, she proceeded to make a series of violent chicken scratchings on a yellow pad. "Okay! Let's get to plannin'," she sang. "It wasn't raining when Noah built the ark!"

Everyone nodded and shrugged. If Hattie said so.

"Now then, shall we begin with music? We have the piano in the parlor, and our neighbor, Bea, has the harp. Tell me, Olympia, dear, what were Rosanne's favorite hymns?" Hattie's birdlike gaze shot to, and settled on, Olivia.

"I…well…" Brows knit, Olivia racked her brain for an idea. Having never met the woman, it was hard to say. "Something simple would be fine, I'm sure."

Zach, whose presence at the dinner table these days had become a given in everyone's mind, offered his thoughts. "How about 'At the Cross'?"

"Diana Ross?" Hattie considered this suggestion for a moment. "I'm not familiar with her gospel work. But she is good, Jack. I'll keep that in mind." In shaky, labored penmanship, she jotted *Diana Ross* on her list. As an afterthought, she added, *and the Supremes.*

Agnes's head snapped back. Her chin disappearing into the folds of her neck, she scowled, thoroughly scandalized. "Absolutely not! I vote *no* to Diana Ross! I will not be commandeered into playing any of that…that…rock-and-roll racket! Especially in the presence of a man of the cloth!"

Biting her lip, Olivia dared not look at Zach. Trying to picture Agnes jamming in front of anyone was more than her imagination could handle.

"If I'm going to play the piano and sing with Glyniss," Agnes continued, warming to her subject, "we will be sticking to the classics."

Glyniss snorted. "You never were any fun, Aggie. I happen to like Diana Ross. I loved that one she did...oh, you know...what's it called?" She pursed her lips and searched her memory bank. "Wasn't it something like, 'My World Is Empty Without You, Babe'? Didn't Diana Ross sing that? Now, there's a song! *Ta dee dee dee doo doo da dee...Babe!*" she warbled off-key. "Why, I'm sure if we could find the sheet music, Bea and I could—"

Casting her a dour glance, Agnes cut Glyniss off. "Am I the only person in this room with a thimble full of propriety? A modicum of taste? You can't sing 'My World Is Empty Without You, Babe,' at a funeral!"

"Why not? I think it would be perfectly apropos. Am I wrong?" Glyniss looked around the table for moral support.

Olivia, wanting to make peace, tried to interject. "Well, actually, I think what Zach was trying to say—"

"Personally," Agnes steamrolled ahead, sniffing haughtily, "I'm partial to 'Amazing Grace.' With Bea on the harp, Glyniss, you and I could do a credible rendition with an hour or two of practice. I'm sure we can be ready to perform by Friday afternoon."

"But we do 'Amazing Grace' for *all* our friends' funerals, Agnes. Can't we do something a little more...upbeat, for a change?"

"Upbeat?" Agnes raised a supercilious eyebrow.

"I think what she means is—" Olivia ventured, only to be verbally flattened once more.

"A memorial service is no place for folderol. It's serious business, Glyniss. That's what's the matter with young people today, they are so busy trying to be...*upbeat.*" Agnes spat the word as if it were an obscenity.

"Here we go again," Glyniss muttered.

Olivia glanced up at Zach and pulled a helpless face.

All smiles, he winked at her, amused at the clucking ballyhoo.

What a sweet man to put up with this chaos on his free time. *He really is one of a kind.* Heart leaping beneath her breast, Olivia smiled back.

After five years at the boarding house, she should have guessed this would happen. Agnes and Glyniss rarely agreed on any topic. She should have warned Zach. Told him that this meeting might go on an hour or so longer than originally planned. Perhaps then he could have bowed out. Spent the evening doing something more constructive. Like watching a game show on TV.

But she couldn't say she was sorry that he was stuck here with her. Spending an entire evening sitting right next to Zach, unobtrusively studying his rugged profile, was just too much fun to regret.

"No, Glyniss, I do not think Gladys Knight and the Pips are a viable alternative! Use your head! What the devil is a *Pip*, in the first place?"

Adjusting her glasses Hattie studied her to-do list, as if unaware of the bickering going on around her. "Colonel, I assume you'll want to be in charge of decorations?"

"Ye-hssss, ma'amhackkkooie!" His wheezing shriek was affirmative. Long, wispy gray hairs, which sprang from the sides of his skull, floated on the breeze of his bronchial attack. The parchment skin of his brow wrinkled as he fumbled endlessly within his breast pocket for his notes. After a tense moment, he withdrew a stack of Hattie's old shopping receipts. He'd jotted a number of lists on their blank backs. Smacking his lips, he sucked at his ill-fitting dentures and began to share his plans.

"I've set up a base of operation in my barracks. This is where I shall brief my task force as soon as we break this evening." He pecked the air with a wobbly finger in Sean's direction. "Private, under my command, you and your men make up the decoration battalion." His watery pale blue gaze included Ryan and Zach in this grouping. "The four of us men should be plenty. At oh-six-hundred tomorrow morning, we'll form a scouting party to the Dumpster. Is that clear?"

Sean and Ryan exchanged rueful glances with Zach. Scouting the Dumpster before sunup and rummaging for party favors sounded even worse than boot camp. But they nodded, wanting to see Hattie happy.

"Good!" the Colonel cried. "Hattie, I've made a list of the particulars." He squinted at the various receipts. "Flowers...streamers...balloons...invitations...an American flag..."

Olivia's eyes widened. Would he really find any of those things in the Dumpster? And, if he did, would they be usable? Unable to control the direction of her gaze, she glanced at Zach who sat in the chair next to hers. Big mistake. For he seemed to find this whole process every bit as...*unusual* as she did. Inclining his face to hers, Olivia could feel his warm breath fan the little hairs at the side of her head.

Balloons? he mouthed, a perplexed frown on his face. *At a memorial service?*

Lifting her shoulders, Olivia gestured her own wonder.

"Very good." Hattie scratched away at her list. "Let's see then. The children will draw pictures of their mother since we have no photographs, and the Colonel"—she fanned the air over her shoulder—"will mount them on an easel up front. I think a nice wreath would look lovely somewhere in that grouping."

"Consider it done!" The Colonel rapped the table with his gnarled knuckles.

Hattie's pencil swung to Julia and Sean. "Beulah and Don, dearies, could you two greet the guests? And, Brian, if you will be so kind, you can be in charge of seating people as they arrive."

Ryan shrugged good-naturedly and nodded in assent.

Zach leaned ever closer to Olivia, bringing his mouth up to the shell of her ear. She shivered. If they sat any nearer to each other, people might think they were becoming an item. Were they?

Goose bumps crawled up and down her spine as he began to whisper. "Exactly how many people are coming to this shindig anyway?"

"I don't have a clue. It sounds like they are planning on inviting some friends."

"Is that normal?"

Olivia trained a droll gaze on him.

"Olympia, you and Jack should probably sit up front with the children. You can say a few words about Rosanne, when Pastor gives you the signal."

"Okay." Olivia nodded agreeably. That sounded simple enough.

"This should be interesting." Zach pulled a comical face. "Waxing poetic about someone we've never met."

Olivia elbowed him lightly in the ribs. "Fake it.

"Bonnie and I," Hattie continued, "will prepare the food before the service on Friday, and then man the buffet table after the services. Beulah, dearie, if you could pour the punch, that would be a real help." Hattie smoothed the list on the tabletop and, after one last perusal, looked up and beamed at her crew. "According to my best guess, we should have somewhere between forty-five and fifty people in attendance.

Zach and Olivia gaped at each other in stunned silence.

"*Fifty* people?" Incredulous, Olivia's gaze moved to Hattie.

Zach grinned. "Pretty good for a woman who had no friends."

• • •

Friday afternoon, Olivia came rushing home from work, just in time to freshen up for the memorial service. Early that morning, she and Zach had gone to the funeral home and overseen Roxanne's burial. Sadly, not another soul had shown up. Being that there was no one else to meet or greet, she'd headed to work. Zach had taken the day off to help with the children.

It had been a crazy day already. Thank God for Zach.

The memorial service was set to start in a half-hour, and already cars were beginning to line the street, making parking a tricky prospect indeed. Sean and Julia were standing just inside the parlor greeting guests, and Ryan, looking dapper in his Sunday best, was already escorting folks to their seats.

To Olivia, Hattie's circle of friends seemed as endless as the rippling effect a falling stone creates in a pool of water. Many of these good folks were loitering in the front hall and parlor area, murmuring in the somber tones that befitted such an occasion. It didn't seem to matter that no one had a clue as to the identity of the person to whom they were paying last respects. If Hattie cared enough to throw a memorial service, that was good enough for them.

Threading her way through the growing throng, Olivia worked her way toward the stairs and caught glimpses of the Colonel's inimitable decorating stylings throughout the house. Clusters of black "over-the-hill" balloons hung from the ceiling in the parlor. The fireplace mantel was swathed in swags of wilting lilies, wired together with coaxial cable and duct tape. Here and there a collection of stubby, half-burned candles were stuffed into empty pop bottles that had been spray-painted black and gold.

Pausing before she bounded up the stairs, Olivia craned her neck around the archway to see farther into the parlor. The furniture had all been pushed against the walls, and folding chairs of every shape, size, and style were crammed into five tight little rows of ten, with an aisle in the center.

Up front, near the makeshift podium, several impressionistic pictures of Roxanne Grady, drawn by her children in a number of mediums, were mounted on a chewed-up corkboard that had been duct-taped to an equally chewed-up easel. The easel, listing precariously to the left, had been duct-taped to a yardstick, as the back leg was sadly missing. A funeral wreath had been fashioned from shreds of the Sunday comic pages. These ragged strips along with more of the wilting lilies had been duct-taped to a wire coat hanger that had been stretched into a circle and hung above the easel.

Poignant tears stung the backs of Olivia's eyes. So much loving care had gone into this occasion. The entire house sparkled from head to toe, and the smells that wafted from the kitchen were mouth-watering.

Agnes, Glyniss, and Bea were in the music room warming their vocal chords and bickering over who was flat. Listening to the throbbing, operatic cacophony that emanated from that room, Olivia winced and figured it didn't much matter who was flat. The audience would be virtually deaf after the first verse anyway.

Clutching the handrail, Olivia took the stairs two at a time. Hopefully everyone was ready. Zach was to handle getting the children's hair cut, and then get them dressed in some Sunday-go-to-meetin'-type clothes that Bea's daughter had donated to the cause.

Rushing down the hall toward her suite, Olivia was suddenly overcome with bittersweet emotion. How on earth would she have managed without Zach? Surely, this whole ordeal would have been impossible. So far, he had been there to pick up all the loose ends with the kids and, at the same time, instill in her a sense of confidence. Of peace.

She couldn't imagine having to care for the children without his steady, rock-solid presence. She trusted him completely. Without a shadow of a doubt, Olivia knew that when she opened her door, she would find three neatly trimmed little children, dressed in tidy black suits.

Which brought to mind a new dilemma. What would she do once Zach finished up his job in the sunroom? Was she getting too dependent on him? Her heart surged at the thought. That's what had happened with John. He and Lillah had become her whole world.

Just as the children and Zach were doing now.

Ah well. She couldn't worry about that right now. Strains of a funeral dirge wafted up the stairs, signaling that things downstairs were heating up. Olivia glanced at her watch. She would have just enough time to put on some lipstick, run a comb through her hair, and head back down. If she was lucky, there might be a minute to speak with Zach privately. To thank him for taking such wonderful care of the children today. Maybe give him a little kiss on the cheek.

As Olivia burst through the door of her room, she stopped short and stared.

"I know, I know," Zach snapped, catching her look of dismay, then turning back to his task. "Don't worry. It'll grow."

"What on earth happened?" Slack jawed, she stared in

wonder at the three ragamuffins who stood looking back at her, eyes wide, the gravity of the situation made clear by Ruth's silence.

His heavy sigh was laden with self-deprecation. "I let the Colonel talk me into allowing him to give the kids a trim. That's what he called it anyway. A little trim. Said there was no sense spending good money on a barber when he had the tools to do the job himself. At the time it made sense, so I agreed."

Olivia shook her head and tossed a pained glance at the ceiling. That was a man for you. But she couldn't chastise. Zach already looked as if he felt lower than a snake's belly in a wagon track. Her heart went out to him. And to the kids. Oh, the poor kids.

Cain looked like he was recovering from a bad case of mange, sporting a military flattop, gone somehow terribly wrong. Moth-eaten patches covered the back of the boy's head, and at the very top, a cowlickish rooster tail still sprouted, obviously having been overlooked by the near-sighted Colonel.

"The Colonel was having some trouble with the little shield/guard thing. That's why there are a few...sort of, er...bald spots," Zach explained, as he fussed with a bow he was tying into Esther's choppy do. "I was thinking I could loan him a baseball cap till we can get him to a real barber in the morning."

Glancing up at her, Zach saw that she had shifted her attention to the girls.

"Dull scissors. Plus, the Colonel didn't have a bowl small enough to fit their heads." His face a high-blood-pressure crimson, Zach paused and covered his mouth with his hand, struggling not to laugh. "The bowl he used kept sliding around, which would account, ahem," he cleared his throat and had to look away, "for the rather crooked edges."

That was an understatement, Olivia thought dryly. The girls looked like the Campbell's soup kids after having gone one too many rounds with a mulching lawn mower. The chopped-up look was not at all enhanced by the fact that the little black suits Bea had sent in no way, shape, or form fit the kids. Poor things. They looked almost worse than the day she'd brought them home. If possible.

"Olivia?" Esther ventured, fingering the spiky edges of her hair. "This dress scratches my tushy." She plucked at the heavy wool with her free hand.

Stepping forward, Olivia lifted the dress and peered beneath. "What happened to your underwear?"

"It's in there," Esther said, pointing to the bathroom. "I got tired of waiting for somebody to wipe me! I was standing like this." Demonstrating, she bent over, her head balanced on the floor, her tiny pink bottom hiked skyward. "And I said," the child shouted between her legs, "'I'm done! Somebody wipe me!' Then I got dizzy. I almost fell over and killed my head."

Zach looked sheepishly at Olivia. "I didn't know she was talking to me."

Oh well. Her eyes swept the motley crew. She couldn't worry about it now, or she'd start to cry. Or laugh. She couldn't be sure which.

"Never mind," Olivia said, shuffling to the closet, her heart riding somewhere down around her ankles. "We have respects to pay."

* * *

It was too much.

Zach felt as if he would explode if he had to sit there another minute. From the look on Olivia's face, he sensed she felt much the same way. Trouble was, there was no escape. They were sitting in the front row, a captive audience to Agnes's endless caterwauling. As she pounded away at the keys, Bea at the harp and Glyniss as backup vocal did their best to keep up. But this was no easy task, as Agnes set the jolting rhythm, pausing dramatically here and there for several seconds and then holding some notes an extra beat just for effect.

The kids wore pained expressions, and their tiny fingers were stuffed into their ears.

"...Howww sweeet the sound-d-d-d-h-a! That saved a wrett-t-tch-h-h-a! like me-e-e-e-e-e!!!" Her pulsing vibrato had more than one audience member wincing.

Luckily for everyone, the touching service was, for all intents and purposes, over. Zach and Olivia had read some poetry and a few soothing passages from the Bible on the subject of mourning. The easel had only fallen over twice, and the wreath was no worse for the wear. Pastor Wythe's message was a comfort, in spite of the fact that only three people in the room knew Roxanne Grady, and they had all been sound asleep. Till the music started.

No. It wasn't until Agnes had commanded the spotlight that Zach felt he could no longer rein in the thunderhead of laughter he felt building in his belly. He bit his tongue till tears poured down his face. When Agnes hit yet another in a stream of sour notes, he suddenly knew he could take it no more. Fortunately, he also knew, without asking, that Olivia also wanted nothing more in this life than to escape. It was obvious by the tears that flowed unchecked down her cheeks.

He nodded at her.

She nodded back.

Together, they grasped the hands of the three grimacing

children and, dragging them behind, bolted down the aisle and out the front door. Sympathetic eyes followed their progression. Hopefully, those attending thought that the little group was suddenly overcome with emotion and needed some time to pull themselves together.

When they'd finally reached the front steps and were confident that they were out of earshot, Olivia and Zach clutched each other and finally gave in to the explosion of belly laughter that had been threatening since the start of the service.

"It was just too much!" Zach whooped. "The sour notes, the bad haircuts, the over-the-hill balloons..."

Together, they sank to the porch steps, slapping their thighs and gasping for air. Delighted to be free of the confines of the stuffy parlor, the kids gamboled around the porch. Even Cain seemed to be in a good mood, now that Copper was on the scene.

For once, it wasn't raining, and the temperature was on the warmish side. Truth be told, it was much more comfortable here on the front porch than in the house.

"You know what the ironic thing is?" Olivia struggled to get her point across between bouts of hilarity. "It's that we went to all this trouble for the sake of the kids, and they were dead to the world from practically the moment we sat down."

"Until Agnes started to perform, that is." His eyes squeezed tightly shut, Zach leaned back against a porch post and proceeded to roar with laughter. This, of course, sent Olivia off into fresh gales of hysteria.

"Did you hear..." Zach wheezed.

"How about when..." Olivia hooted.

Together, they doubled over with glee. Clutching each other's arms, they gasped for precious oxygen, pounded on the porch floor, and entertained each other with stylized versions of "Amazing Grace" that would forever be emblazoned on their brains.

Haltingly, between howls, they recounted the ordeal, which only became funnier with the telling.

And so, that's how they were sitting when a sturdy pair of black dress shoes came into view at the bottom of the stairs. Slowly they lifted their eyes from the shoes, taking in the support hose, the natty tweed suit, and the puzzled frown that hovered above that.

"Hello," Olivia was finally able to gasp. She dabbed at her eyes with Zach's sleeve, since his arm was slung loosely around her shoulders anyway.

"Hello. I'm Mertyl Rogers. From the Children's Services Division." At Olivia and Zach's blank stares, she raised a concerned brow and explained. "Your social worker?"

12

A nd this"—smiling a little too broadly, Olivia flung open her front door—"is my suite."

The three kids, Copper, and Zach following behind her, Olivia rushed into the room and kicked some of the kids' dirty clothes under the cots. She wished she'd had time to make the beds that morning. The only thing keeping her from dissolving into a puddle of quivering mush on the floor was Zach's steadying presence.

She glanced through the doorway at Mertyl.

The woman was so hard to read. Her face expressionless, Mertyl strode into the room and wordlessly surveyed the cots, the dirty clothes, the damp towels in the bathroom, and the unmade beds. The dog jumped up on Cain's cot and curled into a ball. Mertyl opened closet doors, peered around corners, and paced off the available square footage.

Heart thrumming, Olivia groped for Zach's hand. The comforting warmth she found there bolstered her flagging spirits. Although Mertyl hadn't said anything overtly derogatory, an eerie feeling of foreboding told Olivia that the news was bad. Mertyl wasn't going to let the children stay.

Suddenly Olivia felt a fierce wave of indignation sweep over her and settle in her belly. This woman was judging her. Determining whether or not she would make a suitable guardian. How could that be? Mertyl Rogers didn't know her from Adam. How could she know what a wonderful mother she'd been to Lillah? She couldn't. Well, if there was one thing on her side it was that she was a much better mother to Roxanne's children than Roxanne had been. Seething, Olivia glanced at Zach.

He seemed to feel her angst. Squeezing her fingers, he rubbed them with his thumb.

"Relax," he admonished, under his breath, as Mertyl disappeared into the bathroom for a cursory inspection.

"How can I?" Her frantic words were gritted out through tight lips. Tipping her chin back, she stared balefully up at him. "This place is a zoo, and she knows it."

"No, it's not." Zach chuckled.

"Zach!" Peeking over his shoulder, she made sure Mertyl was still in the bathroom. "Agnes is still down there singing! How many verses does 'Amazing Grace' have anyway? And some first impression we made, hanging around outside the memorial service for the children's mother, laughing our fool heads off. What must she think of us?"

"Well, I—"

"I'll tell you what she thinks of us!" Olivia clutched the placket of his shirt, knowing suddenly how Nell probably felt most of the time. This panicky feeling was horrible. "She thinks we're nuts!" With a moan, she allowed her head to thud against the solid wall of Zach's chest. "I can't believe I forgot she was coming this afternoon. With all the excitement of the service, I must have blocked it out or something."

Sensing that Mertyl was on the verge of reentering the room, Olivia's head snapped up. She smoothed Zach's shirt and tried to affect a serene smile.

"Where are the laundry facilities?" Mertyl strode back into the room.

"Laundry facilities? Oh, of course. Yes, I know by the look of things...that is you can't tell...but," Olivia rushed to explain, "we do have laundry facilities. Lots of them. Downstairs in the basement. I was going to do the laundry, but what with the memorial service and all..." Her voice trailed lamely off.

Mertyl cocked her head. "Is that noise I hear"—her face pickled—"dogs barking?"

Was she referring to Agnes's baying from the parlor below, or the puppies that howled from Ryan's room?

"Barking? Dogs?" Olivia's giddy laughter was breathless. Dizzy. She felt faint. Had Ryan's latest class escaped? He'd promised to kennel the police puppies for the service. A bunch of loose-cannon dogs running hither and yon would certainly be the icing on the cake.

"Sounds like dogs, here in the house. Barking." Mertyl pursed her lips. "Are there many dogs living here?"

"Living? Here?" Olivia repeated dumbly. What was the right answer? Were dogs bad for children? Were they good? She didn't know what Mertyl wanted to hear. "I...uh...Ryan, he's one of the tenants here, is a canine behaviorist. He teaches dog obedience courses here at the house now and again."

"Dogs that need discipline?" Mertyl asked, a small furrow marring her wide, flat brow.

"I...guess so."

"Hmm." Mertyl made yet another cryptic note on her clipboard. "I'd like to see the rest of the house, if I may."

"Certainly!" Olivia sang, shooting a horrified look at Zach. Agnes was no doubt still entertaining the troops. "Right this way." To the children she said, "Kids, I want you to stay here and change your clothes. Put on some play clothes. I'll be back in a little while to get you and bring you downstairs for supper."

"Hey, big mean lady," Ruth cried as the adults turned to go downstairs, "watch this!"

Zach coughed and cleared his throat.

Olivia winced. Although she had to agree with Ruth's diagnosis, "big mean lady" was hardly the goodwill necessary at the moment. Helplessly, she watched as the child skipped hither and thither in an attempt to chisel a smile into the social worker's suddenly granite expression.

While her sister danced, Esther tugged on Olivia's skirt. "Olivia?"

"Yes, sweetheart?"

"I don't want poo-poo on my plate this time," she shouted. Seeming to sense Olivia's tension, she made the most of her demands. "It makes the dog throw up."

Mertyl's furrow deepened, becoming a small canyon of sorts between her dull black eyes.

Olivia smiled weakly at the social worker. "Kids." Her chuckle was weak. "Don't they say the darnedest things?"

Mertyl remained silent.

"They sure do," Zach agreed enthusiastically, trying to find a graceful way to salvage the situation.

She shot him a grateful glance. "Okay, you guys." Olivia clapped her hands at the kids. "Get to changing."

"Olivia?" Ruth dragged the bow that Zach had installed out of her hair. "Is Zach gonna cut our hair again today?"

Olivia sighed. "Not now, honey. We'll worry about your hair later." Not wanting to further incriminate the situation, she shut the door and smiled brightly at Mertyl and Zach. "Shall we?" She gestured toward the stairs.

● ● ●

Mertyl got the big tour, which included a parlor filled with long-suffering guests, a still-caterwauling Agnes, rooms decorated in a bizarre caricature of a memorial service, and a completely demolished, still partially mud-filled, sun-room. All the while, Mertyl made notes, her expression shrouded in concern. As the touring trio wended their way through the throng of memorial guests, they were stopped here and there by various folk who took a moment to pass on their condolences.

Mertyl, her impatience written all over her face, would glance often at her watch and fidget with the fuzzy wool on the sleeve of her jacket. When they finally arrived in the dining room where the buffet table had been set up, Olivia spied Hattie fussing over one of the dishes, and led Mertyl toward the elderly woman.

"Hattie?" Olivia shouted above the rumble of the crowd. *"Hattie? I'd like you to meet Mertyl Rogers. She is our social worker."*

Mertyl shot a startled glance at Olivia.

Groaning inwardly, Olivia closed her eyes. Great. Now the social worker thought she liked to yell at old ladies. Olivia grasped Hattie's delicate hand and slowly drew her forward to stand between Zach and herself. "Ms. Rogers, this is Hattie Hopkins, my landlady."

Mertyl nodded.

Hattie smiled in welcome. "Hello, Miss Roberts. Why, we've all been expecting you. You're a true gift from the good Lord, you are!"

Dubious, Mertyl arched a brow. "Rogers. My name is Rogers."

"Yes, of course. Miss Roberts, I've been praying for you for...hmm, several weeks now."

Clearly taken aback, Mertyl frowned. "Oh?"

"Such a blessing, these children have been to our lives. God is so good, is he not?"

"God?" Mertyl looked as if Hattie had just forced her to suck a lemon.

Slowly shuffling around, Hattie gestured to the buffet. "Would you care to join us for a light buffet supper, dear? The sweet-and-sour meatballs are especially delicious."

Mertyl gave her head a tiny shake. "No, really, I don't have the time. But thank you just the same. We must be getting back to work."

"Oh, I understand. Those meatballs used to repeat on my Ernie something fierce too. Nothing worse than the bloating that comes with gas, it's true. Well, you help yourself to whatever else appeals to you." With that, Hattie moved off to converse with others in her ever-broadening circle of friends.

Mertyl simply stared.

Feeling as if she'd been kicked in the solar plexus, Olivia glanced at Zach, seeking comfort. Luckily his sweet, empathetic expression gave a little boost to her sagging spirits.

Things were not going well. Nothing seemed to satisfy the social worker. Not their living quarters, not their lifestyle, not the landlady, not the children's clothing, and certainly not their haircuts.

And, most especially, not the references to God.

Olivia could understand that, having taken a powder on the spiritual front for the past five years herself. But, lately, her loyalties had shifted. And she was afraid it showed. It was obvious that Mertyl was not a religious woman, and she didn't seem at all impressed that Hattie was. Olivia knew some state agencies looked at religious belief as more of a hindrance to a foster/adoption case than an advantage. Would Hattie's innocent words be detrimental? Would her own blossoming belief system?

Silently, as they moved toward the stairs to return to Olivia's suite, she shot a quick prayer heavenward. *Dear Lord, I don't like this woman. Please help me, Lord! I'm afraid of her. I'm afraid she's going to take the kids.*

Perhaps telling God up front that she detested Mertyl wasn't the most politically correct thing she could have done, but she had a feeling God already knew how she felt. She was also suddenly flooded with the feeling that God didn't give a flying fig about political correctness. He cared about the welfare of these kids. That much, she was sure of.

That much, she trusted.

As they ascended to the second floor and moved down the main hallway, Mertyl spoke not a word but only paused here and there to jot her opinions on the clipboard.

Upon returning to her suite, Olivia found things even more chaotic than when they'd left. Her heart sank further, plunging her into a fit of melancholy. The kids were jumping on their cots, screaming and giggling and generally running amuck. The laundry was spread over the floor like a lumpy carpet, and her comforter had been used to build a tent that spanned the space between her bed and the cots. *Oh yeah. Just the picture of perfect domesticity I want to portray.*

After absorbing the chaos for a moment, Mertyl turned and strode back to the main hall and assumed her drill-sergeant posture. "Perhaps we can hear ourselves think a little better out here."

Meekly, Zach and Olivia followed the woman to the hall.

"I don't believe," Mertyl began without ceremony, "that a one-room suite in an adult boarding house is a suitable place for these three children to remain." She sniffed and studied her notes. "I don't see where it's an advantage to anyone." Affecting a sympathetic expression, she lifted her lips and bared her teeth in a semismile at Olivia. "Certainly, you can't like having your home overrun by cots. And quite clearly the children deserve better than this."

Her blood beginning a slow boil, Olivia simply stared at Mertyl. A quick glance at Zach told her that he was feeling as outraged as she was.

"They deserve *better* than this?" Olivia asked woodenly, still not certain that she could believe her ears.

"Certainly." Not one to mince words, Mertyl swept her arm toward Olivia's room. "This is unacceptable by our standards."

Unacceptable? What in thunder did *that* mean? This woman's imperious attitude fried Olivia. Why, she was standing there, casting aspersions on her home. On her lifestyle. On the pile of dirty underwear that was now scattered all over the middle of her floor.

Stiffening, she opened her mouth to protest, but Zach stepped in front of her and interrupted.

"Ms. Rogers, what would you think if I installed a door between Olivia's room and the storage room? We could clear all the stuff out, move it to the attic, and put the kids in there. I'd be happy to build a set of bunk beds for the girls, and I'll put a little bed in the alcove for Cain." He shrugged and smiled boyishly. "I could probably have it done by the end of next week, if I work on it every evening and all weekend."

The social worker's smile was condescending. "No, I'm afraid that simply would not meet the standards."

"I'd make sure everything was up to code," Zach argued, taking the government angle.

"No." Mertyl shook her head, seemingly amused at his suggestion. "I'm afraid there is nothing you can do."

Olivia was suddenly shaking with fury.

Stop me, Lord, she prayed. *If I'm to be silent, stop me now.* Silence.

Okay. Fine with her. She took a step forward that brought her nose to nose with the suddenly defensive social worker. Somewhere in the back of her mind, Nell's words began to echo in her ears.

Point at your particular mountain and command it to... move!

Well, by golly, Olivia thought, as the grain of a mustard seed took root in her heart and began to bloom—Mertyl was a mountain in a natty wool suit. And this persimmon-sucking crab apple would move her sorry behind out of this house right now, or Olivia would know the reason why. Eyes narrowed, she watched as beads of sweat began to appear on Mertyl's upper lip.

Here we go, Lord. Mentally Olivia pushed up her sleeves and prepared to go to battle, like a mother lion defending her cubs.

"Not meet your *standards?* Not meet *your*...standards?"

"Well! As I said—" Mertyl, caught off guard by the fury in Olivia's tone, took a step back.

"I heard what you said, Ms. Rogers." Tossing her head, Olivia flipped wayward locks of hair out of her blazing eyes. "Why don't you tell me where you and your people were when the kids were living like rats in a sewer? Did that hovel, where they slept and ate the stale and rotten food they managed to scrounge out of the garbage, did *that* meet your precious *standards?*" Her face felt hot enough to alarm Smokey the Bear, but she didn't care. She was beyond mad.

She felt Zach step forward and reach out as he attempted to soothe her. To get her to calm down. She hoped it wasn't a sign from the Lord to chill out, because it was too late now. Rudely shrugging his hand off her arm, her eyes narrowed at Mertyl as she went in for the verbal kill.

"How *dare* you tell me that these quarters are not suitable for the children? For the first time in…in…maybe their whole lives, they have had three square meals a day! They have had baths and clean clothes. Their hair is vermin free, and they are surrounded by love. By good Christian people who shower them with attention and affection. For pity's sake, how can that be inferior? Why didn't you step in when the children's mother was prowling the streets for drugs and money, leaving these precious babies alone in the house, sometimes for days on end?"

"I…" Mertyl attempted to answer, but it was futile. Olivia was on a rampage.

"I happen to love these children, Ms. Rogers. I love them as if they were my own." Olivia was shocked to discover that as she spoke these words, she suddenly knew they were true. She knew not when or how, but at some point, she'd fallen madly in love with these three little ragamuffins. "I know that God himself put these kids in my care! Who do you think you are to mess with God?"

"Abd…ahh…" Mertyl sputtered.

Leaning back against the doorframe, Zach shrugged in resignation and, with a what-the-hey grin, folded his arms across his chest.

"I want to adopt these children someday, Ms. Rogers," she shouted, eyes wild, nose running, tears flowing, saliva flying. "I don't know how on earth I'm going to swing it, but mark my words. Neither you nor your office full of…of…" she stomped her foot as she searched for an insult, "*bureaucrats* will stand in my way. Because God almighty himself is on my side, so…look out!" Marching to the door of her suite, she flung it open.

White faced, Mertyl watched her go.

"Good day!" Olivia tossed a crisp nod over her shoulder before she disappeared into her suite, crashing the door closed behind her.

Once inside, Olivia leaned against the solid old door and allowed her tears to flow unchecked. Burying her face in her hands, she sobbed as if her heart would break. She'd done it now. She'd lost the kids.

"I'm sorry, Lord," she murmured. "I blew it."

Quietly, like little mice, all three kids climbed off the bed where they'd been sitting and listening. Then they tiptoed across the room and wrapped their little arms around her waist.

• • •

He'd done the best he knew how, but Zach didn't suppose any of his words of placation hit the spot with Mertyl. Nope, she'd been thoroughly insulted. Poor thing. Her sturdy shoes had carried her down the porch stairs and to the sidewalk so fast, he'd been tempted to check the concrete for burned rubber.

As he stood there watching Mertyl's steaming form disappear down the street in search of her car, Zach thought back to Olivia's spicy diatribe and grinned.

What a woman.

If he hadn't been sure before, he was sure now. He was in love with Olivia Harmon. Instead of causing fear, the way those same feelings had when he was a much younger man with AmyBeth, the very thought of loving Olivia made him feel somehow safe. As if, after a very long journey, he'd finally come home. Funny, he mused, how Olivia could cause such a riot of emotions in him. Sure, he felt safe and loving and secure whenever he was with her. But at the same time she made him feel as if he were completely off-kilter. Out of whack. Excited beyond belief by a simple smile. He shook his head. She could sure be a pistol when the situation warranted.

A wide grin split his face as he thought of the way her bright blue eyes fairly shot sparks at poor old Mertyl. Okay, so she'd been a little over the top. But she'd been afraid for her babies. Olivia was passionate about the kids, and he loved that about her. And more and more, Zach was getting the feeling that she depended on him for strength. And courage. And moral support. And a host of other things he was only too happy to give. He loved that about her too.

But, most important of all the things he loved about Olivia, he loved the firm faith she was developing in God.

Nope. Zach sighed the sigh of a happy man. There wasn't much about Olivia Harmon that he didn't love. Leaning back against the porch post, he crossed his arms over his chest and chuckled. He'd never forget the look on Mertyl's face after Olivia had bid her good day and slammed the door.

It was priceless.

Once she'd managed to recover her stoic poise, Mertyl consulted her clipboard and quickly informed Zach of her plans.

"While it's true," Mertyl had said with an insulted sniff, "that these living conditions are less than suitable for the children, I will consent to leave them here for a while longer. We are short on foster families at the moment, but I expect that to be changing soon. As soon as it is possible, you can be sure I will be looking for a suitable home. One with two parents. When I find this home, I will notify Miss Harmon as to when we will be here to pick up the children and unite them with their new family."

With that, she'd jammed her pencil into her bun and made tracks.

Zach stared into the empty street. At least they had a reprieve, no matter how brief, to do some praying. And to form some plans regarding the children. For that much at least, he was thankful.

As he stood there thinking, the front door opened and Hattie stepped out of the people-packed foyer and onto the porch.

"Why, here you are, dear heart. Better come in while there are still some buffalo wings left." Cane leading, she tottered over to where he stood. "Where is our friend, Miss Roberts?"

"She had to go." He spoke loudly so that Hattie could hear. Smiling, Zach placed a loose arm around her stooped shoulders.

"Shame. She didn't eat a thing." She patted his arm with her free hand. "How are things going with the children?"

Zach sighed and shook his head. "Not so good, I'm afraid. Ms. Rogers wants to take the children away."

The gentle hubbub of the gathering filtered out to them through the screen door. People were inside talking and laughing and enjoying the tasty fare. Zach knew that it would probably be well past the dinner hour before the last guest finally departed.

Overhead, the sky was leaden with heavy gray rain clouds. Now and again, the occasional drop would splat noisily on the steppingstones that made up the front walkway.

Hattie turned on Zach's arm and peered up into his face. "Don't worry, sweetheart. Those children aren't going anywhere. Why, anyone can see they are a gift from God." With fingers long gnarled from arthritis, she reached up and cupped his cheek. "When down in the mouth, remember

Jonah—he came out all right." Eyes twinkling, Hattie gathered her cane and stumped back toward the house. She paused at the door. "Buffalo wings?"

Zach grinned, feeling suddenly bolstered by this little saint's giant faith in God. "Sounds heavenly." Reaching around her, he held the screen door, then followed Hattie toward the buffet table.

Yep, he'd sure been blessed by the precious souls that lived their days under this roof. Crashing into the sunroom was one of the best things that had ever happened to him.

* * *

After a quick trip through the buffet line, Zach went in search of Olivia. He found her in the kitchen, feeding the kids. Her face was blotchy, and her eyes were red and puffy. It was obvious that she'd been crying ever since Mertyl left.

Quietly crossing the kitchen, Zach set his plate down on the table where the children were eating and giggling and extended his hand to her.

"Come on." He drew her up to her feet. "I want to tell you what Mertyl had to say after you left."

"Maybe I don't want to hear it." Olivia sounded no older than Esther when she spoke. The plaintive note in her voice was small and fearful and decidedly lost.

"It's not so bad." Smiling gently, he tucked her hand in his and drew her to the service porch located just off the kitchen. The children watched them go but, for once, did not follow.

There, amid the mops and brooms and cleaning supplies and tidy rows of boots, Zach pulled her into his arms. Immediately, the floodgates opened, and Olivia sobbed as if her heart would break.

"I can't stand this!" Heartbroken, she blubbered into his

shirt. Her tears were soaking large, dark patches in the fabric on his chest and shoulder. "I never wanted to go through this again, but it's just like what happened when John and Lillah died. I feel like I'm losing my family all over again."

"I know." Whispering, Zach slowly rocked her to and fro. "I know."

"I feel all terrified and lonely, and I don't know what to do. I'd like to think that God will work it all out, but I'm pretty sure he's not too happy with me at the moment."

"What makes you say that?"

Olivia reared back in his arms and blinked up at him, tears still streaming down her cheeks. "Well, for starters, the way I yelled at that poor woman. She must be sure that I'm a lunatic now."

Chuckling, Zach pulled her head against his chest, and stroked her long, honey-wheat hair.

"No, she doesn't think you're a lunatic. Adamant, yes. Crazy, no."

Outside, it had begun to rain in earnest. *Raining outside*, he mused, planting a light kiss at the crown of Olivia's head, *and raining in*. He tightened his hold at her waist. From the window in the side door, Zach could see the first of the departing guests opening their colorful umbrellas and rushing to their cars.

Inhaling deeply, Zach held his breath for a moment, then, ever so slowly, he let it out. He could spend the rest of his life quite happily whiling away a stormy day by holding Olivia in his arms. And listening to the three kids in the next room squealing and laughing and practicing the manners that Agnes had been teaching. Yes, this was what life was all about.

"Oh, honey." He sighed, gently rubbing the muscles in

her shoulders. "You didn't do anything wrong. God understands that we have emotions and that sometimes we have to let them out. You've been under a lot of pressure lately. God knows that too. He doesn't punish people. Especially not for saying what they believe. For loving his little children when no one else was willing. He's not mad at you, sweetheart, he's happy with you. He picked you to take care of these children. No one else. You."

"Really?" She sniffed, her small voice muffled by the folds of his shirt.

"Yes. And I'm not the only one who thinks so."

"You're not?"

"Nope. Just ask Hattie. She just told me that we have nothing to worry about."

"We don't?"

"No. She says these children are a gift from God. And she seems to think that anyone can see that." Zach shrugged. "So I say, if Hattie says so, we should take her word for it. You know, she has quite a reputation at our church for answered prayer."

"I wonder why her prayers are always answered?" Olivia was becoming distracted from her angst. The tears were beginning to subside, and a spark of real interest lit her face.

"She has the faith of a mustard seed."

Leaning back, Olivia looked up at him. "Odd you should say that."

"Why?"

"Well, that's sort of where you came in."

Zach's brow knit in confusion.

Olivia smiled. "Never mind. I'll explain another day. Right now, I want you to tell me about Mertyl."

An amused grin crept across his face. "You know, I think you gave old Mertyl something to think about."

"I did?" Olivia smiled ruefully.

"Well, for one thing, you made it perfectly clear that you loved these kids with a mother's heart. I think she respects that. She agreed to leave the kids where they are."

"She did?"

"For now."

"Oh."

"But that's good."

"Why?"

"Well, it gives us some time to pray. And to figure out some long-range goals." He held his breath for a moment. He knew it was far too soon in their relationship to be talking long-range goals, but this was an emergency.

Cocking her head, Olivia sent a contemplative look at him. "True," she murmured.

"You know, Mertyl's not really so bad. In fact, under other circumstances, where you felt a little less defensive, you might even like her. Agree with her. She has the kids' best interest at heart, you know."

She lifted a shoulder to display her skepticism.

"And good old Mertyl may not want to admit it, but I'd be willing to bet she's impressed with your passion for the children. I sure was."

"You were?"

"Always have been. Impressed. With your passion. For things."

"You have?" Eyes flashing, Olivia's gaze tangled with his.

"Mm-hmm."

They were quiet for a long moment, looking into each other's eyes, knowing that something very important was passing between them right then. Something so important and so fragile that they couldn't put it into words.

Reaching up, Zach cradled the back of Olivia's head in

his hand and tilted her face just beneath his. Ever so slowly, he brought his lips to hers and found her mouth pliant, eager, and…passionate. They stood for a while, locked in this tender embrace, saying with actions what words could not.

Zach had never felt so perfect. So complete. Olivia was wonderful. She smelled wonderful, she felt wonderful, she tasted wonderful. He twined his fists in her silky soft hair and moaned. Surely, he'd died and gone to his heavenly reward. Her heart was pounding just as furiously as his own, and he suddenly felt as if he were a kid again.

When the kiss finally came to its natural conclusion— brought on in part by a yelp from Ruth from the kitchen— they pulled apart and stood in each other's arms, smiling.

"We'd better go check on them." Zach didn't move. He wished he could stay where he was and just forget the kids for a few more minutes.

"Probably." Olivia's tone was as wistful as his. "Thank you. I feel much better."

She looked better too.

"Anytime." He growled, teasingly. Anytime at all.

• • •

Though Zach wasn't in the habit of working on Saturday, he made an exception when it came to the sunroom. Winter was coming and, with so many elderly people in residence, a nasty draft was the last thing anyone needed. Besides, working the weekend gave him all that much more time to spend with Olivia and the kids.

His regular crew was making real headway up the hill on the historic McLaughlin House project. The retaining wall was in place, and the house's foundation was being refortified. It was as if the landslide had never happened. He was proud of his guys. They did good work.

On the other hand, the progress in the sunroom was slow. But that's how this kind of thing always went. Shoveling dirt, rebuilding walls, reinstalling windows, rewiring, replumbing, reinsulating; it was all fiddly stuff. He and Mike could work like dogs all day long, and it would appear as if they'd made no progress whatsoever. But they had.

In fact, he thought, glancing at his watch, it was time for a coffee break. Nobody made better coffee than Rahni. Grabbing his coffee cup, he headed for the kitchen.

As he ambled down the hall, he could see Olivia standing just outside the kitchen, peering through the door as it stood slightly ajar.

"Spying?" He stood just over her shoulder and whispered in her ear.

Olivia started. "Oh," she whispered back, "you scared me."

"Sorry."

"That's okay." She grinned. "Shhh." She held her finger to his lips.

His heart kicked into overdrive.

On tiptoe, she strained to reach his ear and his arm automatically circled her slender waist. "Don't go in just yet. You've got to watch this for a second. It's so cute. Agnes and Glyniss are giving the kids etiquette lessons. Trying to get them ready for Thanksgiving." Olivia twisted in his arms and turned back toward the door.

Nodding, Zach rested his chin at the top of her head and prepared to enjoy the show. The smell of her floral shampoo filled his senses, and that, coupled with the warmth that radiated from her soft body, had his heart thrumming so loudly in his ears, he had to strain to hear what was being said.

"No no!" Agnes gave the table a sharp rap with her

forefinger. "Ruth, my dear, you most certainly may not have another cookie until you say the magic word."

"The magic word," Ruth ventured, and reached for a cookie.

"No, try again."

"Ummm…" Ruth looked positively stymied.

Leaning forward, Glyniss whispered in her ear.

"Please?" Ruth wanted to know.

"Yes, dear, go ahead. But next time, I want you to figure it out all by yourself." Agnes sternly eyeballed her sister.

"Oh, Agnes, give the kid a break, she's learning."

"Yes, they are, no thanks to you. You seem to think it's cute the way they smack their lips and lick their chops, snorting and rooting through their dinner like a bunch of pigs at a trough." Her beady-eyed gaze swung to Esther. "This is a prime example of what I'm talking about. Child, chew with your mouth closed."

"What?" Esther wondered, crumbs flying.

"Oh, for goodness' sake. Here." Agnes handed Esther a napkin, and the child dutifully mopped her face. "That's much better."

"Can I have another cookie?" Cain asked, looking longingly at the plate piled high with gooey, rich, chocolate chip and walnut cookies.

"No!" Agnes snapped so that the boy jumped. "The question is, 'Please, may I have another cookie?' and the answer is, 'Yes, you may.'"

Confused, Cain hesitated, glancing at Agnes, then to the cookies, then back at Agnes again.

"Go ahead, sweetheart." Glyniss smiled her encouragement. "Sergeant Agnes has given you permission to eat."

"What are these things?" Esther demanded, picking a walnut out of her cookie and throwing it across the table.

"Do not throw your food when you don't wish to eat it, young lady." Agnes huffed, casting a scandalized look at the offensive walnut. "Instead, if you find that you don't like something, take it out of your mouth and place it in the napkin. Like this." Picking up the walnut bit, Agnes daintily tucked it into her napkin and set it in her lap.

"Watch me," Ruth instructed around a mouthful of cookie. Mimicking Agnes, the child spat a wad of saliva-coated cookie into the palm of her hand, then daintily tucked it into her napkin. "Is that right?"

At the pained expression on her sister's face, Glyniss threw back her head and roared with laughter.

"Not exactly." Agnes sighed. "But you're getting the idea." Pushing the cookies aside, she reached for her cup of tea. "Let's practice not slurping, shall we?"

Back behind the kitchen door, Zach and Olivia huddled together and enjoyed the show. And each other. When the etiquette lesson finally came to an end, both were disappointed. For many more reasons than they cared to admit.

13

The first two weeks of November flew by in a flurry of activity as everyone prepared for Thanksgiving. Zach's goal was to button up the sunroom walls as soon as possible. He wanted to get them insulated, the drywall installed, and the hole in the stair landing repaired before the holidays began, so that he could take a few days off to simply enjoy this time with Olivia and the kids.

Olivia's goal was to establish a routine for the children. She hoped this would help adjustment to life without their mother go as smoothly as possible, especially during this first holiday. She also planned to take a vacation for the first time in years so that she could spend Thanksgiving with Zach.

They hadn't discussed it in so many words, but Olivia knew Hattie had invited him to join them at the table for Thanksgiving, and she couldn't have been happier.

In their time off, in the evenings and on the weekends, Zach and Olivia went ahead and cleared out the storage room next to her suite, acting in faith. Or denial. She couldn't be sure which. If, and when, Mertyl came to take the kids away from her, Olivia decided it would make a lovely sitting room. In the meantime, it would serve as a comfortable bedroom for the kids. So she and Zach moved mountains of furniture up to the attic together. And in the process, they became closer than ever.

Hattie was happy with the changes, feeling that the storage space would make a perfect extra bedroom for future rental use. But for now, she was most delighted to see the kids getting settled into a little nook they could call their own. Cain would even have a private area in the alcove and, with some clever curtaining, he would feel as if he were in his own room. Of course, it was taken for granted by everyone now that Copper would be his roommate.

Ryan had even stopped including the pup in the course for police dogs he was giving for the local precinct. When Olivia had questioned him on this, Ryan had said something about training Copper another time. For now, he felt Copper was doing far more good by staying just where he was. In Cain's arms.

And so, for Zach and Olivia and Hattie and the children, the chilly November evenings had been spent in easy camaraderie, pitching in and cleaning up the storage room.

As they sorted through the contents of the room, Hattie was alternately teary-eyed with nostalgia and amused at the absurdity of this eclectic collection of furniture and memorabilia she had accumulated over the years. The dear little lady claimed that she'd been meaning to clean this old room out for more than two decades, and Olivia believed her. In fact, Olivia wouldn't be at all surprised if it took them at least that long to do the cleaning.

However, even though it was a lot of hard work, it was also a lot of fun. A veritable treasure hunt, actually, for they found things that Hattie had tucked away over the years that she'd quite forgotten she'd ever owned.

The Colonel hovered on the perimeter as they worked, making sure that nothing of value was thrown away. Now and then he would delightedly abscond with an item that was destined for the Dumpster. Cackling gleefully, he'd cart his finds off to his room, certain that sooner or later he would find a need for a broken dress dummy or a set of Elvis-on-velvet oil paintings.

The kids were also delighted with many of these discoveries, for a number of the things Hattie had stored in this room were toys her grandchildren used to play with when they would come to visit.

"Oh, look, Hester!" Hattie unearthed a box of her granddaughter's old things. "Just the right size for you!"

Esther stared with open-mouthed joy when she spied the three-foot-tall walking doll that Hattie held out to her.

"I love her!" She grabbed the doll to her chest, completely captivated. "I will name her Tra-La." Immediately, she stripped the doll naked and dragged her by the hair to Olivia's bathroom, where she proceeded to give it a bath and a shampoo in the sink.

Cain and Ruth were enthralled with the big, red Radio Flyer wagon they'd found tucked under an old chest of drawers. Together, they took turns giving each other and, of course, the wriggling Copper, rides up and down the hall.

"Watch me, Olivia!" Ruth lay in the wagon, legs flailing.

"I see you, honey," Olivia replied as she helped Zach lug one of the heavier pieces of furniture to the attic. "Very good. Just be careful you guys don't go too near the stairs, okay?"

Every so often, the two wagoneers would stop by the storage room to see what other items of interest had been brought to light before speeding back down the hall. Sometimes they would help Hattie by carting a box or two to the bottom of the attic stairs for Zach or Olivia to carry up.

"You know," Hattie told Cain on one such occasion, "this wagon used to belong to my grandson. But I don't think he'd mind a bit if I gave it to a sweet boy like you." She paused and tapped her nose reflectively with an arthritic forefinger. "As I recall, he had a puppy too. Used to go all over town with that dog of his in this very wagon."

"Really?" Cain was delirious with the idea of owning such a beautiful set of wheels. "I can have this wagon?" Suspiciously, he eyeballed Ruth. "All to myself?"

"Well, now, the occasion might come, now and again, when you'd like to share it with your sister." Hattie winked at Ruth. "But I think I have found something Rose will like far better than a red wagon."

"What is it?" Ruth was skeptical. What could possibly be better than the wagon that had just been handed over— lock, stock, and barrel—to her bossy big brother?

"Come here, sweetheart." Hattie beckoned the child to follow her into the storage room.

Ruth's enthusiastic shriek had even Hattie covering her ears. "Tap shoes!"

"These were my oldest daughter's tap shoes," Hattie informed the child, once Ruth had come back to earth. "She took tap lessons for several years, and was actually pretty good, considering that she was such a terribly clumsy, uncoordinated child. Knock-kneed, she was. Oh my goodness, you've never seen the like. Always tripping over something or crashing into something or falling down. Hoo-hoo-hee! Some nights I would simply marvel that she was still in one piece at the end of the day."

"Uh-huh." Ruth nodded, but was far too excited to care about details. Stripping off her own shoes, she quickly jumped into the oversized taps and was tippity-tapping down the hall in record time. "Watch this, Hattie!" Stomping and spinning, she clicked her heels like a frisky lamb on a spring morning.

"Why that's lovely, dearie! Very picturesque!" Hattie sent her praises after Ruth. Memories of days gone by burned brightly in the landlady's misty eyes. "Already, you are better than my own precious little girl."

Pausing at the bottom of the stairway that led to the attic, Olivia and Zach watched the child dance. Olivia leaned back against Zach's body, and his arms circled her waist. A poignant warmth suffused her as they smiled and, with a tilt of their heads, exchanged glances.

It was wonderful for Olivia to see the children so excited and full of life. All three had been amazingly more resilient than she could have imagined. A fact that must have had a lot to do with the love and affection and prayer support they were receiving under this roof.

Yes, this—Olivia knew as she watched Ruth imitate the wild tap dancing the child had seen on one of Hattie's Irish dance videos—this was what family life was all about. The elderly and the young, caring about each other, depending on each other, loving each other.

Too bad it was far too early in her relationship with Zach to discuss such things. She swallowed past the bittersweet lump in her throat, and with a glance at Ruth, she and Zach reluctantly moved apart and set back to work.

• • •

When finally the door between Olivia's room and the storage room had been installed—and the new pine bunk beds built and put in across the room from Cain's alcove bed—both Olivia and Zach were ready for a break.

And Zach had ideas.

After he'd dropped a broad hint here and an even broader hint there, Sean and Julia volunteered to watch the kids that Friday night. They had decided to rent *Mary*

Poppins from the video store and order a pizza. The movie and pizza excited the kids nearly as much as the prospect of popping their own popcorn with Sean and Julia.

Since she had no excuse to stay in, Zach had insisted that Olivia needed a night on the town, if for no other reason than to celebrate the fact that her suite was now twice its previous size. Once she'd finally capitulated and agreed to leave the kids for a few hours, he'd made reservations at his favorite Italian restaurant, hoping that she liked pasta.

• • •

The atmosphere at Tranquilli's was delightfully quaint and, from the look of the cozily supping twosomes scattered around the room, very conducive to romance. The lights were low, the music soft, the seats comfortable. And the smells? Something that transcended the mere confines of this planet was wafting through the dining room, causing Olivia's mouth to water. The tantalizing aromas of fresh-baked bread, onions, garlic, newly chopped herbs, and an assortment of pasta sauces permeated the air. Under that olfactory umbrella of ecstasy, the subtle scent of gourmet coffee perked away, teasing the senses.

Mmm, yes, Olivia decided as the hostess whisked her coat away, going out to dinner was a lovely idea. She was so glad Zach had thought of it. Her eyes darted to his handsome profile, and she was struck by how much his sweet face had come to mean to her.

After having slipped the maître d' a healthy tip, Zach was able to commandeer a charming little table in the corner that overlooked the expansive valley below. Olivia glanced around the dining room and was delighted. Surely they had the best table in the room. Once Zach had helped her into her seat, she peered out the window into the evening sky. It was already dark, so the lights from the little township below twinkled, creating a breathtaking view.

Olivia smoothed her dress and tried to remember how to act on a date. It had been so long since she'd gone anywhere to have fun. That evening she had chosen to wear a soft purple outfit of jersey knit that made her feel feminine and desirable for the first time in years. Then again, she couldn't be sure if it was the dress, or the expression on the face of the man who made himself comfortable across the table, that was causing such havoc with her senses. Candlelight flickered in Zach's mahogany eyes, enhancing the interest she found there.

"I'm so glad we could get out for an evening." Zach's low tone caused a shiver of goose flesh to zoom down her left side, then back up her right. "Can you believe it's been over a month since I crashed into the sunroom?"

Olivia shook her head. "Only a month? Seems like years."

A rather vulnerable, lopsided grin tipped Zach's mouth. "Years? Should I be flattered or insulted?"

"Flattered."

Zach chuckled.

"I wonder what the kids are doing." She cupped her cheek in her hand and smiled at him as the waiter filled their water glasses.

"Hopefully not doing any more damage to the house than I do on any given night."

Olivia laughed.

After the waiter had left, Zach brought his glass to his lips, then, after taking a sip, let it dangle between his fingertips. "Isn't this what all couples do? Go on a date to get away from the kids, then spend the evening talking about the kids?"

"Are"—she cleared her throat—"are we a couple?"

Zach sobered for a moment and lowered his glass to the table. "I'd sure like to think we're headed in that direction."

Olivia felt as if she'd just stuck a fork in an electrical socket as her entire body was engulfed with tingles of delight. "Really?" The solitary word came out strangled. Excited. Nearly giddy.

Once again, she wished that she could open her mouth and some witty, sophisticated line would trip off her tongue. But alas, that was not the way she was made.

Zach nodded and smiled with disarming candor. "Really."

"Me—" Much to her eternal chagrin, her high squeaky whisper was choked, so she paused and, lowering her voice an octave, started again. "Uh, me too."

Zach's infectious laugh put her at ease.

For the longest time, they sat there, staring into each other's eyes and smiling foolishly as their server returned to take their appetizer orders. Completely ignoring him, they were lost in a world of their own, until the poor waiter threw his hands up and announced that he'd return.

"Just give me the high sign. When you are ready. Whenever that will be. Sometime this evening. Hopefully."

They continued to ignore him.

Giving up, he moved on.

"You know," Olivia admitted, "this is the first time I've been on an actual date in over five years."

"I can't understand that. A woman as sweet and beautiful as you, I'd think you'd have dates every night of the week."

Olivia ducked her head and fussed with the paper doily under her glass. How silly. How sweet. She wished he'd ask her out again tomorrow night. "I guess I haven't been ready."

"But you are now?" Zach's voice was full of hope.

"Mm-hmm." She felt a smile stealing across her face and heating her cheeks.

"Why?"

"I don't have any idea. Maybe enough time has passed since I lost my family."

Zach nodded in understanding.

"Or it might have something to do with the fact that I asked Hattie to pray for me. To give me a reason to get out of the house. Maybe you were that reason." She eyed him speculatively. "After all, I could hardly ignore you, the way you came bursting into the sunroom like a member of the Olympic luge team. I mean, if you wanted to get my attention, you succeeded." Plucking her napkin out of her lap, she smothered a laugh behind its folds.

"Well, now, I'd sure like to believe I'm an answer to your prayer." He huffed on his nails then buffed them on his shirt. Sobering, he leaned forward across the table and took her hands in his. "I think you are an answer to mine."

"Why?"

"Well, for one thing, when I woke up after crashing into Hattie's place and saw you smiling at me over the back of my rig, I thought I'd died and you were an angel. And for a minute, I wasn't sorry at all that I'd bought the proverbial farm."

Olivia felt her mouth go dry. The way he was looking at her made her feel positively dizzy. "I…uh"—she began to tear her paper doily into little strips—"did you know that I found the kids the next day?"

She closed her eyes, gritted her teeth. That was an idiotic thing to say, when the poor man was spilling his guts about his attraction for her. But for the life of her, she had no idea how to respond to such advances. She was miserably out of touch when it came to the dating scene.

"Ah. So we're back to the kids."

The amusement in his eyes put her at ease. "See how we are? Just like a boring old couple."

"Hardly boring." Zach wiggled his brows.

"Hard to be boring with three wild banshees livening up the old boarding house." Perhaps she'd be less flustered if they stuck to subjects other than themselves. "I told Julia the kids could stay up late tonight."

"They'll like that." It seemed so natural that he would take her hands in his and play with her fingers. His tone was casual. Jesting. "Did you hear the Colonel reading them a bedtime story last night?"

"No, I was folding laundry. I saw them all crammed into that old recliner with him when I walked by though. Looked to me like he was reading them the encyclopedia."

"He was." Zach rolled his eyes. "He was reenacting World War I for them. Hardly Dr. Seuss."

"So *that's* why they all woke up screaming last night. This morning I had three little bodies plastered to mine."

"Now that sounds like fun! You know…" He stared at her with wide eyes and pouted in mock innocence. "I'm just a big kid, at heart."

"Don't go there," Olivia warned, shaking a playful finger at him.

Reaching up, he grabbed her finger and laced their fingers together again and laughed with her. "Did you see the scooter the Colonel found in the Dumpster at the recycling center?"

"Is that what that was? I wondered. Needs wheels."

"Needs to be taken back to the recycle center. The rust on that thing could give all of us lockjaw."

"Mm-hmm. But his heart is in the right place."

The waiter returned and was finally able to take their appetizer orders and scurry off to fetch their requests. Reluctantly, they had to break off their discussion for a while so that they could study the menu. While they perused,

Olivia told Zach that Italian was her absolute favorite and asked if he had any suggestions. Looking inordinately pleased, he took the liberty of ordering dinner for them both when the waiter returned with their appetizer.

"Did I tell you that I talked with Ryan today about Copper?" Olivia asked once the waiter had collected their menus and moved on.

"No. What'd he have to say?"

"Well, I guess he explained to the guys down at the precinct about Cain and how he's become so attached to the puppy. So they all chipped in and bought the dog for him. Ryan wants to tell him at Thanksgiving."

Zach's smile couldn't have been more touched or loving if he'd been the child's father. "That's great. I think it's just what the doctor ordered for him. I worry more about him than I do the girls. He strikes me as being more sensitive. Although he goes pretty far to cover his feelings."

"I suspect you're right. He does hold his emotions at bay, and I'm sure it's because he's been let down so many times in his short life. But I see a glimmer now and then of interest. Or hope. Or happiness. Or something vaguely reassuring. These little glimpses of improvement don't last long, but they are there. Eventually, with counseling, I have to believe he'll be okay."

"Oh sure. He's a great kid. We just need to give him space."

Olivia loved the way he said *we*. Sometimes she had the feeling that Zach was as emotionally invested in the children as she was. As she studied the adorable little crinkles at the corners of his sympathetic eyes, she wondered what would become of them once Mertyl came to take the children to their permanent home. He would probably be just as devastated as she would be.

Would it bring them closer together? Or would it have the opposite effect?

With a deep breath, Olivia studied Zach's compassionate face and decided to broach a plan she'd been nursing in the back of her mind for quite some time. His opinion meant the world to her. Whatever his thoughts or comments, she would take them to heart.

"Zach?"

"Hmm?"

"You know the other day, when I was telling Mertyl that I was thinking about adopting the kids?"

Laughter rumbling, Zach leaned back in his chair. "You mean when you were reading poor old Mertyl the riot act?"

Olivia pulled a face. "Whatever."

"I could hardly forget. Why?"

"I was serious."

"About adopting?"

"Yes. Am I crazy?

Zach rubbed his jaw and gave her question careful consideration. "No. No, you're not crazy at all. In fact, I think you are one of the most wonderful women I've ever met. And I happen to think that you would make those three kids one terrific mother."

"You think?" Again, the same old lump, preventing her from sounding as suave and debonair as she wished, clogged her throat.

His head bobbed once. There was a look of yearning in his eyes that Olivia hadn't seen in a man's eyes since John had passed away. "It certainly won't be the easiest thing you've ever done, but yes, I think you should do it. Really."

• • •

The delightful evening, spent talking and laughing and getting to know each other, unfortunately, like all good things, came to an end. After parking at the curb, Zach walked Olivia to the front door of the boarding house and paused with her under the porch light while she fished her keys from the depths of her purse.

"I had a wonderful time." Once she'd located her keys, she turned her face up to him and smiled.

He couldn't believe the evening was ending already and wished with all his heart that they could turn back the clock and start all over again.

"Me too."

She was so beautiful, standing there under the dim glow of the single bulb. Zach felt his lungs constrict. What was it about this special woman that made him feel so alive again? He wished that he could think of something to say, to prolong the evening. But he couldn't think of a single intelligent thing.

For an awkward moment, they stood regarding each other, and Zach wondered about the end-of-the-evening etiquette as he tried to conquer his runaway pulse. Surely he should reach for her and give her a good-night kiss. After all, it wasn't as if they hadn't shared a simple kiss before. His gut tightened at the memory of the two of them standing in the service porch, sharing a kiss that had kept him sleepless for more than one night. Ever since the moment he'd taken her in his arms to comfort her, he'd been dying for another excuse to kiss her. Unfortunately, they'd never been alone long enough for him to work up the courage.

He only knew that tonight he had no intention of letting the opportunity pass.

Night sounds filtered to them as they stood smiling at each other. Several blocks away, a car's horn sounded. A light breeze rustled the branches of the trees near the house, causing one branch to scratch at the gutter. In the distance, a dog barked.

"You know"—Olivia tiptoed toward him and lowered her voice—"they are all watching us."

His chuckle was low as he reached for her. "I knew the Colonel and the Ross sisters were peeking out the parlor window. I can see the glass fogging from here."

Olivia nodded, slanting a saucy look up at him. "And Hattie and the kids are watching from the dining room."

He pulled her tight and stole a quick look toward the dining room's bay window. "Wow, you're good." He looked down into her eyes.

She shrugged. "Elementary, my dear Watson."

"Shall we move off into the shadows?"

"What?" Olivia's jaw went slack in mock horror. "And deprive them of the show they've been waiting all evening for?"

"You do have a very good point."

Their gazes tangled and held for a long moment.

"Ready?" Zach murmured, cupping her cheeks in his hands and angling her mouth beneath his. He could feel the pulse beneath her jaw thrumming like the wings of a hummingbird.

"Oh yes." Olivia sighed, her lashes sliding toward her cheeks. "I've been ready for days." Reaching up, she wound her arms around his neck and pulled him close.

"Me too," Zach agreed and, ignoring his audience, proceeded to thoroughly kiss Olivia good night.

* * *

"You're looking pretty cute in that apron, sailor."

Olivia tossed Zach an appreciative wink as she strolled through the kitchen the next day. Saturday afternoon was always baking day, and today Zach and the kids had been drummed into service by Rahni to bake some cookies to fill the cookie jar.

His cheeks stained red, Zach looked up from his labors. Flour was everywhere. In his hair and on his nose, and all over his clothes, the countertop, and the floor. The kids were no better off. To Olivia, he'd never look more appealing.

Glancing ruefully down at himself, he wiped his dough-coated hands on the apron emblazoned with the festive phrase "Kiss the Cook."

"Yeah, well, I'm not sure why I even bothered to wear this silly thing for all the good it's done. Nobody's even kissed me today."

Ruth and Esther—who stood on stools on either side of him—thought this was riotously funny. Lips smacking, they smooched and patted his cheeks and called him boo-boo head and other preschool terms of endearment. Cain, who sat on the floor nearby cracking walnuts with one of Zach's hammers, glanced up and let a faint smile tug at his mouth.

Coming up behind the three at the counter, Olivia wrapped her arms around the girls' waists, and kissed all three of the cooks on the cheek. Then, bending low, she tilted Cain's face and planted a noisy kiss on his fiery cheek.

Very satisfied with the attention, they all went back to their respective chores: Olivia to stripping the beds, and Zach and the kids to filling the cookie jar. The scene was so blissfully domestic, Olivia thought she might just burst from the joy that crowded into her throat.

• • •

The next morning, after Sunday school, Olivia joined Zach and the children at what was becoming "their" pew. Pastor Wythe delivered a moving Thanksgiving sermon on the subject of counting blessings and giving thanks. When he had concluded, the pastor recounted his own list of blessings, then invited folks in the congregation to stand up at their seats and give their own testimonies.

Olivia was moved to tears on more than one occasion as various people stood and told stories of love and salvation and hope. Before she knew what was happening, she found herself suddenly upright and haltingly introducing herself to the congregation.

"Hello," she began, swiping at the tears that had begun to flow during the last story, "my name is Olivia Harmon. I used to attend church here pretty regularly, a long time ago."

Several heads nodded, and smiles indicated that they remembered her and were glad to see her back.

"My husband and daughter were killed in a car accident about five years ago." Closing her eyes, Olivia took a deep breath and held it. Just saying those words still evoked such powerful emotion. Slowly she exhaled and forged ahead.

"For a long time, I was angry with God. I felt that my life was meaningless without my family. I don't know, I guess I thought some great, cosmic mistake had been made and that it should have been me in that car. Not my precious husband and daughter. I'd been left behind to muddle through all by myself, and I was mad."

Her eyes swept over the congregation as she spoke. She had no idea why she was standing here, saying these things, but she was, and it felt great.

"I was miserable. Lonely. Bitter. Discouraged. Down on life. And I'm sure that the people who spent any time at all with me would go away feeling thoroughly depressed. But," she sighed and smiled, "you can only live like that for so long before you need a change of pace."

A wave of amusement passed through the crowd.

"I'm not sure what came over me, but one morning, about a month or so ago, I decided to ask my landlady, Hattie Hopkins, to pray for me. To ask for God's help in getting me back on track again. To help me find peace and a place to feel useful. Well, she prayed, and this was a major turning point for me."

More amusement rippled through the room. This congregation was obviously familiar with Hattie's successful prayer life.

"After all, I wasn't getting anywhere by railing against God, so I thought, why not turn back to him? What did I have to lose? Anyway"—she glanced at Zach and then at the three children who were snoozing peacefully against his side and on his lap—"the Lord heard Hattie's prayer, because before I knew it, I had temporary custody of three of the most beautiful little children I've ever laid eyes on." Her fingers strayed to Ruth's head, where she stroked the child's soft, gold curls.

As Olivia recounted the children's history, her gaze slowly traveled from row to row. The people listened with rapt attention and strained to see her children.

"You can probably imagine my distress. I had nothing for these kids. No clothes, no beds, no toys. Nothing but a little stale love in my shriveled heart and some wonderful people the Lord sent along to help. And you know, it's amazing how God can work. I haven't been so happy and so filled with love since my family died.

"In the long run, I don't know what's going to happen. I can't see the big picture. But if there is one thing I do know, it's that God sent me these children for a reason. If I am able to end up adopting them, that would be wonderful. If not, well, I still thank God for giving me the chance to feel like a human being again. To love. To be loved. This

Thanksgiving," her eyes darted to Zach's, "I feel truly blessed because I've finally learned a very difficult lesson about life.

"I've learned that I don't always have the ability to see the long run, like God does. When someone dies, my first reaction is to say that it's not fair. To rebel and grow angry. Because, in my limited scope, I think I know what's best for that individual. How long they should live. How happy they should be." Olivia paused and shrugged. "But how do I know what God had planned for that person's life? What we think of as a tragically short life on this planet may be the perfect life in God's eyes. The perfect amount of time to accomplish what needed to be done. No more, no less."

Zach smiled at her, tears brimming in his eyes.

"My daughter, Lillah, was only with us for four years. Yet, in that time, she taught me to have a mother's heart. She gave me inexplicable joy, nearly unbearable sorrow, and prepared me for the job God had set for me to do during my time here on this old earth. I'm still not exactly sure what that job is, but I know that it involves children in pain. In need. Children with sorrow-filled hearts. Children that a mother like me can understand and love."

Agnes and Glyniss, sitting several rows away, sniffed and dabbed at their eyes with lace-trimmed handkerchiefs, and Hattie nodded along, as if she understood every word. Even the Colonel, who sat thoughtfully clicking his dentures, seemed touched. Olivia's hand trailed from Ruth's silky head to Zach's firm shoulder. He laid his hand on top of hers and squeezed.

"So, this Thanksgiving, I give thanks for a new lease on life and for family." Olivia smiled around the room, her eyes flitting to the various boarders with whom she lived and finally landing on Zach and the sleeping angels at his side.

"No matter how God placed them in my life."

14

Thanksgiving arrived long before anyone was ready. So in order to prepare for the day's rather strenuous culinary activities, alarm clocks were synchronized the night before, and with a promise to pitch in and help, everyone turned in early. When the first rays of dawn filtered through the curtains on Thursday morning, all the boarders—like a sleepwalking gaggle of honking and clucking geese— crowded into the kitchen.

Zach, hair tousled and carrying a thermos of strong black coffee, joined the throng, letting himself in through the service porch door. He scanned the kitchen till his gaze landed on Olivia. Relaxing once he'd spotted her, he ambled over to where she stood and pulled her close for a good-morning kiss on her temple. His heart flip-flopped as she lifted her chin and planted a kiss of her own on his cheek. Nobody seemed to find this greeting between the two a bit unusual, especially after their date last Friday night.

Taking it for granted that Zach would be there, Agnes, who was passing out aprons, slapped a fresh one into his chest. Then, pecking his forearm with a knobby finger, she ordered them to break it up and to go scrub their hands. He grinned and winked at Olivia. Though Agnes's tone was gruff, there was a twinkle in the old girl's eyes.

With a lingering touch, Zach slowly unwound his fingers from Olivia's and moved to the sink to do as he was bid. Olivia followed. Nudging him aside, she crowded in next to the sink and put her hands with his under the warm spray. As he soaped his hands, and then hers, he pondered the oddly comforting feeling that he'd finally found his place in the world. And that place, he now knew for certain, was right here, by Olivia Harmon's side. After they'd finished up at the sink, Zach and Olivia filled cups from his thermos and waited patiently, hands linked, to be told what to do.

At the top of her voice, Agnes assigned duties and numbered everyone off into various work crews. "Glyniss! You, Hattie, Rahni, Sean, and Julia are in charge of the turkey!"

Glyniss arched a brow and spoke in a deadpan manner to her crew. "I'll try not to exhaust you all at once."

"Ryan and Zach," Agnes pointed to the sink, "start peeling potatoes. Kids and Olivia, you're all with me over at the baking table. Colonel, you can begin decorating. Let's go! We only have eight hours to create a masterpiece." She gave the whistle she wore at her throat a sharp blast. "Let's be courteous, efficient, and hard working, shall we?"

Wide awake, the kids were thrilled with their appointment to the baking area and added to the fracas in their own ways. Cain with Copper, Esther with her giant doll, and Ruth with her furious tap dancing on the tiled floor.

"Watch this, everybody!" Ruth would occasionally shout, then demonstrate a complex step, the likes of which Fred Astaire had never seen.

"Very good, honey," Olivia would praise.

"Mm-hmm!" Zach would chime in.

They were the picture of proud parenthood, and Ruth flourished under their adoration.

Once everyone had been assigned a task, they all began to prepare for the feast and decorate the house in the tradition of the season. The bird was expediently stuffed with Rahni's special mouthwatering cornbread-sausage-raisin-hazelnut dressing. Potatoes were peeled; sauces and gravies and vegetable dishes were prepared. Relish trays crowded the refrigerator. Spirits were unusually high—there was so much to be thankful for this year.

Over at the baking table, the Colonel had drifted from his decorating endeavors to temporarily head up the dessert team. As squadron leader, his self-appointed job was making sure that the pies and cakes and other confections that came out of the oven were all quality tested. That and, of course, to generally get under everyone's feet.

"Mmm...mmm.... hmm..." His pale blue eyes would roll with rapture. Lips smacking, he'd chop off bits of cake here and sneak bites of pie there. "Not bad!" He'd mumble his approval around a mouthful of dessert and loose dentures. "This could use a little more of the pink frosting." He waved at a cake Agnes had just frosted.

"Out!" Agnes had finally bellowed, upon discovering that her desserts were beginning to look as if they'd been chewed by a pack of ravenous mice. Brandishing her rolling pin, she chased the cackling man out of the kitchen.

The Colonel didn't mind. He had plenty of decorating to do. Fancying himself to be Martha Stewart on a shoestring, he commenced to create an atmosphere befitting the holiday.

Candle stubs came out of hiding and were plunged into lumps of crafting clay and then smashed into the center of the table on a paper plate, yellowed with age. Indian corn and some of the less moldy gourds from Hattie's garden were duct-taped into a circle of sorts around the candle

214

arrangement. The night before, the elderly man had fashioned paper turkeys—to be implemented as part of the centerpiece—out of used napkins he'd collected from dinner plates over the last few weeks. All things considered, they really weren't that terribly unattractive. Overlooking the bits of dried food and lipstick was no problem, as these things only gave the bird's wild plumage a little...character.

Then the paper turkeys were duct-taped to the main conglomeration of odds and ends. And when the candles were set to flame, the entire thing was a sight to behold indeed. The children were agog with wonder.

By the time everyone had finally finished their respective chores and then showered and dressed for dinner, the turkey was done, and it was time to eat.

The grand total at the Thanksgiving dinner table reached an all-time holiday high of thirteen, Zach being the only person in attendance who did not actually live at the boarding house. But he felt as if he did, with as much time as he spent there and as much emotion as he had invested under this roof.

Before everyone took their seats, Ryan had an announcement to make. Once the crowd was quiet, he smiled at Cain and handed him a package. "This is from the police department."

A flicker of fear flashed across the child's face, and he froze.

Setting the package on the table, Cain shook his head. "I didn't do it, honest." He looked balefully around the room, hoping to be believed.

Ryan chuckled. "No, kiddo. You're not in trouble. This is a present. For you. From the guys down at the precinct. Go on, open it. You'll be glad you did."

Cain reached for the package and slowly tore the wrap

off an old shoe box. Inside, there was an assortment of dog supplies—a leash, flea powder, a brush, and some leather chew toys.

Puzzled, Cain looked up at Ryan. "This is for me?"

Ryan shook his head and gestured to Copper who lay faithfully at the child's feet. "For your dog."

"My dog?" His mouth dropped open, and then, for the first time since he'd come here over a month ago, Cain laughed. "You mean I can keep him?"

"You and your sisters, yes."

The fact that he had to share his beloved pet with the girls didn't faze the child, so overjoyed was he. Laughing and jumping up and down, Cain grabbed Copper and, pulling out an extra chair, proceeded to seat the gangly pup at the table next to his own plate. This, oddly enough, did not seem to bother Agnes.

"Us too?" Ruth asked in wonder. "He's our dog too?"

"Yep." Ryan grinned. "But since every dog needs a master, I think Cain should handle that responsibility. He'll be in charge."

A mere technicality, in Ruth's mind. "I want to name him Rosy Cheeks."

"No!" Cain snorted. "That's a stupid name."

"It is not, you big dumbhead."

"Children!" Agnes bellowed. "No profanity at the table please." Waving her arms, she took charge. "Everyone, sit, sit, sit. This turkey ain't gettin' any younger."

"Speak for yourself, Agnes," Glyniss quipped, as everyone moved into their preassigned positions.

Zach held Olivia's chair for her, then helped the kids settle into their seats. Taking his own place at the table, he joined hands with Olivia and Esther and bowed his head for Hattie's Thanksgiving prayer.

"Zach?" Esther leaned against him and whispered loudly into his face.

"What, honey?"

"I want you to hold me."

An easy grin overtook his features. "Come here," he said softly, lifting the child into his lap and wrapping his arms around her little waist. In his peripheral vision, he could see Olivia watching, a sweet, loving smile on her face.

"Are we gonna pray now?" Esther was becoming familiar with this routine. She wriggled until she found a comfortable position against his chest. Ruth slid over one chair, taking Esther's empty spot so that she could be next to Zach.

"Yes, honey. Bow your head like this." He ducked his head and tightly closed his eyes.

Every night at bedtime, he and Olivia had been teaching the children to pray. And every night, they would go around their little circle and talk to Jesus, taking turns blessing people, asking for forgiveness, and making their requests known to the Lord. Even Cain would issue a clipped sentence or two, on behalf of his mother. It was a very precious time, and Zach wouldn't miss it for the world.

"Okay." Esther whispered in a noisy, huffing voice that could most likely be heard in the next room. "Who is gonna start?" This was a question she asked every night.

"Today, Hattie will." Zach placed a finger over his lips, trying to encourage her into silence.

"Okay. Then me," Esther announced. "Then Ruth, then Cain. Then you and then Olivia." Speculatively, she peered around the table. "Then him." She focused on the Colonel.

"Good, good. Hush now, sweetie. Hattie is starting."

"Then her, then her, then him, then him, then her..." Esther continued assigning prayer order with her stubby forefinger.

"O dear heavenly Father," Hattie began, "we have so many things to be thankful for this year—"

"Okay, my turn," Esther announced, and plunged in over Hattie, "Aaand, Jesus, thank you for the polar bears, because they won't bite me because I'll just say 'RRRAAARRR.'" Expression fierce, she growled at the ceiling. "Aaand we're eating turkey with"—her nose wrinkled, she pointed at the bowl of Rahni's special dressing—"that yucky stuff."

Around the table, eyes popped open and focused disparagingly on Esther.

Hattie continued praying, oblivious to Esther's prayer choreography. "Father. This year, we are so blessed by these three darling children that you have sent to Olympia."

"Okay!" Esther pointed at her sister. "Now, Ruth, you go."

"Shhh, honey," Olivia admonished, "Hattie is still praying."

"Go, Ruth!" Esther insisted.

"But she's not done," Ruth protested.

"She is too. You go."

"We thank you, Lord, for answered prayer," Hattie went on, only to be upstaged by Ruth.

"Jesus, I love my tap shoes. Amen."

"You say that every night." Cain's lip curled in boyish disgust.

Agnes's eagle eye swung from Esther to the older children, and she affected a menacing glare.

"So? I love my tap shoes."

"I hate 'em."

"You're mean! Olivia, he hates my tap shoes."

"Shh!" Olivia smiled weakly in apology at Agnes, then hissed at the children. "Stop fighting!"

"—and even for the puppy, Lord," Hattie went on. "And most especially, for the complimenting man."

Esther pointed at her brother. "Okay now, Cain, you go."

"I'm not goin'."

"Why not?"

"Cuz we're supposed to be quiet."

"Shhh!" Exasperated, Olivia clapped her hands.

"See?" Cain's tone was triumphant.

"But it's your turn!" Esther wriggled with impatience. "Then, Zach, you go."

"Ahhhemm." Zach cleared his voice in an effort to hint to Esther that she needed to zip a lip.

"—for everything that has fallen into your perfect plan," Hattie spoke with reverence, "we are all so truly grateful. And we are also thankful for continued good health. We are so humbled that you've brought us through yet another year, safe and sound—"

"Go, Zach!" Esther was frustrated beyond endurance. Lolling her head against his chest, she reached up and poked an exploratory finger into his nose.

Unable to help himself, Zach threw back his head and laughed. The kid was on the right track, how could he refuse? Leaning toward Esther, he whispered, "Rub-a-dub-dub, thanks for the grub, yea...God!"

"—into the future for another wonderful year. Amen." Hattie opened her eyes and beamed at her family.

Ruth and Esther, having found Zach's prayer hilarious, giggled with delight and heaped silly names upon his head.

"You're such a poopy diaper," Esther shrilled, squirming with excitement. "Poopy hair! Poopy face!" She screeched and hollered, rolling her head back and forth. "Poopy, poopy, poopy."

Lips quivering in amusement, Agnes did her best to sound gruff. "Esther, you know what I told you about your language."

"Yes ma'am." Esther hung her head in contrition.

Zach caught Olivia's eye, over the child's head, and they smiled, loving Esther's innocence and pure heart.

The food was delicious, and Zach couldn't remember ever having a meal that he enjoyed more. As he filled his belly and his spirit, Zach came to the realization that some-day—sooner than later, he hoped—he and Olivia would become a real family. Like Olivia, he'd had some remarkable healing take place recently.

Oh, he still missed AmyBeth very much. Going through the holidays without her sweet smile and loving arms still hurt something awful. He'd been very happy in his life with AmyBeth. He'd counted on many comfortable years of quiet, easy camaraderie together with her. During his marriage to AmyBeth, Thanksgiving was always a small affair, including perhaps AmyBeth's mother or his folks when they could afford to travel from Canada.

But even their wild and woolliest Thanksgiving had never been anything like this. He glanced around at the chaos that prevailed in the dining room. He loved it here. Never had he enjoyed himself so much.

Yes, he thought, feeling happier than he could ever remember, *I can see the beginnings of a wonderful future with Olivia and the children.* For that opportunity, Zach Springer was most thankful that Thanksgiving.

The rest of the meal proceeded without incident, with the exception of one small fire in the middle of the Colonel's centerpiece. It seemed that a candle had tipped, catching a piece of duct tape on fire, which in turn caused the gourds to roll into the rest of the candles and... well, after a concerted effort by everyone who still had water in their glasses, the fire was safely a thing of the past.

Olivia and Zach were holding hands and teasing the children about having to eat more dressing when the phone rang.

Rahni answered. It was for Olivia.

Shrugging, she excused herself from the table and ran to her room to pick up the call.

* * *

"Tell me what's wrong," Zach encouraged, as he ushered Olivia out of the children's room and into the sitting area of her suite later that evening. He left the door between the two rooms slightly ajar, so that they could hear any unusual stirrings in the children's slumber. It had been a big day, and though the night was still relatively young, the kids were exhausted.

Olivia closed her eyes against the well of raw emotion that had been gnawing at her gut for hours now. The last thing she wanted to do was tell Zach what she had learned in her conversation with Mertyl that afternoon. Surely it would devastate him too. She didn't want to talk about it. Instead, she wanted to go to the beach, dig a hole in the sand, and bury her head. And her heart.

Zach took her by the hand and led her to the wing chairs grouped in front of her small fireplace. Propping her feet up on an ottoman, he draped a throw over her legs. Then, before sitting down next to her, he gave the fire a few vigorous stirrings with the poker and brought the flames to life once more.

"Something has been worrying you all day." His eyes were filled with a tenderness that had her near tears.

Leaning her head back against an upholstered wing, Olivia lifted her heavy lids to gaze in his direction and willed her head to stop pounding. "Yes," she murmured. Even speaking the words was too much effort.

"Can I help?"

"You already are helping." Sucking a deep breath into her lungs, Olivia turned her eyes to the fire, then exhaled wearily. "Just your being here helps immensely."

He was silent, as was the room, with the exception of a crackle or pop from the dancing flames. For a long time, they sat without speaking. But finally Olivia knew she could remain silent no longer.

"Mertyl called."

"Ah."

"She said she had…" Olivia swallowed and waited for the trembling in her lip to subside, "…good news."

"Uh-oh."

"Yep. She found a family who will be willing to take the children. They are a lovely married couple. They live in a great big house with a fenced-in backyard. She says it's just what the children need."

"Is that what they need?" Zach's tone was sardonic.

"I guess. Mertyl says she has a few more details to iron out, but things are looking…good. She's going to stop by tomorrow and let me know when they will be by to pick up the kids and deliver them to the foster family."

"Oh, for the love of—" Zach sputtered, pounding his fist on the arm of his chair. Unable to help himself, he leapt to his feet and began to pace in front of the fire. "What about what the *kids* want? What about what *you* want? What *we* want? Don't these people ever take that into consideration?" Propping an elbow against the mantel, he hung his head and stared into the fire. "Did you tell them that you were interested in adopting the kids?"

"Mm-hmm. Mertyl doesn't seem to think that is such a good idea."

"Why not?" He swung his head in her direction and stared at her through bloodshot, worried eyes.

"Because I'm not married. Because I live here. Because she already has a family who fits the bill. I don't know. There are lots of reasons, I guess." Olivia valiantly battled the tears. "You know, the thing I don't get is why would God answer my prayer, just to snatch this gift away again? It doesn't make any sense." She blinked back the tears that threatened.

Sighing, Zach pushed away from the mantel. "I know, honey. It seems unfair. But I also know God does not work that way. He doesn't give something, only to grab it back." Zach ran a hand through his hair and stared at the wall. "Something is going on here. Something we don't understand. Maybe we'll never understand. But I think that there are things we can do." His gaze turned to Olivia. "Things God expects us to do."

"Like what?" Olivia queried in a small voice. The idea of letting go and having faith terrified her. What if she let God handle this problem and he didn't want the same things she wanted? What about that? "I don't want to lose these kids, Zach! I'm scared. What if there is nothing we can do?"

"We can pray."

"We've been praying!" She leapt to her feet to face him. "That's what got me into this mess."

"Oh, honey." Zach took a step, closing the gap, and gathered Olivia into his arms.

Olivia loved the warm comforting feel of his steady heartbeat against her cheek.

"You know, you yourself said that God was on your side. That he wanted you to have these children."

"I don't even know why I said that." Olivia moaned into his shirt. "I was insane."

Zach chuckled. "No, you weren't. I think for once you were listening to God's plan for your life. Why don't you give him a chance to work out the details?"

"He did! He's giving them a backyard with a fence and a dad."

"True," Zach murmured. "But maybe not in the way you expect."

Too tired to argue, Olivia simply allowed herself to be rocked and comforted by the man she loved.

• • •

Neither Olivia nor Zach realized that a small, five-year-old boy—with tears streaming down his face, and clutching the ruff of a puppy—sat huddled near the crack in the door, listening. It wasn't until the next morning, when they found him missing, that they began to suspect that he may have overheard.

15

He doesn't have a proper coat for this weather!" Olivia was frantic as she helped Zach stuff himself into the foul-weather garb he'd grabbed from the cab of his truck. "The only thing he's got to keep him warm is that oversized Windbreaker and"—her eyes pooled with anxious tears all over again—"his puppy."

Having crammed his head into his knit hat and zipped his jacket up under his chin, Zach turned and pulled Olivia into his arms for a quick hug. "Don't worry. Everything's going to be fine."

"How do you know?"

"I have a feeling."

"That's not enough."

Cupping the back of her head in his hand, Zach pressed his lips to her forehead. "Keep praying, okay?"

"Of course," she whispered through trembling lips as she sagged against his chest.

With a final pat on her shoulder, Zach stepped toward the door and looked at Ryan and Sean. "Ready?"

"Yep." Ryan and Sean nodded. They held up their cell phones.

"Good." Zach put his hand on the knob of the massive front door and addressed the somber crowd of boarders that had gathered in the foyer that Friday morning. "If we find him, or hear of anything, we will call. If you hear, call one of us. The police are all out looking, too, so it shouldn't be long before we know something. In the meantime, keep the phone lines clear so that we can stay in touch, okay?"

"Okay." Olivia stepped forward. "Don't forget to go back to that convenience store. The one where I found the kids, over on Twenty-second."

"We'll go there first. And we'll check his old house too."

"In the meantime, we'll set up a command post here at the base!" The Colonel waved his arms to gain attention. "I'll man the radio. Where is the radio? Do we have a radio?" Crisply about-facing, he wobbled off in search of a radio. His excited, raspy wheezings could be heard long after he'd left the foyer.

Olivia ushered the three younger men out to the front porch. She stood shivering as they crossed the icy walkway to their respective vehicles. "Are you sure I can't go with you?"

"Yes, I'm sure." Zach tossed his phone and his thermos into the cab of his truck. "Stay here with the girls. You're needed much more here."

"Call me!" She shouted in order to be heard above the inclement weather.

With a nod, Zach swung in behind the wheel, slammed his door and, leading the way, backed out of the drive and into the street. Olivia stood watching and shivering till they'd disappeared, then moved woodenly back into the house where she stood in front of the parlor fireplace and tried not to cry.

Feeling at loose ends, Julia and Rahni had gone to the kitchen to prepare pots of coffee and tea and a plate of breakfast pastries for everyone. Julia had wanted to go with Sean to look for Cain, but Sean had insisted she stay home. The driving sleet and snow that pelted down from the heavens was no place for a pregnant woman, let alone a little boy. Rahni, also, had very much wanted to help, but with her limited understanding of the language—and the area—had decided it best to stay home and keep everyone else nourished and as comfortable as possible.

Agnes and Glyniss herded the girls into a corner of the parlor to play a game of Chutes and Ladders that they had unearthed from the storage room several weeks earlier. Before she'd joined her sister and the girls, Agnes honked noisily into her monogrammed handkerchief and blinked through watery eyes at Olivia.

"Don't worry, dear," she began, then stopped and shook her head. "No, you go ahead and worry. How silly of me to tell you not to. I'm worried sick myself. That poor boy, out in the elements without so much as a—"

"Agnes!" Glyniss hollered at her sister from the corner, a beleaguered expression on her face. "The girls are waiting."

"Of course." Agnes threw herself at Olivia, hugged her fiercely, then taking a stoic breath, turned to the girls. "Ruth! Esther!" she bellowed, suddenly returning to her perennial role as a schoolteacher. "Stop fighting over the spinner! Remember what we talked about last time?"

Olivia stared unseeing at them while they played. As she warmed her hands near the flames, her mind whirled with such an array of emotions, she feared she'd faint. She still couldn't believe it. Cain had run away. Her sweet little boy. Why? Just when he was finally beginning to make some headway too. The last few days had been especially wonderful, for the boy had really begun to open up on an emotional level.

Olivia peeked over at the girls. In spite of her best efforts to shield Esther and Ruth from her emotions, tears began to slide unchecked down her cheeks. She simply couldn't understand why Cain had done it.

Unless…

A niggling fear that he may have overheard her and Zach talking last night worried the back of her mind. She tried to remember what they might have said, but everything was such a blur. Biting back a sob, Olivia dabbed her eyes with her sleeve.

The girls hadn't seen him go, so the exact time of his departure was questionable. From the trail he'd left, they'd only been able to deduce that he'd taken a sweater, an old Windbreaker, a knit cap, a bag of cookies, some dog food, and an old backpack that had been sitting on the floor of the hall closet for ages.

"Dear heart." Hattie's voice came from just beyond Olivia's elbow, and startled her out of her reverie. "I can see that you are frightened. You know, I always say, 'if your knees are knocking, kneel on them.'" She smiled tenderly. "Many years ago, one of my boys—I can't remember which one now—ran away when I was a young mother. I'll tell you, the only thing that got me through was turning my troubles over to the good Lord." She cast a reverent glance at the ceiling. "Luckily, we found the child the next morning, sound asleep in the doghouse where he'd taken up residence with Daisy and her puppies. It was an answer to prayer, I'll tell you."

Olivia smiled weakly at her little landlady. The last thing she felt like doing was praying. Screaming? Yes. Throwing a tantrum at life's injustices? Sure. Falling apart and sobbing uncontrollably from fear for Cain? Maybe a little later. In private. But praying? How could she pray at a time like this? She didn't even know where to begin. Besides, the mood she was in, she was afraid of offending God. She wasn't too sure about this strange plan of his, whatever it was.

On the other hand, perhaps a prayer would take her mind off her troubles.

"Okay," she agreed, not wanting to hurt Hattie's feelings. The little lady meant well.

"Come along, then, dearie."

Hattie tugged her over to the small grouping of antique chairs that surrounded the coffee table. Once they were settled, Hattie clutched Olivia's hands and wasted no time before she began. "O dear heavenly Father, we come to you with troubled hearts. We are very concerned about your precious boy, Payne, Lord. You know, Lord, this reminds me of the shepherd who lost his little lamb. We know that you're more concerned for that little boy right now than the rest of us could ever be, and for that, Lord, we are so grateful..."

As Hattie prayed, Olivia felt the familiar waves of goose flesh race up and down her body and across the back of her neck, and suddenly a peaceful feeling began to warm her belly.

Until the doorbell rang.

Olivia's head sprang up. Could Hattie's prayer have been answered so soon? She glanced down at her hands that were still clasped tightly in Hattie's.

Sitting closest to the door, Agnes went over and opened it to find Mertyl Rogers standing on the front porch.

Olivia's eyes slid closed. She couldn't believe she'd forgotten this woman's visit again. "Lord, help me."

Hattie continued to pray.

"Is Olivia Harmon here?" Mertyl's matter-of-fact voice filtered in from the foyer.

"Yes." Agnes nodded. "Would you care to wait? She is in the parlor speaking to the Lord."

"Pardon?" Mertyl was clearly wondering if she'd heard correctly.

"She is having a word with the Lord," Agnes repeated. "On behalf of the boy. Please come in. I'm sure they will be finished in a moment."

Tentatively, Mertyl followed Agnes into the parlor, her eyes darting about, as if looking for a glimpse of "the Lord."

Obviously unaware that they had a visitor, Hattie continued to pray, "Lord, we know that you have been working with Payne, bringing him to Olympia and the complimenting man and the puppy. That you have been healing his little heart. We can see the changes, and bless you for that—"

Olivia glanced up at Mertyl, her hands still caught tightly within Hattie's.

Mertyl simply stared.

The doorbell rang again.

Please, Olivia pleaded with God, *let it be good news*.

Stumbling out of the hall closet and into the foyer, the Colonel pulled open the door.

It was Nell. Eyes wild, she rushed past Mertyl, over to where Olivia was sitting with Hattie.

"Oh, you poor thing!" Gasping, Nell enveloped Olivia in a bosomy hug as Hattie continued to pray. Nell's damp coat wrapped around Olivia's head and clung to her face and hair, effectively smothering her.

The furrow between Mertyl's eyes deepened.

"—know that you are with us, Lord," Hattie went on, unaware of the sudden burst of traffic in her parlor. "And we pray that you will—"

"I heard the news!" Nell panted, pawing through her

coat until she located Olivia's face. Dragging her coat off Olivia's head, she did her best to smooth her friend's hair back into place. "I came over as soon as I got your message."

"Here's the radio!" the Colonel cried. "I knew we had one!" Triumphantly, the old man shuffled into the room, teetering precariously with each step. "Here she is! Now we can set up a command post." His curious gaze swung to Mertyl, and he paused and shifted his sagging load a little higher on his scrawny chest. "Who are you?"

"My name is Mertyl Rogers and I—"

"Ms. Rogers is our social worker," Olivia announced, by way of introduction to everyone.

"Private Rogers? Give me a hand, will you? I'm in the process of setting up a command post for the missing child."

Not knowing what else to do, Mertyl jumped forward just as the Colonel was losing his grip, and she caught the other end of the ancient ham radio. Once they'd lowered his load to the middle of the coffee table, he patted and crooned at the old radio as if she were a beautiful woman. Then, joints cracking and popping like so much firing artillery, the Colonel dropped in slow motion to his knees and began to search for an electrical outlet. Mertyl backed out of his way as he crawled by.

"I was just sick with worry!" Wide eyed, Nell studied Olivia, strangled giggles of terror escaping her throat. "How are you doing? Have you heard anything? How long has he been missing? The poor boy!"

Mertyl took a step closer and stared pensively at the odd group. Over in the corner, the girls argued with Glyniss about whose turn it was. Rahni swept into the parlor, followed by Julia, and together they silently prepared the sideboard for the small repast they'd prepared. The Colonel found power for his radio, and suddenly the room was filled with odd squealings and static.

"—and pray that you bring the boy safely back to us, Lord—"

"Excuse me," Mertyl interjected, her face suddenly even more concerned than usual, "am I to understand that…the boy…is *missing?*"

Nell stared at her. "You mean you didn't know?"

Mertyl rolled her eyes. "I should have. I knew this was not the proper environment for these children. Unfortunately, we were short on foster parents, but that is not the case anymore." Her worried gaze flicked to Olivia, then to the still-praying Hattie. "Have you called the police? Or are you simply relying on God?" There was a load of derision in her question.

"Well, I, uh," Olivia stammered, her anger rising. She was glad that Hattie held such a tight grip on her hands—Mertyl was skating on thin ice.

"Of course they've called the police." Nell's snorts and giggles reflected her offense. "It's not as if they wanted the boy to run off, for heaven's sake. What kind of parent do you think she is anyway?"

"I'm beginning to wonder." Mertyl sank into an empty chair.

"Can't you see how worried Olivia is? Do you think your judgmental attitude is helping anything? You know, sometimes you social wo—"

"Nell," Olivia murmured, closing her eyes. *Why, Lord? Why did Nell have to choose now to lose her fear of speaking out?*

"I don't know exactly who you think you are, but I—" As Nell squared her shoulders and proceeded to give Mertyl a piece of her mind, the Colonel rotated the dials on his radio, shouting into the mouthpiece.

"Come in? Anyone there? Come in? Come in? Anyone roger this?"

"—Lord," Hattie murmured, "I know that you have the perfect plan. I believe you are taking action, even as we pray. I trust that you will work everything out to your divine purpose. That you know what is best. That you, precious Savior, are always in control and, most especially, that you love us. Thank you, Lord, for taking the time to incline your ear to our humble requests. Amen. Oh, and, Lord, in case I haven't told you lately, I love you."

"Roger? Roger! Battle-ax!" the Colonel shrieked into the mouthpiece, then abruptly shut off the radio.

Mertyl Rogers's suspicious gaze honed in on the old man.

Having thoroughly put Mertyl in her place, Nell turned her attention back to Olivia.

And then there was silence. Even the girls over in the corner were quiet.

Olivia couldn't bring herself to look at Mertyl.

Long, torturous moments passed, and no one said a word.

Finally, unable to bear the suspense any longer, Nell leapt to her feet. "I'm going out there to look for that boy. Wish me luck!"

Olivia rushed after her into the foyer. "Nell! No! It's a blizzard out there! What if you panic?"

"I won't panic!" Nell trotted out to the front porch before she could lose her nerve.

"How do you know?"

"I don't know how I know, I just know. For some reason, I have the funniest feeling I'm better."

"I don't know about that, Nell." Olivia was dubious.

"I do. Call it a miracle. I'm going." Looking like Rambo after waking up on the wrong side of the bed, Nell tossed her head and flamboyantly tightened the sash on her coat. With a last, confident grin at Olivia, she marched to her car, revved the engine and, fishtailing wildly, sailed out onto the street.

Hands folded, Olivia murmured a quick prayer. "Be with her, Lord." With a heartfelt sigh, she closed the door and moved back into the house.

• • •

Olivia was simply sick. Now Nell was missing too. Ten minutes ago, after about two hours of searching, Ryan, Sean, and Zach had come back to the house to give unsuccessful progress reports and to change their damp clothing. Mertyl was still sitting like a lump in the middle of the parlor, occasionally jotting notes in her notebook and making cryptic calls on her cell phone.

Feeling as if she might just jump out of her skin from worry, Olivia prayed as she'd never prayed before.

Lord, I don't know why this is happening. I feel totally out of control. You know I hate that feeling, Lord. I'm scared. So very scared. I'm trying, Lord, to have the faith of a mustard seed. I'm trying to know that you are going to keep Cain and Nell safe out there in this terrible weather. I'm trying to believe that you don't give us more than we can take, she rambled on, mumbling fervently under her breath as she peered out the parlor window into the snow that was now blowing sideways, *but I feel it only fair to warn you that this is about it. I really feel as if I'm just about to explode, Lord. I know, I've had lots of practice at waiting and wondering and being devastated, but I'm hoping that just because I'm good at it now, doesn't mean I have to go through it again.*

Finally, just as the men were preparing to step outside for a second round of searching, the doorbell rang once more.

Olivia rushed to the foyer in time to see Officer Menkin step into the room with Cain under one arm and Copper under the other. Once inside, he set his load at his feet.

Her trembling hands covered her mouth as Olivia cried out with joy.

"Cain!"

The boy took one look at her and, sobbing as if his heart would break, he flew into her open arms.

"I...huh...huh..." He brokenly tried to communicate around his jagged breathing and wrenching anguish. "I...I...don't want to move! I want...to st-st-stay here with you! Don't make me go!" Face buried in Olivia's shoulder, the child wrapped his little arms around her neck and hung on for dear life. "I don't want a n-new mom and dad. I don't want a f-fence. I want to stay here. With you. With Zach. With her." Tears squirted from his eyes as he pointed at Agnes.

"Well, I'll be." Glyniss gazed at her sister, teary eyed.

Overcome with emotion, Agnes trumpeted noisily into her handkerchief.

The members of the boarding house, old and young alike, were all grinning foolishly with relief, exchanging watery glances and sniffing.

"Of course you do, honey," Olivia crooned, rocking the boy back and forth. Her eyes, swimming with tears, strayed from Officer Menkin to Mertyl—who was staring agog with disbelief—and finally to Zach where their gazes locked in wonder.

In thanksgiving.

In love.

"Shhh. Somehow, we'll work it all out, sweetheart."

Zach stepped forward, and the little boy held his arms out to the man. "Hey, tiger. You had us really worried."

Olivia shifted her precious bundle to him, then moved to stand near the unflappable Officer Menkin.

"Where did you find him?"

Officer Menkin spread his legs for balance and cleared his throat. Pinching his nose, he marshaled his concentration and began to speak in his monotone.

"I was headed southbound on Twenty-second when a screaming banshee of a woman flagged me down in the middle of the road. Because of the blizzard conditions, visibility was nonexistent, and I nearly ran her over. But," Officer Menkin allowed a small smile to crack his frozen features, "she didn't budge. So I swerved and ended up stuck in a drift. She wasn't into waiting for help to come pull me out, so she pushed me back out onto the road herself. Never seen such brute strength."

The room was silent as everyone listened to Officer Menkin tell his tale.

"The lady told me she'd found a boy and his dog near a Dumpster behind a convenience store. Matched the description of your boy here, so I decided to bring him by after I took her home so that she could change her clothes and warm up."

"Did she tell you her name?" Olivia wanted to be sure to thank this wonderful woman.

Officer Menkin flipped through his notes. "Let's see. As I recall, it was somebody who goes by the name of…Nell?"

Olivia closed her eyes and smiled reverently. *Thank you, Lord.* Nell had gone over to the convenience store on Twenty-second after she'd been so afraid of that neighborhood? It was a miracle. It seemed Nell would be all right after all. In more ways than one.

Feet shuffling, Officer Menkin, having finished his business here, began to back toward the front door.

"I can see that you've done great things with these kids. He's"—the policeman pointed to young Cain—"he's not the same kid at all. It's really amazing." Looking decidedly misty, he blinked to compose himself, then abruptly exited into the inclement weather.

Once he'd gone, all eyes swung to Mertyl.

With a stoic breath, she nodded. "I'd best be on my way, now that everything is all right on this end." She patted her briefcase in a most efficient manner, her tone clipped. "I'll be in touch."

However, when she looked at Cain, there was a softness in the woman that hadn't been there before.

"Do you need a ride?" Zach asked.

"No no. I have all-wheel drive and studded tires. But thank you." She nodded crisply, but it was obvious she was touched by his offer. "I'll go talk to my people. We"—she cleared her throat—"will take the boy's feelings into consideration." And with that, she stepped after Officer Menkin into the blizzard.

• • •

Later that same Friday afternoon, Olivia and Zach spent some time alone with Cain. The emotional dam burst, and all of Cain's fears of abandonment surfaced. Olivia sat on the edge of his bed and, holding the little boy in her lap, she rocked him back and forth, stroking his hair. Zach pulled a chair up next to them and tugged Cain's small, booted feet into his lap. After removing the boots, Zach rubbed his feet and encouraged the child to talk out his fears.

"I don't want to go back to our old house..." Cain sniffed. "George is mean."

"Oh, honey." Olivia nuzzled the top of his head with her nose and cheek. "You never have to go back there."

237

"I want to stay here!" He turned pleading eyes up at Olivia. "Tell them to make me stay h-here." His small body still shuddered from time to time, leftovers from his crying jag. "I don't want to be fenced in an old backyard. I don't want a new dad or mom. I like it with you guys. Esther and Ruth don't want to go either."

Zach and Olivia exchanged glances over the top of the boy's head. They soothed him the best they could, but each privately wondered how they could accomplish this feat. Raising Cain and his sisters would take far more than good intentions. It would take commitment, hard work and...an act of God.

• • •

After all three kids had boarded the train to dreamland, Zach and Olivia sat in the wing chairs in front of the fireplace in Olivia's room and speculated about how they were going to keep the promises they'd just made to the little boy who slept so soundly in the next room.

Though immensely relieved that Cain and Nell were both home safe and sound, Olivia was fretting. Okay, she reasoned, God had come through on that front. He'd answered her pleas all day long. But was it in his plan that she and Zach parent these three children? She couldn't begin to know. It seemed that there were so many strikes against them.

"I don't make enough money."

"Pardon?" Zach pulled his eyes from the mesmerizing flames and stared at Olivia.

"I can't take care of—" She paused and lowered her voice. It wouldn't do to have Cain hear what she had to say at this point. "I can't take care of three little kids on my paltry salary. I can barely make ends meet by myself and still put away enough for my retirement. That's why I live here. Because I can't afford to live by myself. John," she began, then paused to pull her emotions under control, "John and I owed a lot of money when he died. It's taken me the last five years to simply break even."

"What about all the food and clothes that came pouring in this week after you spoke to the church? That must help offset some of the cost."

Olivia shrugged. "Sure. For now. But what about the future? What about schooling and counseling and other expensive things these kids are surely going to need?"

"Well, someday, sure. You're going to need more money. That's the way it is with kids. But you don't need to worry about that bridge till you cross it. God will provide."

"I know that, but I'm a worrier."

Zach grinned. "What good does worry do?"

"None."

"Right."

"But what about my home?"

"What about it?"

"It's not what they are looking for. I'm simply not what they are looking for. I'm not even married, for heaven's sake." Agitated, Olivia threw off her afghan and rose to her feet. "It's hot in here. Are you hot?" Without waiting for his response, Olivia crossed the room, flung open the French doors that led to her little veranda, and stepped into the frigid, bracing air. She needed air. She needed answers. She needed them now. Crossing her arms over her chest, she rubbed her forearms with vigor. It was cool out here.

Lord, she prayed as she stared up into the starry patches that twinkled down between the clouds, *please, give me an answer. I'm floundering*. Again, the familiar wave of goose flesh traveled down her arms, and she wasn't sure if it was from the cold or from God's presence with her out on the veranda.

Zach came up behind Olivia, enveloping her in a heavy afghan, and wrapped his arms around her from behind. He held her for a long, silent moment, slowly swaying back and forth, waiting for the perfect moment to speak. Taking a deep breath, he turned her in his arms and rested his forehead against hers.

"I was going to wait until Valentine's Day to do this." He smiled and, reaching up, cradled her face in one of his hands. "But I figure now is a much better time."

Olivia peered up through the shadows into his eyes and saw a love there that stole her breath. "You were?"

"Mmm. I was."

"Oh." Olivia sighed. "What is it you were going to do on Valentine's Day?"

"I was going to ask you to marry me."

Olivia's breath caught in her throat. He wanted to marry her? Her heart pounded like a jungle drum. He wanted to marry *her*? The giddy feeling of wild excitement vanished as soon as it had come. Was he doing this for the kids? Would he have proposed at all, if not for the kids?

"But I figure it would be too late by then."

"It would?" The last vestiges of her excitement fizzled. Ah. Well. Too late. Perhaps he wasn't proposing after all. Her muzzy brain searched for a meaning behind these words.

"Yep. So, instead, I'm asking you now."

Olivia frowned. "Asking what?"

Shaking his head, Zach's chuckle resounded pleasantly throughout his chest. "I'm asking you to marry me. Now. As soon as possible."

16

Zach looked down into Olivia's face and wondered what she was thinking. There were shadows of doubt marring her usually sweet expression.

"What do you say?" Zach winced at the vulnerable, nearly pleading note in his voice. He was wearing his heart on his sleeve, but he didn't care. Suddenly it meant everything to him that she say yes.

"I…uh…" Olivia blinked and swallowed. "I say…no."

"No?"

Zach was stunned. He hadn't considered that she might say no. In all the times he'd practiced his proposal in front of the mirror, in all the times he'd fantasized about this joyful moment, in all the times he dreamed of a future with his sweet Olivia, the answer had always been yes.

Yes!

Not no.

He'd been sure that after so much prayer and supplication, that this was what God wanted. *God? Isn't this what you wanted?*

"No," Olivia whispered, her eyes filling with tears all over again.

"But…but…" Zach could only stare at her. This was not working out according to his fantasy at all. "Why?"

"Because…I…" Her face crumpled. "Oh, Zach. I need some time to think. Can you understand that?"

At this point, Zach couldn't understand diddly-squat. But if she needed time to think, then she should have time to think. He passed a hand over his jaw, then around to the back of his neck. "Uh, sure. You, uh, go ahead and think all you want. I'll just go home…now."

Olivia nodded wordlessly.

"Call me?"

Again she nodded.

"Tonight."

"Yes."

"Okay." He planted a tender kiss at her temple.

As Zach left the boarding house that evening, shrouded in melancholy, he prayed.

• • •

Olivia peered out the window, watching as Zach very slowly pulled out of the driveway and into the street. Suddenly, she felt lonelier than she ever had in her entire life.

Why on earth had she said no?

Because she knew that she could no longer make life decisions without first consulting the Lord. Especially enormously confusing decisions such as this. No, she couldn't make up her mind all by herself. This was far too big a decision. She needed God on this one.

After all, he'd brought her this far, hadn't he? If she were perfectly honest, God's plans seemed to be working out far better than any she'd ever made. It was when she interfered that things didn't go so well.

Gathering the afghan that she still wore around her

shoulders, Olivia stepped back to the fireplace and sat down for a time of communion with her Lord.

"O Father"—her throat was tight, her eyes stinging—"I didn't go into this wanting another family. I simply wanted to get involved in some sort of charity work. I don't know if I'm ready to be a mother again. I already lost one daughter, and today I nearly lost Cain. I don't know if I'm cut out for this kind of stress. But here I am, hopelessly attached to these kids. And to Zach. It's such a mess."

Lifting and dropping a shoulder, she watched the sparks in the fireplace whirl up the chimney. "I don't know that I want to go back to the depression and boredom of the last five years, either."

She swallowed, trying to sort everything out in her mind.

"Lord, on the one hand, I love Zach."

Her gaze dropped to her hands in the soft firelight.

"On the other hand, I loved John, and look where that got me."

Balling her hands into fists, she pressed them into her cheeks.

"I love the kids. But I loved Lillah, too, and that broke my heart."

A thought came to her that she hadn't processed yet. "Do you think I feel guilty or disloyal because I've found love again?" She frowned. "Do *you* think I'm being disloyal?"

She strained to hear some message from God. Nothing. Olivia sighed.

"Do you think Zach is proposing to me for the sake of the kids?"

No answer.

"How about my money? Do you think he wants to marry me for my money?" She was teasing, hoping God had a good sense of humor.

He must, she decided. After all, he gave her three motley kids and a house wrecker for a charity project.

Suddenly another question came to Olivia's mind. "Lord, why would any sane man want to take on three little kids and a poor, rather pigheaded woman for a lifelong commitment? Do you suppose it's because he loves me?"

A wave of goose flesh rumbled down her right arm, then up her left.

"Should I marry him?"

The tingly bumps flashed down her spine.

"Should I call him?"

Even her scalp tingled.

"Okay, okay, already!" She giggled, burrowing even further into her afghan. "But I just want to make it clear that this is your idea." Her whole body literally vibrated with excitement.

* * *

"It's me."

"I know." Zach clutched his cell phone to his ear, not wanting to miss a single word. He hadn't expected to hear from her till morning.

"Can you come over?"

"Now?"

"Yes. Right now."

Zach looked out his windshield at the desolate street. He'd simply pull a U-ie. "Uh, sure."

"Great. Where are you?"

"Right outside your house."

Olivia's laughter danced into his ear. "What are you doing out there?"

Zach grinned. "I stopped to pray right after I left your driveway."

As he'd prayed, he'd discussed his love for AmyBeth and how hard it had been to let go. He'd confessed his disappointment that she hadn't been able to conceive a baby. He said good-bye to his past and hello to his future, whatever that may hold. He told the Lord of his love for the three kids but, most especially, of his passion for Olivia. And then he did the hardest thing he'd had to do since the day he'd buried AmyBeth. He'd let go of Olivia and the kids and placed them in God's hands.

If God wanted him to have them, he would.

Of that, he was sure.

"Good thing you were praying," she whispered.

"*Good* thing?"

"Very good."

"Really?" He wondered exactly what she meant.

"Really."

"Come open the door. I'm standing on your porch."

• • •

Olivia fell into Zach's embrace, and he kicked the front door closed with the heel of his boot.

"I'll marry you."

"Just like that? What if I've changed my mind?"

Rearing back, Olivia peered up into his face in consternation. "Did you?"

"No." Laughing, he cradled her head in his hands, and before she could remonstrate, sealed her mouth shut with a kiss that had her toes curling inside her slippers.

"What changed your mind?" His mouth was feather light against hers.

Thoughtfully, she nibbled his lower lip. "I prayed about it."

"Mmm," he groaned. "I prayed you'd pray about it."

"I prayed you'd pray that I'd pray about it."

"I give up." He drew her back with him against the foyer door. Pulling her against his chest, he planted tiny kisses on her cheeks and brow and lips. "You, my beautiful wife-to-be, are one wonderful woman."

"What makes you say that?" Coquettishly, she wrapped her arms more firmly around his neck.

"Everything. You're perfect for me. I couldn't envision a better life partner or mother of our children."

The tingles were back. "You really are a complimenting man," she said saucily.

Zach pulled back and eyed her. "What is the deal with this complimenting man thing anyway? I've heard Hattie pray about that more than once."

Olivia giggled. "You, silly. You are an answer to her prayer."

"Me? I'm not much on compliments."

"Ah, but I think you complement me perfectly."

"Yeah," he mused before claiming her mouth for another kiss, "you do have a point."

"Zach," she managed, when she could speak again, "what about the kids?"

Leaning his forehead against hers, his sigh fanned her cheeks. "We'll pray for God's will. If we are lucky, we will get to keep the kids. If we're not so lucky, we'll simply have to make some of our own."

Olivia nestled a little closer. "Sounds," she said on a sigh, "like a little bit of heaven."

Epilogue

Valentine's Day in McLaughlin, Vermont, was especially exciting that year. And not simply because Julia had chosen to give birth to her and Sean's daughter on that day. Although everyone in the boarding house was over the moon at the news and planned to rush to the maternity ward later in the evening.

After the wedding.

For, at two o'clock that brilliantly sunny afternoon, everyone from the boarding house—with the noticeable exception of Sean, Julia, and baby Caroline—was at the McLaughlin Community Church witnessing the joining of a family.

The adoption plans had sailed through with so little fuss that Olivia and Zach both knew without a doubt that God's hand was on every detail. How else would the curmudgeonly Mertyl have gone to bat for them over and over and pushed through paperwork that usually took months to complete? Obviously, the Lord knew that the right woman for the job was Mertyl.

The fact that Zach had promised to remodel his existing house to accommodate his new family and to fence in the backyard for the kids was the impetus it had taken to win Mertyl to their camp. She was even amenable to the fact that—for several months after the wedding, while he was remodeling—Zach and his new family would live at the boarding house.

Hattie was thrilled with the arrangement. The sunroom was complete and even better than before, and the little landlady had ideas about some shelves here and there. Perhaps expanding the service porch to accommodate more food storage would be a good thing.

Mertyl saw no problem with any of these plans, as long as they eventually moved into a home of their own. Zach and Olivia had been faithfully praying for the woman for several months and were pleased to see her sitting next to Nell in the crowd of well-wishers.

The wedding ceremony was one of a kind.

The kids stood up with Zach and Olivia, their faces beaming as their soon-to-be parents took their vows. Agnes, Bea, and Glyniss had collaborated on a medley of gospel hymns and some songs that the kids had picked out. Luckily for Agnes, the children's taste did not run toward Diana Ross. Even the Colonel had been allowed to help, to some degree, with the decoration. The Elvis-on-velvet paintings had been confined to the darkest corner of the lobby area, and anything that smelled badly or contained rust was relegated to the outdoors.

Zach's partner and friend Mike stood up as best man, and Hattie was tickled pink to act as the matron of honor.

It was not a huge wedding, although Hattie had insisted on inviting at least fifty of her closest friends. And, of course, they'd shown up, bearing gifts for the new little family. After all, who could say no to attending a reception/buffet at Hattie's place after the wedding? Especially when Rahni was cooking delicacies from her native land.

After the vows had been exchanged and Zach and

Olivia had been pronounced not only man and wife but mother and father, Zach thoroughly kissed Olivia. Then they both turned and embraced the giggling, wriggling, wiggling children.

Hattie moved slowly to the pulpit, and eyes brimming with tears asked the congregation to join her in prayer.

"Dear heavenly Father," she began reverently, "we take this joyous occasion as an opportunity to thank you for answered prayer—"

"Okay," Esther shouted, "now me! Jesus, thank you for my new mom. I love her. And thank you for my new dad. I love him. And I love the panny-o"—her gaze shot to the piano—"and the flowers and the candles, but I *don't* like those pictures out there," she pointed to the lobby, "of that dancing man in the white suit. He's baaaaad."

"—you have fulfilled our every heart's desire, Lord. To see your miracles in action is such a blessing to us all. I pray for your continued blessing on this little family—"

"Okay, now," Esther commanded, "Dad, you pray. Then Mom, then Cain, then Ruth, then Aunt Agnes." Turning toward the crowd, the little child began to point at each broadly smiling face. "Then her, then him, then her, then him, then her, then her, then..."

"—thank you for loving us. Amen. Oh, and," Hattie added as an afterthought, "just in case we've been too preoccupied to tell you yet today, Lord, we love you."